I0761620

PLAYS WELL WITH OTHERS

BOOKS BY LAUREN MYRACLE

NOVELS

Plays Well with Others

This Boy

The Infinite Moment of Us

Shine

Peace, Love, and Baby Ducks

Bliss

Rhymes with Witches

THE INTERNET GIRLS SERIES

ttyl

ttfn

l8r, g8r

yolo

PLAYS WELL WITH OTHERS

LAUREN MYRACLE

BLACK STONE PUBLISHING

Published in 2025 by Blackstone Publishing
Cover and book design by Sarah Riedlinger

Printed in the United States of America

First edition: 2025
ISBN 979-8-8747-1083-5
Fiction / Thrillers / Domestic

Version 1

Blackstone Publishing
31 Mistletoe Rd.
Ashland, OR 97520

www.BlackstonePublishing.com

For Tricia Ready
shiny stickers, steadfast heart—
hope in darkest drafts.

It’s all fun and games until someone loses an eye.

THELOWDOWN.COM

Your premier source for keeping up with what's going down.

Disgraced Charity Director Has Nothing to Smile About

October 19, 2024 • Culture • 4 min. read

Tempers flared this week when the director of a humanitarian organization declared that "people with birth defects don't deserve special treatment." Whether you're new to the debacle or simply confused about how a small-town do-gooder ended up on the world's most hated list, here's everything you need to know about Jake, Shelby, and Adam, their twisted love triangle, and the bizarre role frozen vegetables (yes, you read that right) played in this sordid tale.

Two days ago, Jacquelyn "Jake" Nolan went online to accuse former friend Shelby Bryant of sleeping with her husband. The message Jake left on Shelby's Facebook page included this cryptic zinger: "Anyway, hope you had fun f*cking my husband behind my back, while I had frozen peas on my breasts."

Some context:

Once close, Jake and Shelby bonded over their volunteer work at the Brahman Foundation, a nonprofit organization focused on improving healthcare in their hometown of Fort Collins, Colorado. Local success paved the way for greater outreach, and under

Jake's direction, the Foundation launched an international program to aid infants with cleft lips and palates.

In February of 2022, the Miles of Smiles team made their inaugural trip to Guadalajara, Mexico, performing over twenty palate repair surgeries. Jake's husband, Adam Swift, served as the team's anesthesiologist, while Shelby—who was born with a congenital condition known as a microcleft—served as the group's education and support services provider. Jake, despite professing herself a champion of the program, remained in Colorado.

Fast-forward to this past Monday, when Jake broke the internet with her unhinged tirade. Thanks to Colorado public records law, we can confirm that Jake's tantrum came on the heels of her soon-to-be ex-husband's request for a divorce, and thanks to an exclusive interview with Shelby, we can likewise confirm that Shelby and Adam *are* romantically engaged. (Shelby, it should be noted, took pains to clarify that at the time of the Miles of Smiles trip, their relationship was purely professional.) Given this collision of events, we can (almost) understand Jake's meltdown. What woman wouldn't unravel upon learning that her husband was ditching her to be with her best friend?

But Jake lost all sympathy when she moved from haranguing Shelby on Facebook to harassing her via a long and poisonous email . . . an email that Shelby turned around and published on X (formerly Twitter). The excerpts included deeply inappropriate remarks about people born with congenital abnormalities, with Jake going so far as to say that "people with clefts are ugly, inside and out." Jake then doubled down by informing Shelby that "[she] will always and forever be ugly to the bone."

The backlash was swift and savage.

Kim Sung-hyun, administrator of the largest worldwide cleft lip and/or palate support group, tweeted that Jake was "the worst kind of hypocrite, giving lip service to supporting the cleft and palate community while actively punching down on the very people she claims to support." The #lipservice movement exploded as celebrities, influencers, and bloggers amplified the viral campaign.

It is hard to imagine a more brutal online thrashing, and harder still to foresee a path forward for Ms. Nolan. After being canceled so decisively, is it possible to come back? But as Shelby sees it, her one-time bestie is the architect of her own ruin.

"Adam told Jake the honest truth, which is that he and I are in love," Shelby asserted. "I'm sure that hurt. But the vital work of helping cleft-affected babies shouldn't be overshadowed by the dissolution of someone's marriage, which, let's face it, happens every day."

Jake, who was asked to step down from her position at the Brahman Foundation, declined our request for an interview. Perhaps she has at long last learned the lesson passed down by kindergarten teachers everywhere: If you don't have anything nice to say, don't say anything at all.

COMMENTS

SusanB
Wow—fired from volunteering! That's a first!

DClady
Jake is clearly a glassbowl, but does she deserve a public lashing with millions of onlookers?

madkingrichard
Yes

pinchme
Not defending a toxic ableist, but Shelby had to know she was throwing Jake to the wolves when she shared Jake's private email. I wonder if it was a smoke screen to hide her own sins . . .

madkingrichard
JAKE NOLAN SAID BABIES WITH BIRTH DEFECTS ARE UGLY TO THE BONE. Friend's motives are irrelevant.

LOAD 2401 MORE COMMENTS

TEN MONTHS LATER

1

JAKE

I absolutely, positively did not say the terrible things Shelby claimed I did.

Except for the part about Shelby fucking Adam behind my back. I did say that, and I said it online, where nothing dies and no one is granted the right to be forgotten.

As for the other things, I suppose I said them too, but the situation was more complicated than Shelby acknowledged. She failed to mention that while she and Adam were sneaking around having their affair, I was giving birth to Adam's and my dead son. She failed to mention the excruciating mastitis I developed, my breasts as hard as concrete from the buildup of undrunk milk.

"Bind your breasts and take the antibiotics," my ob-gyn instructed, tapping out a script for cephalexin. "I'll throw in a prescription for Diflucan, in case you end up with a yeast infection."

(Oh, I did.)

She suggested ice packs to bring down the swelling. "If you don't have an ice pack, use a bag of frozen vegetables," she said. "Your milk will dry up. You just have to ride it out."

A year to the day after I lay in the hospital delivering my dead son, Adam left me for Shelby—or rather, he booted *me* out and invited

Shelby to take my place. Shelby, surprise, surprise, failed to mention that detail as well.

I was an idiot. I said hurtful, foolish, idiotic things. I allowed my pain to cloud my judgment, and I'm so very sorry.

But put yourself in my shoes. Think of it as a thought experiment, just for kicks. You're going about your normal life, and things aren't great. Things are pretty shitty, to be honest. Your pregnancy has been labeled "high risk," you've been consigned to bed rest, and your husband, Adam, reveals himself to be woefully inadequate at giving you the support you need.

"I don't know if I can do this," he says when he takes in the beached whale mass of you spread out on the marital bed.

"Do what?" you say. After all, it's you who will ride out the five remaining weeks of your pregnancy in this bed, not him.

He rakes his hand through his hair, his demeanor that of a haunted man. "I don't know. All of it!"

(You hate him a little, because as a child you experienced things that would traumatize Boo Radley. You know what it is to be haunted. But Adam knows very little about your past, and that's how you plan to keep it.)

"Adam, you *can* do it," you say. You take his hand and wait for his eyes to lock on yours. "You're strong. We're strong. We'll get through this."

Your best friend, Shelby, puts on a better performance. Determinedly upbeat, she brings you trashy magazines, saltines, and vast amounts of the peppermint tea she's so fond of. Special peppermint tea, a blend created by Shelby herself and sewn into tiny sachets, a whole tin of them delivered to you with happy squeals when she first learned you were pregnant.

Tea, in the early weeks of your pregnancy, was Shelby's goofy way of taking care of you. Now that you're high risk, the tea becomes serious business. You'd prefer Dr Pepper and a Pop-Tart or three, but Shelby denies you these small pleasures. "Too many artificial ingredients," she says, pressing a hot mug into your hands. "This is natural. It will calm your nerves."

So, things are hard. But you've been through worse. You keep on keeping on, while Adam shakes his head tragically and Shelby brings you tea. Tea, apparently, is the answer.

Then, in a game of devil's dominoes, you lose your baby, your husband, *and* your best friend, tac tac tac, one after the other. (Tea was not the answer. You hurl the remaining sachets at Adam and Shelby, who stand hand in hand and bear the assault with red-rimmed eyes. "We're so sorry," they tell you. "We're so very, very sorry.")

They "give you some space."

You use it to make bad decisions.

You double down with worse decisions.

You're flogged on the world stage, where insults come at you like knives, especially the rusty-bladed ones reserved for women. Your name takes a quick lap around the talk show circuit. There's a *Saturday Night Live* sketch about you. You become a meme.

Are you still with me?

Imagine the depths of your humiliation, rage, self-loathing, and grief. Multiply it by hell. That's what it felt like, give or take death by a thousand cuts.

I nursed those cuts for just under a year, hiding from the world in an apartment I rented month to month until the construction of my new house was completed. I say "*I* rented," but it was Adam's money that paid the bills. I say "*my* new house"—and it is mine, and I will cling to it ferociously—but it was purchased with Adam's money.

Midway through my second trimester, he and I signed a contract for a property that didn't yet exist, securing the seventh of eight planned homes in a project helmed by a well-known developer.

"The Sweetwater Bungalows marry classic craftsman style with modern convenience," boasted the brochures. "Close to Old Town Fort Collins and Colorado State University, these homes will be erected in a legacy neighborhood with mature trees and a bike trail. Schedule your virtual tour today!"

The bungalow we purchased wouldn't be finished for two years. We didn't care.

"What's two years?!" we said giddily. "It's our dream house!"

Fuck you, Adam. It's my dream house now.

I met him while I was still in college. We married before I got my degree. I was young and naïve and desperate to please. Adam encouraged me to do volunteer work, because that's what the other doctors' wives did. I spent my days taking care of others and my nights taking care of him. That was my career, and yes, I am retroactively aghast. I was one dumb bunny.

After the shit hit the fan, I wised up. Not immediately. I was too raw. (I'm still raw, but I've gotten better at hiding it.)

But after Adam asked for a divorce, I found a way to harness my fury and play nice. I was chastened. I was penitent. I sat through three grueling sessions with a divorce mediator who would have been a great preschool teacher in another lifetime. She was a small, tidy woman with a gray bob, and she listened and nodded and acted as a conduit between me and the man I once loved.

"What I'm hearing Adam say, Jake, is that he isn't proud of how your marriage ended," Celia said. "What I'm hearing him say is that he and Shelby didn't *choose* to fall in love. Is that right, Adam?"

"It just happened," Adam told her miserably.

Another case of "Oops, I fell and landed between another woman's legs," I thought. *Why is there never a Caution When Wet sign around when you need one?*

What I said was, "It was hard for you, too. With the pregnancy." I refused to speak Liam's name aloud. "And then, afterward, I fell apart. I see that now."

Celia nodded sagely. "What I'm hearing Jake say," she said to Adam, "is that she acknowledges her own role in how things played out, and that she's sorry."

She swiveled back to me. "Is that an accurate representation of what you're feeling, Jake? *Are* you sorry?"

I was sorry, all right—for falling for Adam in the first place. For welcoming Shelby with open arms when Adam invited her to a work party I hosted, at the house I used to live in, the house on Hemlock Avenue where Shelby now lives. She moved in with Adam a week after he filed for divorce.

The Hemlock house may not be a craftsman bungalow, but it's no shack. At any rate, Shelby has plans for a top-to-bottom renovation. The improvements she implements, in conjunction with the property's coveted Old Town location, will turn the Hemlock house into a gem. Its value will be twice that of my little bungalow within the year, Shelby will make sure of it.

After I moved out, Adam changed the locks, but tucked a spare key in the same hiding spot as always. One night, after the light in Adam and Shelby's bedroom went out, I lifted the paver stone with the chipped corner, and there it was.

In Celia's stuffy office, I slid my hand into my pocket and thumbed the spiny ridge of the copy I made. I bowed my head and said, "Yes, I'm sorry. So, so sorry."

My groveling dovetailed with Adam's guilt, resulting in a divorce agreement that awarded me the Sweetwater bungalow, half of Adam's retirement funds, and monthly alimony payments for the next seven years. Generous payments. I'm still working as a freelance editor—if I can call myself that with one client, no degree, and very little experience—so I have that small infusion of income as well. Financially, I'm set for the foreseeable future.

I stand in the sunlit bedroom of my brand-new Sweetwater bungalow and do a slow turn. There are boxes everywhere, some of which are full, but most of which are empty and need breaking down. The movers dropped everything off yesterday. I've made an impressive start. A fresh start, facilitated by the fact that my new neighbors know me only as "Jake." I was only ever internet famous, not recognizable-on-the-street famous. Or infamous. Whatever.

I can walk into the sunlight without fear of being run out of town, and after nearly a year of hiding and crying, this forward momentum is long overdue. My mom, were she here to see it, would breathe a sigh of relief.

"Life is tough, Jakey, but you're tougher," she'd tell me when I was little. "Keep putting one foot in front of the other, and everything will work out. Okay, my good girl?"

That's what she told me when my half brother, Toby, died at the age of four. She held me tight and sang her favorite Carter Family song, pressing my cheek to her chest. "'Keep on the sunny side, always on the sunny side. Keep on the sunny side of life.'"

My mom died when I was in college. She's with Toby and Liam and June Carter now. As for me, I'm no longer a little girl, and I've given up on being good. I gave it my best shot, but it got me nowhere.

So I've set my sights on something new: revenge.

2

JAKE

Something else my mom used to tell me: "Jakey, sweetheart, not one of us is nearly as important as we think we are."

She said it with the best of intentions, I swear.

I'd come home in tears over some small thing—not a single person at school had complimented my new haircut, for example—and my mom would urge me not to take it to heart. It wasn't that my classmates hated my haircut. They probably just hadn't noticed it. Everybody was too busy with their own lives to have excess energy for mine.

She was telling me to keep things in perspective.

What I heard was, *Oh, sweet girl. You thought you mattered?* My cheeks would burn, time and again, because I did think I mattered. I kept thinking it despite boatloads of evidence to the contrary.

Then came #lipservice, and perspective flew straight out the window. Suddenly everyone had an opinion about my life, or at least about the parts they could get to.

Some things, thank God, have remained private, even though sharing them would have likely shifted public opinion in my favor. But I kept Liam out of it. I protected him, because I am his mother. That's what mothers do.

I go to the cardboard box marked *Important Papers* and remove the smaller white box within. I sit on the edge of my bed and run my thumb over its textured surface, steeling myself.

I remove the lid and take out the first item, a piece of card stock featuring a falling autumn leaf. Falling autumn leaves were everywhere during my stay at the hospital, laminated indicators of death. A leaf was hung on the door of my room, warning nurses not to pop in with a smile and a cheery, "How's our new mommy? And how's baby?" There was a leaf on the front of my medical file. There was a leaf clipped to the top of my chart. There was even a leaf taped to the wheelchair I was rolled out in the day I was discharged, in case my slack features and empty arms failed to communicate that my stay on the maternity ward hadn't been a joyous one.

Printed on the card are the words, *In Memory Of,* followed by Liam's name, weight, length, and date of death. Below are two tiny footprints and two tiny handprints. The labor and delivery nurse pulled a pad of ink from her scrubs and took the prints while I watched, manipulating Liam's lifeless limbs as if he were a doll. Adam had to leave the room. He blanched and choked out the words, "I can't," before rushing into the bright hall.

My thumb covers Liam's handprint completely. That's how small his hand was. "I love you, little guy," I whisper.

Next out of the box comes a handmade onesie the size of an iPhone case, with matching booties and bonnet. It's fussy and frilly, and I hate it almost as much as I hated those laminated leaves. But some compassionate soul in a bereavement group knitted it for my child. I can't throw it away.

The final item in the box is a nubbly purple blanket. I smiled when I picked it out at the store, imagining Liam clutching it with a chubby fist and gumming the silk trim. I touch the trim now, as I lift it from the box. It's soft beneath my fingers.

The doorbell rings, and I jump. I've slept here for all of one night, and the only sentient being I've encountered is a neighborhood cat whose owners aren't big into grooming him, as his fur is matted and he smells of urine.

But cats don't ring doorbells, so who could it possibly be?

The bell chimes again.

I pad across the room and peek out the second-story window. A curvy, adorable redhead grins up at me, a plate of cookies in her hands.

"Shit," I say, dropping to my knees.

"Hello?" Strawberry Shortcake calls.

Seconds tick by.

"Hel-*lo*-oo!" she calls again.

She saw me, and now she thinks I'm up here hiding. Because I *am* up here hiding. Shit, shit, shit.

I repack the white box, fit the lid in place, and tuck it on the top shelf of my closet. I jog downstairs, combing my hand through my hair.

"Hi!" Strawberry Shortcake says when I open the door. She nods toward the opposite end of the street. "I'm Mabel. I'm in the very first bungalow. Can I come in?"

"Sure," I say, though she's already breezed past me.

Mabel looks to be in her early thirties, same as me. She wears cropped jeans, pink polka-dotted kitten heels, and a pink floral top that shows off freckled cleavage. Her red curls are tumble-perfect, and her figure fills me with familiar envy. Next to Mabel, I look like a ten-year-old boy.

I follow her through the house to my kitchen, where we exchange pleasantries. Mabel, it should be said, is far more pleasant than I am. People make me skittish these days.

My pre-scandal friends responded in one of two ways when #lipservice upended my life. The majority disappeared not with a bang, but a whimper. No, a sigh. They were as quiet as the outgoing tide, erasing their footprints as they tiptoed away.

Jake Nolan? I hope she's doing well, poor thing.

Those things she said, though . . .

I know!

I worry for her, don't you?

These women give me quick glances if they chance to run into me, then make a beeline to the other side of the store.

A second, smaller group of former friends—purple-haired Lucy comes to mind—went to the opposite extreme, becoming rabidly interested in All Things Jake. On the day *The Lowdown* article dropped, Lucy appeared at my dumpy rental with wine, Thai food, and a sympathetic ear.

"Oh, *honey*," Lucy said when we got down to the nitty-gritty. "Is it all just a big misunderstanding?"

"Is what a big misunderstanding?"

Lucy leaned in. I leaned in. Her eyes shone with what I mistook for compassion. "About Shelby and what you said about"—she winced and circled a finger in the vicinity of her mouth—"you know?"

"Her cleft lip?" I groaned and fell back against the sofa, half laughing and half crying. We were into our second bottle of wine. "Lucy, Shelby doesn't *have* a cleft lip. She only says she does for attention!"

That wasn't exactly true. Shelby was born with what's called a microform cleft. I shouldn't have made light of it, then or ever. But a surgeon fixed the anomaly when Shelby was an infant, leaving her with a sliver of a scar. A sliver of a *sliver* of a scar, less noticeable than the hair that sprouts from my chin like clockwork every month.

Two days after Lucy came by bearing food and wine, *Medium* published a piece in which a "close friend of Jacquelyn Nolan's" was interviewed for an exclusive tell-all.

"Jake said Shelby pretends she has a handicap to get attention," my anonymous friend complained. "Which, for the record, I totally disagree with. Jake is gaslighting Shelby, and it's problematic."

Lucy is problematic, and her purple hair, too.

No. Her hair was cute.

But yes, I have become cautious around people. As for Mabel, she doesn't seem to have a cautious bone in her body. She plunks the cookies down on the granite island, her words spilling out in an endless stream. In the span of a few minutes, we've covered the weather, our matching floor plans, and the upcoming neighborhood get-together hosted by Todd and Lisa, the retired couple who live next to me.

"It's this Sunday," Mabel says. "You'll be there?"

I puff up my cheeks, then blow out. I'm not here to make friends, but I'm not out to make enemies, either. "Yeah, sure."

"Great!" She steps into the great room. "Ooo, I *love* your sofa."

"Let's go outside," I say. I grab the plate of cookies. "Shall we go outside?"

It's the beginning of August, and warm. We sit beneath the eaves in weathered blue Adirondack chairs, and I nibble on a sugar cookie as Mabel tells me about everyone on our street. She has a faint Southern accent, her vowels rounded and her consonants soft. Georgia, possibly, or Alabama. Not backwoods North Carolina. I'd recognize backwoods North Carolina in a heartbeat.

"All the Sweetwater Lane peeps are great," Mabel says. "The people who live behind us and around us? Not so much. For years, this land was privately owned, just a big open field, so the people who were here before us see us as interlopers."

I shrug. "The world moves on."

"But the bungalow owners have banded together. We're our own little neighborhood within the neighborhood."

"When did you move in?" I ask.

"June of last year," Mabel replies. "My husband, David, loves that he can bike to campus on game days. He's a Rams fan."

The Rams are CSU's football team. I say, "Yeah, my ex is, too." Then, to get it over with, I add, "We got divorced last fall. One of these days, I'll have to find a job, but for now, I'm focusing on me."

Mabel gives the requisite sympathetic nod.

"What about you?" I ask. "Do you have a job? Kids?"

Mabel launches into easy patter, and I learn that her husband works for a med tech company in town, while she teaches ceramics to seniors at City Park Pottery Studio. She says nothing about kids, which tells me everything. My ribs loosen. I'm glad I'm not the only childless woman on the block.

"It pays nothing," Mabel says of her pottery job, "but I get free access to the studio." She taps the cookie plate resting on my thighs. "This is for you to keep."

I lift the plate's edge. "You made this? It's gorgeous."

Mabel waves away the compliment. "It's fun. It's a hobby. I've given one to just about everyone. Now that you've moved in, there's only one house left."

We swivel our heads to the eighth and final bungalow, tan with brown eaves. A Sold! sign is planted in the yard.

"The new owner is a single mom," Mabel says. "Her name's Vanessa. She's got a son in the same grade as my stepdaughter."

I feel prickles everywhere. "You . . . have a stepdaughter? What's her name?"

"Bethany. She's ten."

"That's a fun age," I say. I could be remarking on Mabel's nail color, I'm that casual. "Do you two get along?"

"Absolutely. Really, really well, actually."

"A rare non-evil stepmother. Nice."

Mabel twists her mouth. "I hate how that's the first thing everyone thinks." Something in my expression must give her pause, because she says, "Hold on. Do you have one?"

"An evil stepmother? Oh . . . ha. No."

She lifts her brows. "You sure?"

"I . . ." *Did not mean to bring up my stepmother*, I want to say. I don't talk about Carrie. I never have, not even to Adam. We were married for six years, and he never knew I had—have?—a stepmother.

He never knew about Toby, either.

"She wasn't evil, just young," I tell Mabel. I do some quick calculations and realize that Carrie would have been in her early twenties when she married my dad, younger than I am now. I was five when she and I met, a tiny interloper with needs of my own. "She said guests should bring their own toothpaste."

"To who? *You?*"

"I was like, 'I'm not a guest. I'm my father's daughter.'"

"Good for you!"

"I didn't say it out loud," I admit. "I did, however, use her decorative soaps and dry my hands on her fancy hand towels."

"Her fancy *guest* towels. Well played."

I remember the cloying scent of those little soaps. They were as smooth as wax when they were dry, but slick as pond scum once they'd been used.

"Do you get along now, you and your stepmother?" Mabel asks.

"We never see each other."

"How come?"

"No reason to."

"Right," Mabel says. She plays with the pendant hanging from her necklace, a miniature key with filigree in the shape of a heart. Once upon a time, I had a similar necklace. The key I wore was one I found in a box in the attic of my dad and Carrie's house, a vintage brass skeleton key that, in a fairy tale, would unlock a secret garden or a pirate's chest.

I strung it on a piece of leather cord and wore it around my neck, convinced it had magical powers. I lost it two decades ago, along with my faith in happy endings.

"She and my dad split up," I explain. "She sends me birthday cards, but addresses them to 'Mrs. Jake Swift,' who isn't me."

Mabel furrows her brow.

"Because of the divorce. 'Swift' is my ex's last name. I kept my own, which is Nolan."

And stop now, I tell myself.

Mabel's phone dings. "Oh, joy," she says as she checks the screen. "My nemesis just posted a comment on GoodNeighbors."

"Your nemesis?"

"She goes by WarriorMom." Mabel mimes a finger gag. "Are you on GoodNeighbors? No? Omigod, it's the best. People huff about dogs being off leash and cats pooping in sandboxes and unruly youth setting off firecrackers in the middle of the night." She says "unruly youth" like it's a delicious, ironic caramel.

Mabel rises. "Anyway, duty calls. I've got to leave a petty comment in response to the petty comment she left me."

"What did she do to become your nemesis?"

"WarriorMom? She left a *very* aggressive post about how everybody should stop feeding the damn squirrels. She thinks they're too fat already."

"And that elevated her to nemesis status? You must really like squirrels."

"No! I mean, yes, I do, but . . ." She laughs and rolls her eyes. "I said that feeding squirrels was fine. They're cute. WarriorMom fired back in all caps that wildlife is called wildlife for a reason and said that the real pest in this situation"—she indicates herself with her thumbs—"is me."

"She said you're worse than the squirrels?"

"She sure did."

"I hate the internet."

"Right?" Mabel says.

The vagrant cat jumps onto the porch and lands with an *oomph.*

Mabel steps back. "Oh! Hi, kitty." She looks at me. "Is . . . that your cat?"

"That is *not* my cat."

"Phew, because that is—"

"One ugly cat. I know."

His pelt is clumped and greasy, and he smells worse than ever. I spot what looks like a brown marble wedged into the fur near his nether regions. Only that is no brown marble. That is . . .

I grimace.

"Mrawwh!" the cat complains.

"You don't recognize him?" I ask Mabel. "You don't know who he belongs to?"

"No clue, sorry."

"He keeps coming around. I think he's hungry."

Mabel regards him dubiously. "I don't think he's going to waste away, if that makes you feel better. He's got some pounds on him."

"What should I do? Should I call animal control?"

"Or take him to a vet? Maybe he's chipped, and a vet could find out who his owners are?"

The two of us stare at the lumpish gray mass of him. He flattens his body against the floorboards and stares back, a plaintive warble emanating from his barrel-shaped chest.

"Gracious," Mabel says. She tears her gaze away. "But make an account on GoodNeighbors, so you can downvote WarriorMom and upvote me. I'm 'Miss Manners,' because of my first name. You know, 'Mabel, Mabel, if you're able?'"

"'Get your elbows off the table?'"

"Bingo," she says. "What were my parents thinking? Did it not cross their minds that everyone over the age of fifty would trot out that gem the minute they heard my name? Not to mention—and I'm being serious, I've had a lifetime to think about it—how absurd that expression is. What would it take for someone to *not* be able to get their elbows off the table? Sudden onset upper body paralysis? An MI5 agent jumping from behind the curtains and handcuffing their wrists to the table?"

She frowns. "I don't know what an MI5 agent is, actually. Just that there's a TV show about them."

"British spies," I supply.

"Ah. Spies. Good for them." Mabel waggles her phone as she trots down the porch stairs, careful to give the cat a wide berth. "Find me online. Upvote all my comments. Oh—and welcome to the neighborhood!"

3

MABEL

Before marrying David, Mabel inhaled everything stepmother-related she could. Novels, self-help books, movies, TV shows, podcasts—Mabel educated herself to arm herself. She knew stepparenting came with challenges, but secretly, she assumed that Bethany would adore being her stepdaughter. Who wouldn't? Mabel is a peach, a bona fide Georgia peach! Mabel likes almost everyone she meets, and they almost always like her back.

The stepmother-themed material warned Mabel to expect rough patches even so, especially if a prickly tween was in the picture. Especially a prickly female tween, Daddy's little darling.

The stepmother, for example, would cook the stepdaughter's favorite meal, only to find that whatever dish she prepared was stupid and disgusting and all wrong, just like the stepmother. And on and on, until the breakthrough moment when the stepdaughter got her period and needed womanly advice or developed a crush on a boy—or a girl—and couldn't go to her darling, clueless dad about it because, gross!

There'd be laughter. Maybe a few tears. The stepmother would never take the place of the stepdaughter's real mom, and she'd acknowledge this out loud. But she'd wonder (also out loud) if perhaps, one day, the stepdaughter might find it in her heart to think of her as sort of . . . a bonus mom?

Spoiler alert: yes. In the books Mabel read, the stepdaughters and stepmothers always worked things out, feeling their way toward an imperfect relationship that was perfect for them.

Either the books are full of shit, or Mabel isn't the peach she thinks she is. (Also worth noting, ten-year-old Bethany isn't very likable. At least Mabel doesn't think so. And Mabel likes almost everyone!)

She pulls dinner out of the oven: roasted chicken, baby potatoes seasoned with olive oil and salt, and a spinach casserole oozy with sour cream and parmesan cheese. She cheated a little, buying a rotisserie chicken from Whole Foods and shoving the bag in the outside trash bin, but she made the potatoes and spinach casserole from scratch.

Everything looks and smells delicious, and Mabel feels for a moment like a proper wife-slash-stepmom. She steps into the hall and calls, "Suppertime, darling family!"

David emerges first, tromping down from the upstairs office with the slightly disoriented look he wears whenever he's pulled out of his work.

"Hello, gorgeous husband," Mabel says, placing her hand on his cheek and stealing a kiss.

He grins. "Hello, gorgeous wife."

Yes, they're *that* couple. The ones who are just as much in love three years after getting married as they ever were, the ones who communicate constantly through quirked lips and knowing looks, who exchange fleeting touches when passing in the hall.

"Smells great," he says, pulling Mabel's chair out for her.

"Thanks."

They smile at each other. Mabel does a mental countdown, and just on schedule, David sighs and steps back into the hall.

"Bethany!" he calls, because Bethany never comes for Mabel. "Come on downstairs, sweetie!"

At the table, David divides his attention between his wife and his daughter, working hard to create the illusion they're a functioning unit of three. He already knows that Mabel took Bethany to Lee Martinez

Park this afternoon, where there's a small working farm. He also knows that despite Mabel's hopes, but in line with her expectations, the outing was a bust.

Still, he perseveres, saying, "Feeding the goats must have been fun, Bethany. Sounds like you and Mabel had quite an adventure!"

"There was a Frigibax at the railroad crossing," Bethany replies sullenly.

"A Frigibax!" David marvels. "Is that a Pokémon?"

"One of the super rare ones, only *she* wouldn't let me catch it." Bethany jerks her chin at Mabel, in case there was any doubt.

"There was a train," Mabel explains. "The Pokémon was on the other side."

"We could have got there in time if she'd hurried. But *no-oo-o*." Bethany makes the word a dragged-out accusation. "She had to use the bathroom before we left the farm. She had to refresh her *lipstick*."

David's face reddens. He says, "Bethany, don't be rude."

Mabel smiles tightly. If she were a better woman, she would squeeze his thigh beneath the table to say, *Babe, I get it, it's fine*. Only, it's not. She's finding it more and more difficult to forgive her husband for his daughter's insolence.

When Mabel and David first married, Mabel tried too hard with Bethany. When that didn't work, she pulled back, determined to be bland and pleasant if it killed her. (It almost did. Her "bland and pleasant" phase was short-lived.) Mabel has since moved on to actively resenting her darling husband's darling daughter, a petty response if there ever was one. Mabel is the grown-up! Bethany is the child!

Mabel hates herself for not being better. Unfortunately, she hates Bethany, too, for being such a pill.

No, she doesn't.

Yes, she does.

No. She. Doesn't. She throws back a slug of wine and plonks down her glass.

"So," she says to her curdled stepdaughter. "Are you excited to start school?"

Bethany scoffs.

Oh well, I tried, Mabel tells herself.

"I met our new neighbor," she says, turning to David. "She's nice! No kids, just got divorced. She liked my sugar cookies."

"Baby, everyone likes your sugar cookies," David says.

She looks at him fondly. "Aw, my sweet man."

"My sweet woman."

Bethany loudly rolls her eyes. Yes, she is that good.

"I feel like I know her from somewhere," Mabel pushes on. "Her name sounded familiar. Jake Nolan?"

David pauses, his fork halfway to his mouth. "The woman from the charity scandal?"

Bells of recognition ding. #lipservice, is that what David's referring to? It involved babies with cleft lips, as Mabel recalls, and one of the doctors sleeping with one of the organizers behind the other organizer's back . . . ?

Holy shit, the organizer was Jacquelyn "Jake" Nolan.

Mabel's neighbor, Jake, is the woman who got cheated on!

#lipservice was as salacious as #kidneygate for a while, that online drama about a woman who donated a kidney to a stranger and the friends who made fun of her behind her back. But #lipservice was more recent, and though it played out on the national stage, it happened in Mabel's hometown, which made it special.

More details swim to the surface. #lipservice went viral when the person who started the cleft lip charity (Jake!) found out about her husband's affair and threw a big stinking fit, only to be shamed into submission when the mistress told her side of the story, sharing details that turned the narrative upside down.

What unforgivable sin had Jake committed? Mabel can't remember, although she's pretty sure the husband ended up divorcing Jake and riding off into the sunset with the mistress.

Jake was remarkably blasé about it in front of Mabel this afternoon. *Oh, yes. I got divorced and now it's just me, perfectly happy and living by myself.*

Good for Jake, Mabel thinks, because it's nobody's business but her own.

And Mabel's, now that Jake is her neighbor.

Jake, who ate Mabel's cookies. Jake, with her sweet smile and tousled blonde hair, who talked to Mabel about decorative hand towels and overfed squirrels!

"I totally didn't make the #lipservice connection," Mabel says to David.

"She didn't mention it?"

"Would you, if you were in her shoes?"

"Hopefully I never will be."

Mabel pats David's hand. "Of course not. You're a straight arrow."

She assumed Jake was a straight arrow, too. But, considering Jake through this new lens, perhaps there were markers of old wounds after all. A certain wariness in Jake's eyes . . . and what was her comment when Mabel brought up her GoodNeighbors feud?

"I hate the internet," she'd said with flat despondency.

Poor Jake!

David spears a baby potato. "She made some pretty callous remarks about kids with birth defects, as I recall."

"Did she?" Mabel almost asks. She swallows the question, telling herself she'll satiate her curiosity later, when she's alone. She doesn't want David, in his calm and measured way, suggesting she exercise caution in pursuing this new friendship. Whereas David senses drama and stays away, Mabel perks up and scoots closer.

(And if Jake turns out to be bona fide bad news . . . ? Well, Mabel will cross that bridge when she comes to it. *If* she comes to it.)

"The last bungalow won't be vacant much longer," she comments, deftly redirecting the conversation. "A mom and a son are moving in. I'm sure they'll want to get settled before the school year starts. The son's a rising fifth grader at Sweetwater Elementary, same as you, Bethany."

"Who is it?" asks Bethany.

Mabel knows his name from the most recent Sweetwater Bungalow HOA meeting. "Billy Stillson," she says.

Bethany turns the spongy color of paste.

"Do you know him?" David asks.

Now, mottled splotches rise on Bethany's cheeks.

"Hmm," says Mabel. "Might you have a crush on this Billy?"

"No!" Bethany exclaims.

Mabel and David trade glances.

"Stop doing that! Stop looking at each other!" Bethany's chair scrapes the floor as she shoves away from the table. She dashes to the hall, pounds up the stairs, and slams her bedroom door.

David flinches.

Mabel tosses her napkin onto the table. The meal was mainly over, anyway.

"She's just a kid," David apologizes.

"I know."

"She's sensitive."

"I know." Mabel shoos him away, knowing he's anxious to go to her. "Go on. I'll take care of this."

David stands, kisses the top of her head, and says, "No, you won't. You cooked. I'll do the dishes. Promise you'll leave them?"

"Sure, babe," Mabel says—and she means it. She doesn't mind making David suffer a little for Bethany's behavior.

He's up the stairs in a flash, rapping on Bethany's door. It swishes open and is pulled shut, quietly this time.

Mabel falls against the back of her chair, knowing all too well that David is a fool for his needy daughter. Theirs is a thorny relationship, and Mabel, of late, has found herself wondering if David is capable of disentangling himself. Maybe not. The briars are dense.

On David's first day back at work after Bethany's birth—this was before Mabel was on the scene—David's wife called him at 9:15 a.m. and demanded he return home. "The baby" wouldn't stop crying, Gigi told him. "The baby" was driving Gigi crazy.

When David shared this story with Mabel, he said that when he answered Gigi's call, he could hear Bethany in the background, wailing. Then came the thunk of a door, and Bethany's screams were muted. Gigi had gone outside, leaving their infant daughter on her own.

"I've got meetings all morning," David told Gigi, checking his watch and doing frantic mental gymnastics. "I can be out the door by one."

"Come home now, or she won't get fed," Gigi informed him, and then she hung up.

It was an early lesson for David in manipulation and desperation—both Gigi's and his own—and Mabel understands, intellectually, that David has some shit to work through. For that matter, so does Bethany. Gigi moved to New York when Bethany was five, while the divorce was still being finalized. Joint custody was never on the table. Bethany stayed with David because Gigi didn't want her.

Mabel *wants* to want her sulky, sullen, door-slamming stepdaughter, but Bethany's rejection has so far proven an effective roadblock. Mabel and David are both too thin-skinned to push past the brambles, it seems.

She pushes up from the dining room table. She rinses her plate and silverware and loads them into the dishwasher, but leaves the rest for David.

Her thoughts circle back to Jake. Mabel has never met anyone who's been canceled, not until now. It's rather exciting. She grabs her laptop, gets comfy on the sofa, and opens a fresh browser window, eager to do a deep dive on her new neighbor.

4

BILLY

Ten-year-old Billy follows his mother up the front porch stairs of what will soon be their new house. Nanette, the real estate agent, unlocks the heavy front door and ushers them in. This is their "final walk-through." If anything's wrong, now's the time to speak up.

As Nanette jabbers away, Billy moves, dreamlike, from room to room of the house his absentee father is paying for in some complicated way. Billy's mom has dreamy eyes too, because of how fancy everything is. Her bedroom isn't just a bedroom. It's a ground-level master suite with a walk-in closet and a private bathroom with a whirlpool tub and a glass-walled shower with a rainforest showerhead.

They tour the kitchen, the great room, and the office, which has wide windows that look out over the far end of Sweetwater Elementary School's expansive playground. Billy's house is opposite the baseball diamond with its two steel batting cages. There's also a large open field where PE classes are held, a basketball court, and a cluster of brightly colored playground equipment. There's a swing set, a climbing structure, ducks on springs, and a pink plastic playhouse furnished with toadstool chairs and a toadstool table.

"Will you be going to Sweetwater Elementary?" Nanette asks when she sees what Billy is looking at.

"I already do," Billy says.

"Our old house is in the same district," his mom explains. "He'll be a fifth grader! My little boy is growing up!"

She ruffles Billy's hair, and Billy's chest swells. It's the new house, he's sure of it. The *bungalow*. If they'd lived here before, maybe Billy's dad wouldn't have left. Maybe Billy's mom would have had only good days, never bad days, and no need for the basement with the lock on the wrong side of the door.

Billy's mom steps toward the window. She's so pretty, a thousand times prettier than all the other moms. She takes in the row of bungalows and says, "What can you tell me about the neighbors?"

"The woman next door just moved in," Nanette says, consulting her notes. "Single, no kids, *very* pleasant. A retired couple lives one house down, and—that's right." Nanette lifts her head and gives them a gummy smile. "They're having a back-to-school party, and you two are warmly invited."

"Mmm," says Billy's mom.

"Billy, you'll like this," Nanette continues, pulling her finger down the piece of paper. "In the first bungalow is a girl your age. Her name is Bethany, and it looks like she goes to Sweetwater, too."

Billy knows Bethany. She's a shy, awkward girl who was briefly famous when her mom got COVID and had to go to the hospital and be on a ventilator. All the teachers made a big deal of it, even though Bethany's mom lives in New York and Bethany only sees her on holidays. All the kids stood around Bethany, and someone made of video of them saying, "Hi, Bethany's mom! Feel better soon!"

On the day of the video, when Billy got home from school, he sat on the edge of his bed and pressed his hands against his knees. If a father died, that was one thing. A kid could survive without a father. But a mom? Not having a mom would be like putting your eye up to a hole and seeing nothing but darkness. Maybe the hole was a stain on the carpet, or maybe it was leaning too close to the bathroom mirror, but if you fell inside, you could never climb out.

Nanette claps, and Billy startles. "Shall we head downstairs?"

The basement is enormous, with carpeted floors and painted walls and deep-set window wells that let in plenty of sunlight.

"I don't know if you're too old for trains, Billy, but this would be a great space to set up a train track," Nanette says. "Or a game console, if you're into gaming?" She turns to Billy's mom. "Vanessa, you could install a home gym."

"What a great idea!" Billy's mom says. "Billy and I could work out together. What do you say, bud?" Billy imagines the two of them getting super fit and strong. After their workouts, they could high-five each other and drink Gatorade.

"Can we get a bench press? And a treadmill with a screen attached for watching TV?"

His mom wanders farther into the basement. "What's in here?" she asks, opening a door.

"That leads to the storage area." Nanette strides over, her heels leaving pockmarks in the carpet. "It's also where you'll find the water heater and the furnace."

"I see," Billy's mom says from within the room.

"The water heater can be adjusted so that the temperature never rises above a certain point," Nanette says, her voice muffled. She talks and talks, explaining in detail how Billy and his mom will never need to worry about bathwater coming out too hot once they set the dial some special way.

Billy edges toward the staircase. It's not a *bad* basement, this new basement. If they turn it into a gym, it could be a great basement. But they probably won't. His mom gets excited about things and then loses interest.

"I'll be upstairs!" he calls.

"Pop in here first!" Nanette calls back. "I'll show you how to change the HVAC filter, since you'll be the man of the house."

Billy pretends he doesn't hear. He's halfway up the stairs when his mom steps out of the storage area.

"*Billy*," she says.

Billy freezes. Then he turns and jogs back down the stairs. "I'm here, sorry, here I am!"

His mom grabs his elbow. “You do *not* ignore someone when they call you,” she says in her just-for-him voice, low and mean.

“Mom, I’m sorry. Ow!”

She shoves him forward. “Go to and listen to whatever Nanette has to say.”

“Mom, I will. I’m going!”

It’s just a basement, he tells himself, trying to regulate his breathing. *It’s not* the *basement. We’re leaving that basement forever.*

“There you are!” Nanette chirps. She points to things and tells him things, and Billy does his best to take it in. The water heater is curved and white. The furnace is a clean gray rectangle. There are no bowls of dog food. No two-liter bottles of water.

“This here is a hot switch for the lower-level outlets,” Nanette says. She flips a switch, and the windowless room turns black.

Billy backs up fast and bams into the furnace.

“Oh, Billy, I’m sorry,” Nanette says, flipping the lights back on. “I didn’t mean to scare you!”

“You didn’t,” Billy says, trying not to think of cold darkness seeping over hard, white ribs.

Billy’s mom has joined them back in the storage area. Billy sees Nanette shoot her a troubled glance. “Well . . . but . . . do you think you got all that?” she asks him. “Do you need me to go over it again?”

“No, I’m good. I got it all.”

His mother jabs him.

“Thank you for explaining,” he adds.

Nanette beams. “Fantastic! Then I think we’re about done.”

The three of them exit the storage area. As Billy plods upstairs behind the two women, he overhears his mother apologizing on his behalf.

“He’s still afraid of the dark,” she confides.

“Oh dear,” Nanette says. “Well, he’ll grow out of it; don’t you worry.”

“I know. You’re right. It’s just . . . he’s such a big boy, sometimes I forget how little he still is.”

Billy goes to the front room and steadies himself in the afternoon light pouring through the windows. It’s three thirty, and the school bell rings even though it's summer. In Billy's imagination, kids of all shapes and sizes spill from the school doors, a scramble of bodies and hair and shoelaces. They cross the playground, push down the steel fence, and surge across the street. They swarm his front yard and press their faces to the windows of his house.

Something pulses in Billy's throat. Next week school starts, and the playground will be full of sheep.

5

JAKE

Adam and I met at Children's Hospital Colorado. Adam was a resident, and I worked part-time at the hospital gift store during my last semester at the University of Denver.

Me: a fresh-faced twenty-year-old. Adam: a smart, handsome doctor. The power imbalance was there from day one, so maybe our relationship was doomed from the start. Maybe it wasn't Shelby who led to our downfall.

Except it was.

Adam is more to blame than Shelby, yes. Adam broke his vows. Adam did the cheating.

But without Shelby, he'd have had no reason to.

After Adam finished his residency, I dropped out of college and followed him to Fort Collins, where he'd landed a job at Poudre Valley Hospital. Shelby was a drug rep for northern Colorado and joined Adam's social circle soon after we arrived. She showed up for Friday drinks. She frequented our parties. She charmed all of us, glamorous and sexy and unafraid to pair a sheer-white blouse with a jet-black bra.

Shelby was a woman, whereas I was a child, pretending to be a woman. But I wasn't jealous of Shelby, not at first. I was in awe of her, as starry-eyed as a high school freshman trotting behind a worldly senior, happy to carry her backpack or fetch her a bag of Takis from the vending machine.

She taught me how to curl my eyelashes, and that thumb-smeared lipstick worked as well as blush when rubbed across my cheekbones. She pulled me aside at bars and shared the latest doctor gossip. She ordered us Irish car bombs. She said, "Chug! Chug!" When at last I swallowed the dregs, she thrust her fist into the air and cried, "Yes!"

I was an idiot for Shelby, just as I was an idiot for Adam. I see that now. But while Adam recognized my naïveté and found it sweet, Shelby sized me up, smiled her wolfish smile, and used my stupidity against me.

She wanted Adam, and she took him. Fine. It's done.

But she wanted more, so she took more, while I mewled helplessly, belly exposed.

She must have loved it when my email arrived in her inbox, that foolish outreach sent in the depths of my distress. Indifferent to the notion of context, Shelby posted fragments of it online, carefully curated rage bait too salacious to ignore. Then she sat back and watched as the world obeyed her directive. *Condemn Jake Nolan, or be condemned alongside her. Go on, do it. Think of the worst insult you can throw at her, then go one step further. It's fun!*

During the early months of my exile, I hunkered down in my crappy month-to-month rental and moped. I wept and beat my fists against my pillows, which were the wrong pillows, floppy and too soft. The good pillows remained at the Hemlock house, with Adam and Shelby.

As time ticked on, I began to plot—though I remained tucked away in my shitty apartment. To a degree, it was a matter of practicality. The apartment complex was south of Harmony, in a high-density area not developed with pedestrians or bicyclists in mind. If I wanted to return to Hemlock Avenue—to spy, to lurk, to wreak havoc—I'd have to take my car, and once there, I'd have to park my car on the wide, tranquil street.

All of my former neighbors know my bright yellow Beetle. What if someone reported me to Adam and Shelby?

So I bided my time, waiting until I was settled in my Sweetwater bungalow. From my new address, I calculated, it would be an easy bike ride to Adam and Shelby's.

Sure enough, it is. I wheel my bike from the garage, hop on, and within fifteen minutes, I'm in my old neighborhood, the warm air lifting my hair and whipping it about. I glimpse my former house out of the corner of my eyes, but I don't look at it directly. I pedal past, playing hard to get.

One block up, I take a right onto Professor Lee's street, and a second right when I reach the professor's driveway. I park my bike and am welcomed inside within seconds, safe from prying eyes.

"Jake," Professor Lee says warmly. His narrow face breaks into his signature smile, mischievous and delighted, and I catch a peek of the little boy he must have been. He grew up in Malaysia, where he spent his childhood fishing and scaling coconut trees. He's in his eighties now. His movements are stiff and slow. Still, his exuberance for life shines through.

"Come in, come in," he urges. "Look at your rosy cheeks! Would you like some tea? A Coke?"

"A Coke sounds great, thanks," I say, and he nods and shuffles into his 1990s-era kitchen, which has remained the same since his wife died five years ago.

Professor Lee's house is directly behind Adam and Shelby's, his backyard separated from theirs by a three-railed fence. When I lived in this neighborhood, the professor and I chatted daily. We talked about his cat, the weather, how well his tomatoes were growing, that sort of thing. These days, I see him less frequently, but his friendship remains precious. Professor Lee has always treated me with kindness, before the scandal and after. Not once has he made me feel abhorrent.

"So, are you in your new house?" he asks after handing me a glass of Coke poured over ice. He hitches his khakis at the thighs and takes a careful seat on his worn sofa. "How are you adjusting?"

"I'm good, everything's good," I say. I take a sip of soda and scan the room. "How's Cindy Pawford? *Where* is Cindy Pawford?"

Professor Lee chuckles. "She's upset with me for slipping a bit of coltsfoot into her food. I suspect she's under my bed."

Professor Lee is a botanist. He used to teach at the university. Now that he's retired, he spends his time concocting herbal remedies for his elderly cat's various ailments. He also works on his memoir, which is why I'm here.

Well. Which is partially why I'm here.

"Why did you slip coltsfoot into her food?" I ask.

"It's an expectorant. Did you know that?"

I shake my head.

He thumps his chest. "Her breath has been shallow. If there's mucus in her lungs, the coltsfoot will help."

"Ah," I say. I tell him about Lump, which is what I've started calling my unwanted feline friend, and he echoes Mabel's advice to take him to the vet.

"Whatever you do, don't take him to the humane society." He widens his eyes. "They do good work. Don't get me wrong. But if he's not a kitten—"

"He is not a kitten, I guarantee you."

"Then he'll be euthanized."

I change the subject.

We visit for a little longer. When I set down my empty glass, he goes to his office and returns with the new pages he has for me, another chunk of the memoir I doubt will ever be finished.

"You'll like this chapter," he says, tapping the page on top. "It covers the fieldwork I did in my thirties when I returned to the Malay Peninsula."

I trade the pages he gives me for the ones in my satchel, which I've marked up with blue pencil. I'm hardly an editor, but my degree, had I finished, would have been in English. Anyway, Professor Lee doesn't want an editor, even if he thinks he does. He wants an audience, and that I can be.

"I don't know if it can outdo this one," I say. While I correct Professor Lee's grammar errors and make occasional suggestions to trim wordy passages, mostly I fill the margins with smiley faces, exclamation points, and comments suggesting that readers might enjoy knowing more about this plant or that.

I accepted this job before the divorce, before everything. I took a break during my darkest times, but I'm happy to be back. I'm fond of Professor Lee. Plus, he pays me a hundred dollars an hour.

We wrap things up, and I hug Professor Lee goodbye. Outside, I put the unmarked pages in my bike bag. I check to make sure he's retreated into his house and no neighbors are looking my way. Then I cross his backyard, hop the fence, and stroll across my former lawn, head down, hands in pockets, moving quickly.

When I reach the back door, my adrenaline spikes. I know Adam and Shelby aren't here, thanks to the energy monitor Adam installed in the house. As I never showed any interest in his technological toys, Adam never revoked my access.

8:45 A.M., GARAGE DOOR OPENED. 8:47 A.M., GARAGE DOOR SHUT, the app told me. There aren't cameras in the house. That would be creepy. But there's a single security camera above the front door. A quick check of this morning's video clips showed Adam and Shelby departing in Adam's Explorer together.

I am positive I am alone, just me and my former house. I will not be bested by my good-girl nerves.

The key slips into the lock like butter.

6

JAKE

I haven't decided how I'll punish Shelby for casually destroying my life, but I trust that ideas will present themselves. I'll feel my way forward, just as I'm feeling my way through their cluttered mudroom. Shelby's things are strewn everywhere. Messy, messy Shelby.

I step into the brightly lit main room. Everything is white: white sofas, white carpet, white end tables. It's hideous and should be put out of its misery. A glass of red wine would do the trick. But, no. Too glaring. Better to stick to smaller transgressions that Adam will blame on Shelby and Shelby on Adam. Stupid, spineless Adam. Traitorous Adam.

The last time I was in this room—well, not the very last time, but the most memorable of those last times—was the previous fall. It was a year to the day after I'd given birth to our dead son, a date that pulsed in my heart but seemed to have slipped from Adam's memory altogether.

It was a Thursday. Adam asked if I wanted to go to his department's boozy get-together the next day. It would be at the Gilded Goat, a brewery I loved.

"You should come," he said.

I blinked. Was he really asking me to go out drinking on our dead son's birthday?

Adam had developed a new way of looking at me, a sideways glance meant to remind me that here he was, being patient with me again. He gave me that look that evening.

"A beer, Jake," he said, spreading his arms. "I'm asking if you want to have a beer with me tomorrow night, that's all."

"Tomorrow is Liam's birthday," I said. I expected him to go still, to draw in a breath. To be horrified he'd forgotten.

Instead, he sighed and pressed his hands flat on the granite countertop. He said, "Jake. Our son died."

The heat of my glare surged like a flash fire. *Yes, you absolute asshole. I know.*

Adam exited the room, shaking his head.

The next day, he told me he couldn't do this anymore. Be with me. Stay married to me. "I keep telling myself, 'Just a little longer. Don't make things worse.' But that's just it—things *can't* get worse, can they?"

Then, tearfully, he confessed to his affair with Shelby, only he didn't call it that. He told me that he and Shelby had fallen in love. "We didn't mean to," he said. "It was bigger than both of us."

As I stand in this house that used to be mine, I feel ill, not only because of the painful memories. I feel ill at the knowledge that once upon a time, and by my own volition, I was married to a man who cheated on me with my best friend and then described their betrayal, unironically, as "bigger than both of us."

After he announced that he wanted a divorce, he looked at me, waiting for a response. He twisted his wedding ring. He said, "Jake?"

"The first time you fucked Shelby," I said. I watched him hard. "Was it before or after Liam was conceived?"

Adam bowed his head and was silent for long enough that I knew the answer before he voiced it. "When I learned you were pregnant," he said gravely, "I made the choice to give our marriage a second chance."

"So you were fucking Shelby even *before* I got pregnant." My head spun. "When did it start? How long has it been going on? Since you and Shelby first met? Since Shelby and *I* first met?"

"I can't see how those details matter. What matters—"

I barked a laugh. "Oh, tell me. Please. What matters, Adam?"

Adam adopted a martyred air, arranging his features to communicate neutral compassion. No, not compassion, but pity, like what you feel for a crazy person who's weaving down the street and arguing with invisible companions. You think, *Such a shame*, and you hurry to the other side of the street.

I drop onto Adam and Shelby's pristine white sofa, kick off my sneakers, and stretch out. I rest my bare feet on the throw pillow that Shelby, perhaps, tucks beneath her cheek when she naps. I rub my soles up and down, pleased to think of the sloughed-off skin I'm leaving behind.

Did Adam rehearse his trite and formal speech? Did he practice before the mirror to get his forlorn expression just right? And, good Lord, was it intentional, his decision to confess his infidelity on the anniversary of Liam's death? Maybe Shelby planted the idea. She'd have known I'd be an emotional wreck. Did she hope it might be easier for Adam to wash his hands of me if I fell into histrionics?

But, yes. Adam put on his martyred air and said, "At any rate, with a child in the picture—"

"'With a *child* in the picture'?" I repeated. How pompous he was, how pious. "With a child in the picture, you were willing to stick it out. Is that it? Should I congratulate you on being such a stand-up guy?"

"I wanted to be a father," Adam pushed on. "When Liam died—"

"Stop."

"I stuck around, even so. But you, Jake, you opted out. You chose Liam over me."

"Stop it! Stop saying his name!"

Adam shed the martyred air. "Our marriage is dead, Jake. It's time we made it official."

He left for the bar, to down beers with his colleagues. With *Shelby*, who would look at him soulfully and rub circles on his back. "Oh, you poor darling," she'd say, furrowing her perfect brow. "Was it just awful? But you did the right thing. You know you did."

After Adam sped away, a blinding rage consumed me.

I texted him. "You want a divorce? Fine. But don't EVER mention our son again. Liam is not a footnote in your sleazy story."

Next, I pulled up Shelby's Facebook page.

"So here's something I just learned," I typed. "My husband, **Adam Smith**, has been sleeping with **Shelby Bryant** behind my back—and all this time, I thought she was my friend. Are you out there, Shelby? Are you reading this?"

Because you were there for me when I learned Liam was dead, I wanted to say. *You* cried *with me.*

"Anyway, hope you had fun fucking my husband behind my back while I had frozen peas on my breasts," I typed. I hit Send and flung my phone across the room.

Regret crashed down almost instantly. I scrambled for my phone and tried to delete my comment. The comment stayed put. Shelby had already demoted me to "read-only," I'd later learn, which meant I could view her page, but I couldn't post, modify, or delete comments. My rant would remain front and center for days, and reactions were already rolling in.

Shelby, what's going on?

I don't know if you've seen what Jake posted, but you should probably take her comment down. DMing you.

Jake seems really upset, did something happen?

And, of course, a zillion variations of, *Frozen peas? WTF?!!!!*

I'd messed up, but I was unable to acknowledge the error, not on Facebook.

I tried calling. Shelby didn't pick up.

I considered texting, but in the end went with an email, so I'd have more room to explain. Shelby didn't respond, opting instead . . .

Well. I'm a dog returning to its vomit, aren't I?

Shelby cherry-picked bits of my email and shared them on X. "@jakenolan believes that 'people with clefts are ugly, inside and out,'" she posted. "As a person with a cleft myself, I'm really struggling. Why would anyone be so cruel?"

I bark out a laugh as it occurs to me, all these months later, that

Shelby is far better suited to be Professor Lee's editor than I am. She can bend words to her will as easily as snapping her fingers.

She wouldn't have taken the job, though, even if she'd been offered it. She visited the professor with me once, and once was enough.

"I think I'll pass," she said the next time I invited her along.

I'd lifted the bowl full of tomatoes from my garden. (Shelby's garden, now.) "I'm just going to pop over and give him these. It'll take all of ten minutes. You sure you don't want to come?"

"I'm sure, Jake," she said, irritation sharpening her tone.

I blinked. "Why? Don't you like him?"

"He's fine. He's just . . . *old*. He has old man smell." She waved me off with a flap of her hand. "You go. I'll stay here and make cocktails. Adam'll be home soon, yeah?"

And off I skipped, good little Jake with my bloodred tomatoes.

So stop being good, I tell myself, swinging my legs up and off the spotless white sofa. *Be ruthless.*

I prowl the house, more familiar to me than my spanking new Sweetwater bungalow. Shelby is messier than I'd expected, an unfortunate flaw for someone who's chosen an all-white decoration scheme. Cereal boxes have been left on the kitchen counter, and unwashed dishes sit in the sink. Adam's favorite coffee mug is among them, a kitschy gift from a patient that says, *I Knock People Out for a Living.* The sight of it triggers a traitorous prick of tears.

It would be gratifying to smash the mug against the floor, but I don't. Nor do I upend the cereal boxes or go crazy with a bottle of red wine, because they'd be sure to investigate, coming home to a riotous mess like that. They might not be able to prove it was me, but they'd have their suspicions. (And, after all, they *might* be able to prove it was me. Forensic science advances every day.)

I search the cupboard for Shelby's fancy tea, thinking of sprinkling vinegar over those stupid sachets, or salt. Alas, it seems she's over her tea obsession. I do find a tin of gourmet hot chocolate and a bottle of fancy honey; a tall, elegant bottle corked like champagne. I thumb off the sticky cork, lay the bottle on its side, and close the cabinet door.

I climb the stairs, curling my lip at the dust bunnies collected on the steps. Shelby has hung new photos on the wall. One is of her and Adam grinning from a rooftop bar. Another shows the happy couple enjoying a day at the lake. Shelby's wearing a white bikini I know too well, while Adam sports a swimsuit acquired post-divorce. Did Shelby pick it out? It's printed with tiny crabs and doesn't suit him.

I flick each frame, knocking them askew.

In the primary suite, a sure of power courses through me. This is Shelby's inviolate space, and yet here I am, violating it—just as she violated me.

I tour the room, trailing my fingers along Shelby's belongings, the new Shelby-inspired bedding as white and sterile as the décor downstairs. On Adam's nightstand sits an open bottle of lube. I upend it, watch the silicone goo slide out in slow, viscous ribbons. It's not as pretty as the honey, but it makes a satisfying mess.

Small mischiefs are all I allow myself. When guilt creeps in—like after riffling through the ceramic bowl of jewelry on Shelby's side of the bathroom and accidentally sending a diamond earring down the drain—I remind myself: they brought this onto themselves.

It's better this way, I decide. Only one diamond earring gone, not both. Shelby will search and fret, accusing Adam of moving it. Adam, stung by the injustice, will snap back, blaming Shelby for being so careless.

But it gave me a scare, seeing that glittering jewel disappear into the dark mouth of the sink.

I slip out the door and lock up behind me. Shelby may have painted me as a monster, but she hasn't a clue how monstrous I can be.

7

JAKE

On my way home, I cruise by Grandview Cemetery to visit my mother's grave. I lock my bike and set off down a footpath flanked with trees, a rarity in Fort Collins, where everything is either tawny prairie or blue-gray foothills. The cemetery, with its lush landscaping, is the only place in town that comes close to evoking the dense North Carolina woods where I spent my childhood summers.

The forest in Boone wrapped around my dad and Carrie's house like a living thing. It enchanted me, though it could turn moody and menacing in an instant. One moment, cheery sunlight danced on bright leaves; the next, a passing cloud snuffed out the light.

My dad no longer lives in Boone. He took off after he and Carrie split up. I don't know where he is, and I'm not interested in finding out.

By all indications Carrie is still there, as the return address on the birthday cards she sends me hasn't changed in twenty years. How does she stand it? Eating in that kitchen day after day, her gaze pulled to the yard which ends where the forest begins . . .

No.

A right off the main path, then a left, and I'm at the gray headstone engraved with my mother's name. *Nicole Elisabeth Nolan*, it reads, although everyone but my father called her Nikki. He called her Nicole, always, and when I came along, he called me Jacquelyn, never Jake. He had a thing against names he considered trashy. "Nikki" topped the list, up there with "Ricky," "Misty," "Dawn," and "Nevaeh."

"His face, when I suggested we name you that!" my mom told me.

"You thought about naming me *Nevaeh*?" I exclaimed, delighted and horrified. I was seven at the time and obsessed with baby names, having recently learned that Carrie was pregnant and I would soon have a brother.

"I threw Esmerelda into the mix, too. And Maeve."

"Maeve?" My eyes practically popped out, and then I caught on that she was teasing me. "Maeve is not even a name, Mom."

"Oh, it is," she said. She hunted down a well-worn paperback called *A Treasury of Baby Names* and said it was mine to keep, telling me it was the book she'd pored over when she was pregnant with me.

"Nevaeh was the name I campaigned hardest for," she told me. "'Just think, John,' I said. 'Our little girl could be named heaven spelled backward!'"

"Ew!"

My mom laughed. "I was just winding him up. In those days, I still could."

"You couldn't later on?"

She retreated inward for a moment and was gone to me, before pulling herself back with a little laugh.

"There was a time when your father could take a little teasing, before he got it into his head how important he was," she said. The shadows she'd dredged up remained, just behind her irises. "But the real Nevaeh . . . have I ever told you about the real Nevaeh, Jake?"

The "real" Nevaeh went to the same high school as my parents, my mom told me, though she was three grades younger. "And Lord, did she have a crush on your father. Nevaeh thought John walked on water, and John took full advantage of it. He had that girl under his thumb."

As teenagers, my parents were forever breaking up and getting back together. During one of their "off" stretches, my dad and Nevaeh briefly dated.

"Except I'm not sure 'dated' is the right term," my mom said. "It was just . . . it wasn't right. Anything he asked her to do, she did, and I don't mean bussing his lunch tray or cheering for him at his wrestling meets, either."

"What *do* you mean?"

She'd looked surprised, as if she'd temporarily forgotten that I was just a second grader and had no idea what sorts of things a boy might ask a girl to do.

"Nothing, honey. Just, from then on, your dad brought up Nevaeh every time he and I got into a fight. He'd tell me he should have married her instead of me. Said he would have if he'd been able to get past her name."

"That's dumb," I said. I caught my lower lip between my teeth. "And kind of mean, too."

"You know what, sweetheart? It was," my mom said. "But he was just a kid. We both were. We've both done a lot of growing up since then, I'm sure."

I wonder, now, how much my mom knew about what went on at my father's house when I was there without her. All those times she took me to the airport, sending me off to Boone while she stayed here in Fort Collins, did she worry?

I'm sure she did. Only, what could she do? A decree in their divorce agreement stipulated that I spend my summers with him—and anyway, it's not like I told her much about what went on there when I returned to Colorado every August.

I think she tried to warn me about him, in her own way. She tried to leave room for any conversations I might want to have about him, while at the same time not bad-talking him for the sake of bad-talking him. He was my father, after all.

On my way out of the cemetery, I pass a freshly dug grave. It's marked with an aluminum plaque on a flimsy stake, a placeholder until the headstone arrives.

I glance at the name and stop short. *Nolan.*

Chills scuttle up my spine, and the guilt I refused to acknowledge at

Adam and Shelby's house seeps back in. I broke into their home. I messed with their things. I cast Shelby's diamond earring into a watery grave.

Who's dumb and kind of mean now? Who hasn't grown up, apparently, despite pretending otherwise?

It's not a warning, I tell myself. It's not my mother chiding me from the great beyond. I bark a laugh and stride away from that sad, sloping grave marker. There are Nolans everywhere. It's a common name. Nolans are born and die every day, just like the countless John Smiths and Jill Millers scattered across the globe, living their lives without obsessing over when death will come.

I hurry from the graveyard, hopping onto my bike and pumping so hard my quads burn.

8

JAKE

My neighbors, Todd and Lisa, are sitting on their front porch when I get home.

"Jake! Hello!" calls Todd, who has a fondness for Hawaiian shirts and what I assume is whiskey. He's got some in a lowball, which he lifts to me in a toast. Lisa is drinking rosé from a large bowl of a glass. She smiles at me.

"Hi, you two," I call back.

"We heard foxes last night," Todd says. "Did you?"

I hop off my bike and wheel it closer, keeping my hands firmly on the handlebars. With any luck, Todd and Lisa won't invite me to join them—or won't expect me to say yes if they do.

"Foxes?" I say. "I don't think so."

"Lisa thought it was a lady screaming," Todd says. He nudges Lisa's shoulder. "Didn't you, Lise?"

Lisa is large and lovely, with a thick gray braid and colorful earrings. "It scared me!" she says. "I thought, 'Should I go to her? Does she need help?'"

"It was only a fox," Todd says. "Or foxes, plural."

"Says you!"

Todd chuckles. "Trust me, Lise. Those were screams of pleasure."

My smile is growing rubbery. I start up the driveway with my bike. "Welp, see ya!"

"You bet!" Todd says. "Our party on Sunday—you'll be there?"

I give him a thumbs-up. My bike wobbles and my hand flies back to grab it.

Inside, I fuel myself with a handful of salted almonds, then grab a shot glass and open the cabinet above my fridge, perusing my limited selection of alcohol. Todd and Lisa have inspired me. I select a bottle of Suerte and wiggle free the cork. I tried for a time to give up tequila, because I can't think of tequila without thinking of Shelby, who once upon a time was a "shot girl" for Tequila Arrojó.

But I like tequila, and Shelby has already taken so much from me. So I buy Suerte, Herradura, or Patrón—never Arrojó—and label my habit defiance.

There's unpacking to be done, but I'm not in the right headspace.

It's not because of the cemetery—or the "breaking and entering," which is putting too fine a name on it. I broke nothing (did I?), and I entered with a key. Still, distraction is what I want, not long stretches of emptying boxes while my thoughts are left untended, free to poke around in dark corners.

I settle onto the front room sofa, wake up my phone, and open GoodNeighbors, the battleground where Mabel and her nemesis wage war. WarriorMom, Mabel called her.

Mabel assumes I'm not on GoodNeighbors, but I most certainly am. GoodNeighbors, Facebook, Instagram—I'm everywhere. I'm just no longer Jake Nolan. Who in their right mind would want to be Jake Nolan?

I killed my pre-scandal accounts and created new ones, using an identity I bought on the dark web. A hundred bucks got me a profile photo of a cute brunette, a handful of candids for credibility, a phone number, and a linked email address. Enough to jump through all the verification hoops. It was as simple as child's play, my first foray into illicit behavior.

Lola DuBois has twenty notifications on GoodNeighbors, none of which have the slightest thing to do with me. Or Lola.

HANNA KORF'S POST IS TRENDING:
IS IT NORMAL TO SEE MARMOTS IN TOWN?

RACHEL MCENTEE AND TWO OTHERS
POSTED TOP STORIES IN YOUR DIGEST.

That sort of thing.

I type "Miss Manners" into the search bar, but my attention is pulled elsewhere before I hit Enter. From outside comes the rumble of a large vehicle, followed by the bang of doors and the rise of male voices. I lower my phone and lean forward. Down the street, slightly to my right, a white truck with *Little Guys Movers* painted on the side is parked at the curb.

I pad to the window overlooking my front porch. Craning my neck, I lean forward to catch a view of my new neighbor's house. From this angle, I can see the walkway that leads to her porch and a sliver of her driveway, which runs between our houses.

The moving van is parked on the street. On the sidewalk stands a woman with a ponytail, one arm folded over her ribs, the other gesturing as she gives directions.

This must be Vanessa, the single mom. Next to her is a sturdy boy, his thumbs hooked through his belt loops—Billy, a rising fifth grader, just like Mabel's stepdaughter.

The movers heave a bed frame up the porch stairs, and Vanessa winces as a corner scrapes the railing. She calls out to the two men, punctuating her remarks with angry eyebrows. The movers set down the frame. One says something to Vanessa. The other lifts his hands in exasperation, as if to say, *Lady, c'mon. We're doing our best here.*

Billy gives his mother a worried frown. Vanessa shakes her head impatiently.

The unloading continues. An upholstered chair. A vanity. A full-length mirror.

I return to the sofa, where I take a sip of tequila and resettle myself. Keeping half an eye on the goings-on next door, I pick up where I left off, launching my search for Mabel's online moniker. A long list of posts presents itself, going back years. I click on one at random.

Miss Manners
Anyone know where cake decorating classes are offered? I've checked Michaels, but no luck.

I try another.

Miss Manners
Need a recommendation for a good HVAC company. Thx!

Outside, a mover pulls a paddleboard from the back of the truck. It's pale blue with a purple elephant painted on the front, stylized with the intricate diamonds and dots of a henna drawing. I'd find it lovely, if I liked paddleboarding.

Shelby likes paddleboarding. All summer long, she posted endless pictures of herself in that infernal white bikini, paddleboarding on Horsetooth Reservoir. (Using my real name, I can't access Shelby's social media accounts, but as Lola, I can hate-stalk Shelby all I want. Lola and Shelby are "friends," a conquest that took such little effort as to be slightly disappointing. I started on the fringes of her friend group, connecting first with those whose accounts weren't private. I left comment after comment, all of them relentlessly positive. "OMG OBSESSED," for example, about one woman's new jacket. "#jelly!" on another woman's pics from Costa Rica. Once my friend group overlapped significantly with hers, I put in a friend request. It took all of a day before my request was granted.)

In the real world, before the scandal, I complimented Shelby's white bikini. "Dang, Shelby, you look *amazing*," I said. "If I wore a strapless bikini, the top would slide right off."

"Oh, Jake, you're sweet. But you do *not* want big boobs, believe me," she replied. She regarded her full, round breasts, then shifted her gaze to my chest, flat as it ever was. "I'd rather have no tits than big tits, I'm not even kidding. You have no idea how much staring I have to put up with."

I pour myself a second shot of tequila. Mabel, I see, has weighed in on a variety of topics over the last few months, from where to get the best Mexican food in Fort Collins—Buena Vida, I concur—to how she feels about roundabouts. Mabel thinks they're great, but that people need to slow down. I find them terrifying and am never sure of the blinker etiquette.

I spot a slew of exclamation marks and sit taller. I've found Mabel's first spat with WarriorMom. It played out last fall when another neighbor launched a debate about whether college kids should be allowed to go trick-or-treating. Mabel said sure, as long as the college kids were respectful and deferred to the "little ones." WarriorMom was of the opposite opinion. "Halloween is for kids, not teens and young adults," she posted. "College kids are TOO OLD!"

Mabel retorted with, "Buzzkill!" But she included ten laughing-crying faces, presumably to let WarriorMom know she was teasing. Or *kind* of teasing?

I scroll and scroll, finding a whole lot of nothing until December, when a woman named Maria posted that Big Al's Trees would be accepting old Christmas trees in their parking lot from December 26 on and that her twelve-year-old niece was running an apple cider cart if anyone wanted to stop by.

"Oops!" Maria said in a follow-up post. "Her pronouns are they/them now, so I guess not a niece! Still, great apple cider!"

And then. *Ooh-wee.* I can see from the thread that Mabel and WarriorMom are about to go at it.

A tiny voice in the back of my head says, *Really? You, of all people, are going to take pleasure in their online spat?*

Hell yeah, I am. I'm going to schadenfreude the hell out of their online spat.

WarriorMom

Are your niece's parents okay with this? Please tell me they're not.

Miss Manners (aka Strawberry Shortcake, aka Mabel)
The apple cider or they/them?

WarriorMom
If the child is a girl, then she's a girl, end of story.

Miss Manners
Let people use whatever pronouns they want. If it were my daughter, I'd support her/their choices.

WarriorMom
Oh, sweetie. You'd probably support her "choice" to run wild in a restaurant, too, wouldn't you?

Miss Manners
You don't know me, sweetie, so please don't comment on my parenting.

WarriorMom
Sweetie, I'll say whatever I like.

Miss Manners
Just like you'll say whatever you like about someone else's gender? Sweetie?

Two women trying to out-sweetie the other? *Le cringe.*

From that point forward, WarriorMom made sure to comment on all of Mabel's posts, and vice versa. They're both ridiculous, but WarriorMom is more so. When Miss Manners—or rather, Mabel—lands a good hit, I laugh out loud.

I don't know how long I'm at it before I realize the sun is sinking low and the Little Guys van is gone—Vanessa and Billy, too. What snaps me back to reality is a flash of color and movement.

It's Mabel.

She's outside my house.

No—she's past my house, climbing Vanessa's porch stairs with yet another plate of cookies. Today she's paired a lime-colored blouse with tailored gray trousers. If I ever manage to grow up for real, I'll beg Mabel to be my stylist.

I unfold my legs and return to the window just as Vanessa opens her front door, looking harried and none too pleased. Mabel smiles brightly, launching into what must be an introduction. She lifts the plate of cookies like a prized show-and-tell item.

Vanessa cuts the air with her hands in a sharp X. Mabel hesitates, then steps closer, extending the plate with a hopeful smile. Vanessa speaks quickly and shakes her head—an unmistakable no—then shuts the door in Mabel's face.

I'm sorry, what?

Uncool, new neighbor.

I go to my own door and open it before giving myself time to think. "Mabel! Hi!" I call out, as if I just happened to spot her.

Mabel hastens down Vanessa's porch steps and walks quickly toward me. Her face is bright red. "Oh. Jake. Hi!"

She peels off the sidewalk and heads up my walkway. "Vanessa, our new neighbor, just informed me that a diet high in cookies leads to excess belly fat."

"No," I say.

"Oh, she did. Believe me." There's outrage in Mabel's voice, but beneath it, I detect a tremble.

Also, she's mounting my steps. She's coming straight toward me with a plate stacked high with sugar cookies.

"She told me they lead to type 2 diabetes as well as heart disease," she says grimly. "She basically said that cookies are the handiwork of Satan."

"I . . . disagree," I say.

"Good!" Mabel says, thrusting the plate into my hands. If not for the Saran Wrap, the cookies would have gone flying. "Because it turns out these are for you. Surprise!"

9

MABEL

"Do I get to keep her plate, too?" Jake says when she accepts Mabel's cookies.

"*Her* plate? That, my friend, is *your* plate now."

Mabel tries to shake off Vanessa's toxicity. *Excess belly fat, my ass*, she thinks. Mabel knows she has excess belly fat. Most days, Mabel feels fond of her excess belly fat.

Not when it's pointed out by her new neighbor on the occasion of a friendly pop-by, when Mabel's sole goal was to welcome the new neighbor into the fucking neighborhood.

"You okay?" Jake asks.

Mabel spots an open bottle of tequila on Jake's coffee table. "Can I waterfall it?"

"What's 'waterfalling'?"

Mabel pours a swig of tequila into her mouth, careful not to let the bottle touch her lips. "Thank you," she says as its warmth spreads through her. "And what I just did, that's waterfalling. It's big among ten-year-olds."

"Waterfalling tequila?"

Mabel laughs and waterfalls another healthy sip, returning the bottle to the coffee table a little too roughly. "Sorry."

Jake gestures at the couch. "Sit. Please. I'll get you a glass."

"Ooh, fancy."

Jake heads for the kitchen, and Mabel drops onto the sofa. She slips out of her sandals and props her feet on the coffee table. Then she lowers her feet to the floor, because ladies don't put their bare toes on other people's furniture. Not that Mabel is a lady.

Jake returns with a second shot glass, as well as two San Pellegrinos. She tops off her own glass with tequila and fills Mabel's to the brim. "What just happened?" she asks, indicating Vanessa's house with a head tilt. "Did Vanessa honestly slam the door in your face?"

"Yes! She really, really did!" Mabel exclaims. She pauses. "Wait. Were you *spying* on us?"

Jake makes as if to protest, then grins. "It got me bonus cookies, not to mention a gorgeous artisanal plate."

Mabel tosses back the tequila Jake gave her, her third shot in as many minutes. Why not? David took Bethany to Target to shop for school supplies, and afterward, the two of them are going out to dinner.

"Join us," David suggested. "You could come with us to Target, and then dinner afterward, or you could meet us just for dinner if you'd rather? You could even meet us at the restaurant."

"You're sweet, but no," Mabel replied. "Make it a daddy-daughter night, just you and Bethany."

"Are you sure?"

She grazed the side of his face with the back of her hand. "Positive."

Jake refills Mabel's glass—glug, glug, glug—and Mabel comes back to the present.

"Walk me through it," Jake prompts. "You went to our new neighbor's house, cookies in hand. You knocked on the door. Then what?"

Mabel harrumphs. "I introduced myself and told her which house was mine, and she—Vanessa—pursed her lips and said, 'I know the one. You need to wash your entryway.'"

Jake does a spit take.

"She's not wrong," Mabel allows. "But who says something like that, right off the bat?"

"Not me."

"I did my best to recover, because: manners. I offered her the cookies—"

"The delicious cookies."

"The delicious *homemade* cookies—"

"Lovingly arranged on the artisanal ceramic plate."

"Exactly!" Mabel says. She describes the head-to-toe appraisal Vanessa gave her, the judgment in Vanessa's eyes taking Mabel back to seventh grade PE, when a girl named Julia recoiled at the sight of Mabel in her bra and panties. Even then, Mabel was pleasantly plump.

"And then she refused the cookies you brought her," Jake marvels. "She actually said, 'No, I do not want those delicious cookies you delivered straight to my door.' Even if she didn't want them, why not just accept them and dump them in the trash after you left?"

Mabel makes an indignant sound.

"Or give them to her son!" Jake amends.

"Good point. She could have given the delicious cookies to her son."

"She *should* have given the delicious cookies to her son. Kids like cookies. Fact."

"Do you know who Vanessa reminded me of?"

"Oscar the Grouch?"

"Ha. Yes. And also my husband's ex, Gigi."

"Oh dear," Jake says. She tops off both their tequilas. "Out with it, then. Tell me about Gigi."

Mabel pulls a face. "She's Italian and flamboyant and charming. She's also ridiculously beautiful."

"Huh. I don't think Vanessa is Italian, flamboyant, *or* charming."

Mabel purses her lips. "She could be part Italian."

"True."

"But the Italian part isn't the problem."

"What is the problem?"

"With Gigi? For starters, Bethany idolizes her, even though she only sees her every other holiday and for six weeks in the summer. Which they spend in New York, by the way. Manhattan. Gigi owns an art gallery."

"Your husband's ex is a charming and beautiful Italian woman with an art gallery? Unacceptable!"

"She's convinced we're not exposing Bethany to enough culture. She wants Bethany to grow up going to the *the-ah-tah*."

"In Fort Collins?"

"She wants David to sign her up for voice lessons, ballet, drama, you name it. Bethany has zero interest, but Gigi insists that Bethany is a child and, therefore, her opinions don't count."

"Good luck with that," Jake says. She untwists the cap from one of the sparkling waters and hands the bottle to Mabel. "How does David handle all this? Does he stand up for Bethany?"

Loyalty keeps Mabel from telling Jake how dysfunctional David and Gigi's relationship is, not only when he and Gigi were married, but as co-parents to this day. Gigi likes to push David's buttons. Gigi needles him, on purpose, much like Vanessa tried (and succeeded) in needling Mabel with the belly fat business.

"He does stand up for Bethany," Mabel finally says, "but even so, Gigi's . . . a lot. She thinks Bethany needs braces, which she doesn't. She thinks Bethany needs glasses, which she doesn't. But if David doesn't schedule Bethany for every appointment Gigi wants her to go to, Gigi does her best to turn Bethany against him. Like, Bethany will say, 'Mommy says you don't care about my health,' and David will say, 'Honey, of course I do.' And Bethany will say, 'Okay, but Mommy does care, which is why you need to take me to see the orthodontist *this month*. Okay, Daddy? I have *a serious underbite*. If I don't get it corrected, my enamel will crack and I'll get really, really bad headaches and probably *die*, all because you don't care as much as Mommy does!'"

Mabel hears herself and breaks off. "Anyway," she says sheepishly.

"Does Bethany have an underbite?" Jake asks. She experiments, jutting out her jaw so that her lower teeth extend farther than the upper ones. "If she does, wouldn't you know?"

"Yes, we would, and no, she doesn't."

"How does Gigi feel about you?"

Mabel snorts. "She's not a fan. 'Mommy says it's bad to spray perfume on your hair,' Bethany tells me. 'She says that's why your ends are so damaged.' Or 'Mommy says it's bad to eat before bed. After seven o'clock, you should only have water.' This morning, Bethany said, 'You know, Mabel, if you want to hide your cankles, you should wear pants. Mommy said I should tell you.'"

"No."

"Yes."

Jake's eyes flit to Mabel's trousers. Mabel tucks her feet under her thighs.

"Please pretend you have no idea why I chose pants today, and please don't check to see if I have cankles. I do." Keeping her legs folded beneath her like a mermaid, Mabel executes a hip swivel so that she's facing Jake on the sofa. "Yes, I'm mental. I'm aware. It just sucks, that feeling of being judged. You know?"

Jake gives Mabel a pained smile. "I do."

Mabel remains in her bubble of self-pity—which, thanks to the tequila, is rather pleasant—for another self-indulgent moment. Then she remembers whom she's talking to. She blinks and says, "Oh. Shit."

Jake's smile gives way to resignation. "You Googled me?"

Mabel nods reluctantly.

"Any chance I could tell you my side of the story?"

Mabel is irritated to have put herself in this situation and irritated to be muzzy-headed from tequila. She can't blame Jake, though. Vanessa made her feel foolish, and Jake flung her door wide open and offered kindness and a sympathetic ear. Of course, Mabel came in. Of course, she allowed Jake to comfort her. *Oh, you poor thing. Vanessa sucks. We hate her, that cow!*

Now Jake is perfectly positioned to ask the same of her. *Oh, you poor thing,* Mabel will be expected to say. *They're evil, those people who criticized you online. We hate them! They suck!*

She wishes she hadn't done a refresher on #lipservice after all. It had seemed scandalous in a fun way, when David reminded her why Jake's name was familiar. The infamous Jake Nolan, living just down the street!

But what Jake did—insulting people with birth defects . . .

Jake's anxious eyes settle on her, wide and pleading. Sitting criss-cross-applesauce on the sofa, clutching her shins and rocking slightly, she looks like a child. Mabel doesn't want to sympathize. She knows she shouldn't. But if she lets Jake explain, she probably will. And when she does, will that implicate her by association?

She stands abruptly, scooping up her sandals. "Of course, you can tell me your side!" she says, her voice too bright, too forced. A rush of tiny sunspots assaults her. "But let's save it for another day? I have *so* much to do, I can't even tell you."

"Got it," Jake says with a tired smile.

Mabel edges toward the door, monitoring Jake's expression as it morphs into confusion. No, not confusion. Nausea.

Mabel's stomach ripples in uneasy sympathy.

Jake hunches forward, arm clutched to her abdomen. "Oh God. I'm going to throw up."

Mabel's palm flies out like a stop sign. "No, no, no!" she exclaims, her voice threaded with panic. "Do *not* throw up, Jake. If you do, I will."

Jake untangles herself from the couch, hand clasped to her mouth. Mabel searches wildly for a trash can, a bucket, a vase.

San Pellegrino! Mabel grabs a bottle and forces it on Jake. "Drink!"

Jake does, a sheen of sweat coating her forehead.

"Good," Mabel says. She drops her sandals and guides Jake back onto the sofa. "I'll get you more water—and a throw-up bowl, just in case."

Mabel, cursed with a hair-trigger vomit reflex, grew up having throw-up bowls thrust upon her. She understands the urgency. She bangs around in Jake's kitchen until she finds a stainless-steel mixing bowl, which she plants in Jake's lap. She secures it with Jake's hand, curving her fingers around the rim and pressing them there to make them stick.

"I didn't do that to make you stay," Jake says pathetically.

"Sweetie, of course not."

"As impressive as that would be, I'm not able to vomit on command."

"Please don't say the word 'vomit.'"

"Sorry," Jake says. "I might, though. It might just slip out, the word or actual vomit."

"Jake!"

"Unless . . . I talk about something else?" Jake says pitifully, looking up at Mabel from beneath her lashes.

Mabel rubs her temples with her thumb and forefinger. When she sits, she does so gently, careful not to jostle Jake.

"Fine," she groans. "#lipservice, the Jake Nolan version. Spill."

10

JAKE

I've told no one the full story. At first, it was because the online attacks flattened me. After being steamrolled, the temptation to stay buried in the muck was irresistible.

As the furor faded, I stayed quiet, afraid to reawaken the Kraken. People had moved on, finally. I didn't want them rushing back.

So why Mabel? Why now? Partly, it's the tequila. But also . . . I like my new neighbor. I want her to like me back. How can she, though? It's hard to like someone you're supposed to despise, especially when the only story out there justifies the hate.

I start off slowly, and the old sick feeling comes back inside me. As the details come back, I pick up momentum, and soon the story tumbles out of its own accord.

Before Shelby came along, I tell Mabel, Adam and I fit well together. We were a good match, or so I thought. True, I wasn't a college graduate like he was. I dropped out of the University of Denver when I moved with him to Fort Collins. But Adam didn't seem bothered by that distinction, so I tried not to be, either.

Was that the first sign I missed? "Someone who loves you should lift you up, not push you down," my mom once said, not wanting me to make the same mistakes she did. I convinced myself that Adam *was* lifting me up; that instead of pressuring me to go back to school, he accepted me for who I was. Only later did I wonder if he actively liked my lack of status. Not having a career of my own meant I could make a career out of him.

"Waitressing? Really?" Adam said when he came home to find me filling out online restaurant applications.

"I've got to do something," I told him. I hadn't been jobless since I was fifteen. "If I get in at the right restaurant, I can make good money."

"I make enough money for both of us," Adam pointed out. "And you're already doing something. You're taking care of me."

So we played house. It was fun. In the mornings, Adam marched off to work. In the evenings, after a day that involved laundry and dishes but also lazy hours napping or reading in the hammock, I greeted him at the door with a cocktail, a ritual Adam loved. He said I made him feel like a king.

When he grabbed me by the waist and growled, "Come here, woman," before kissing me and cupping my ass, I felt less like a queen than a feisty tavern wench, but I didn't care. I liked being a feisty tavern wench.

When Adam invited colleagues to the house, I gave them the same royal treatment, throwing parties that gained legendary status. That's how I met Shelby, all boobs and hips and tiny waist. I caught Adam admiring Shelby's cleavage, but all the men admired Shelby's cleavage, along with most of the women.

At the end of that party, on the evening Shelby and I first met, Shelby stayed after the other guests left. She helped me clean up, and we chatted and laughed as we cleared the dishes and washed the champagne flutes by hand.

"I like her," I told Adam when it was just the two of us and we were cuddled up in bed.

"Who? Shelby?"

"At first, I wasn't sure. But that was just me feeling inadequate, because she's so drop-dead gorgeous."

"Mmm," Adam commented.

"She is, don't you think? Drop-dead gorgeous?"

"Not compared to you," he said obediently.

I burst out laughing. "Oh, Adam," I said, climbing on top of him and straddling his waist. "Just remember that as gorgeous as she is, my boobs are the ones you come home to. Got it, mister?"

"That's 'doctor' to you, young lady."

"*Doctor*," I repeated. I took his hands and guided them under my T-shirt. "Are you going to show me that bedside manner you're so famous for?"

Soon after, I started volunteering at the Brahman Foundation, a local nonprofit. Nothing fancy, just ten hours a week, helping to match Fort Collins residents with community resources like the food bank and Crossroads Safehouse.

"Jake, you're such a better person than me," Shelby lamented one night over margaritas at the Rio. She, Adam, and I had formed a comfortable friendship. We had dinner and drinks at least once a week.

"My biggest contribution to the world," she went on, "has been providing people with two things." She counted them on her thumb and forefinger. "Booze and drugs."

"Booze?" I said.

"Which, to be fair, isn't *un*important," Shelby acknowledged. "But one day, I'd like to do something a little more meaningful."

Adam leaned back in his chair and fiddled with the saltshaker, tapping it against the edge of the table. "Drugs, sure. You're in sales. You distribute samples. When do you provide people with alcohol? Are you a bootlegger on your days off?"

Shelby laughed. She grabbed a chip, licked it, and held it out, gesturing for Adam to sprinkle it with salt. He did, and she popped it into her mouth. "I used to be a shot girl."

"What's a shot girl?" Adam asked.

"Someone who goes to bars and passes out free shots. In my case, Tequila Arrojó."

"Did you wear one of those holsters filled with shot glasses?" I asked. "Please tell me you wore a holster filled with shot glasses."

"Obviously," Shelby said. "Tank top, holster, and a microskirt that barely covered my coochie." She swung out one leg and traced a line high on her thigh to show us. As her skirt slid up, her bra strap slipped down. She lazily pushed it back in place.

"I told my parents I was in marketing," she said. "Which was kind of true? I mean, I have the same job now, just with a different title and better clothes."

She grabbed another chip, this time holding it out for me to lick. Giggling, I did. She plucked the saltshaker from Adam's hand and salted it, and when she placed the chip salt-side down on my tongue, my chest expanded with a tight, fierce joy. This beautiful creature was my friend, or rather *our* friend, because Adam and I were a couple. A unit. Together, we'd taken Shelby under our wing.

I found out about Shelby's cleft lip on a rare night in, the three of us squeezed onto our one semi-nice sofa (a sofa long gone, now that Shelby's in charge of the manor). We were eating pizza, drinking beer, and talking through the movie we were supposedly watching, an old film in which Joaquin Phoenix played the role of Johnny Cash.

"He's got the whole brooding thing down, doesn't he?" I said, tilting my head and studying the actor.

"'Brooding,'" Shelby scoffed. She picked at a thread on the sofa. "Just because someone's tormented doesn't make them special, Jake."

I'd learned by then that Shelby wasn't always sly smiles and dancing eyes. She could be prickly, even mean.

My father was a mean man. When I was little, one sharp word was all it took to bring me into line. As I grew up, I'd gotten better at holding my ground, and in certain situations doing so felt nearly compulsory. I'd failed when I was a kid, but I was a kid no longer.

"I never said he was tormented or special," I said evenly. I tapped a spot above my lip. "It's his scar. It makes him look mad, even when he's not."

"How do you know if he's mad or not?" Shelby shot back. "And it's not a scar. It's a microform cleft lip."

"Really?"

"*Really*," Shelby said, doubling down on the sarcasm. "I know because I have one, too."

My eyes dropped to Shelby's mouth. So did Adam's. When I squinted, I could make out a tiny white scar above her upper lip. "Aw," I said, "it's cute!"

Shelby leaned back on the sofa and crossed her arms over her chest. "Comments like that are pretty patronizing, actually."

Heat rushed to my face, because somehow the tables had been turned. Now I was the one being mean. "Shelby, I'm so sorry!" I stammered. "I didn't know."

Shelby didn't relent. "It's something I'm self-conscious about, all right?"

"Don't be," Adam proclaimed. He grabbed a beer, popped it open, and handed it to her. "Chicks with scars are sexy."

Later, I hated myself for being so blind. Adam called Shelby "sexy" right in front of me, and I felt grateful to him for smoothing over an awkward moment. As for Shelby, she blasted me for being patronizing, then simpered and cooed when Adam jumped to rescue her. How was calling a scar "sexy" better than calling it "cute?" How was it anything but patronizing for Adam to police Shelby's emotions and call her a "chick," all in the same breath?

But that's how it started. That's how I got the idea for Miles of Smiles. I educated myself about cleft lips and palates. I learned to call a cleft lip a condition, not a birth defect or a deformity. I learned that being born with such a condition affected more than a kid's self-esteem, presenting challenges both with eating and speaking.

My research also taught me that children born with clefts in poorer countries were far less likely to get the surgeries they needed than children in America.

"Let's do something about it," I said to Shelby, after sharing my new knowledge. I was still desperate to make amends. "You said you wanted to do something meaningful. Why not this?"

Shelby, by then, was over her mood. She pronounced herself all in, and we hammered out the details of our nonprofit. I suggested a partnership between the Brahman Foundation and Tequila Arrojó, whose tequila a younger Shelby had peddled in crotch-high skirts and dramatic black eyeliner. We outlined a plan to send a team of American doctors to Guadalajara, where they would train local doctors to perform cleft lip and palate surgeries. Both the Brahman Foundation and Tequila Arrojó signed on, and Miles of Smiles was born.

I didn't go to Guadalajara for the inaugural trip. Adam went, as the team anesthesiologist. Shelby went too, as an Arrojó brand ambassador. I could have gone, but the prospect of being on my own for a week, free to do whatever I pleased, filled me with exhilaration.

In hindsight, my reaction warranted more scrutiny. But at the time, I convinced myself it wasn't about needing space from Adam—it was about needing space for myself, with no one to care for but me.

"You guys are going to have a *blast*. It's going to be amazing!" I exclaimed when my giddiness rose up and overflowed. Then, not wanting to hurt Adam's feelings, I threw my arms around him and added, "But I'm going to miss you so, so much!"

Adam professed that should a business trip ever separate a husband and wife—this was age-old wisdom, he claimed—the wife should make a point of having sex with her husband the night before his departure. "At least a blow job," Adam had recited with little-boy innocence. "It says so in the Bible."

"Is that before or after 'Thou Shalt Also Tend to Thy Husband with Birthday Sex, or at Least a Blow Job'?" I inquired.

Still, the night Adam left for Guadalajara, I slipped off my panties and T-shirt and let Adam take me from behind, the way he liked. Did he get a thrill out of having sex with two women—one his wife, one his mistress? Or was it a smokescreen, a way to keep me from growing suspicious?

As Adam moved inside me, I thought about having the house to myself in the days ahead. When I moaned, I let him believe it was because of him.

The next morning, he kissed my forehead before leaving to pick up Shelby, who was catching a ride with him to the airport.

"Don't get into trouble while I'm gone," he said.

"You neither," I teased. "I made Shelby promise to keep an eye on you."

Three weeks later, I found out I was pregnant.

11

JAKE

When I reach this part of the story, my throat closes, and a salty thickness makes it hard to take full breaths.

"You don't have to tell me," Mabel says. She's soft and vague, no more dangerous than a throw pillow as long as I don't look at her directly.

"No, I want to," I say. I put aside the metal mixing bowl I've been holding. I'm no longer afraid of throwing up, but of keeping it all within.

I tell Mabel about the complications in my pregnancy, Liam's stillbirth, and the depression that followed. I tell her about Adam announcing that he wanted a divorce on what would have been Liam's first birthday, had Liam lived.

"I don't blame Shelby for Adam's infidelity," I say. "That's on Adam. But Shelby hurt me. A lot. When I posted that comment on her Facebook page, it was because I wanted to hurt her in return." I draw my legs to my chest. "It wasn't my greatest moment."

"I had no idea," Mabel says. "Some of the pieces I'd put together, but . . ." She whistles. "That's really shitty, Jake."

Outside, the evening sky is purple, turning the school playground grainy and dim. The shadows thrown by the swing set resemble long, bony fingers. I grab my phone, open Gmail, and type Shelby's name into the search bar. I offer it to Mabel, saying, "This is the email I sent Shelby."

Mabel looks uncertain. "You want me to read it?"

I nod.

Warily, she accepts the phone. I stand, needing to create space between us, and go to the hall bathroom. I brace my palms on the sink, and my reflection stares back at me, a ghost with pallid skin.

I close my eyes, and the roaring in my head sends me back to the summer of my eleventh year, to my dad and Carrie's house in North Carolina. The oppressive forest bearing down, the suck of the creek, the line of emergency vehicles approaching on the gravel road, sirens blaring. Four cop cars, two fire trucks, and an ambulance. The ambulance was white, emblazoned with a red stripe and a blue star. Toby would have loved it.

When they left, it was with sirens silenced, a funeral procession in advance of the funeral.

I open my eyes and name my dread. *Please don't let Mabel feel sorry for me. When I return to the living room, don't let there be pity on her face.*

I don't want her pity. I want her to be on my side.

12

MABEL

Mabel sits on Jake's sofa, holding Jake's phone. She feels like she's holding Monica Lewinsky's dress, that infamous blue dress stained with shame.

Or is that Mabel's conscience talking? *Whatever Jake did, you're just as bad.*

Because of David, and Gigi, and oh Lord, Mabel can't leave Bethany off the list. Does Bethany know the role Mabel played in her parents' divorce? Is that why she refuses to let Mabel get close? Or is Mabel's guilt sufficient unto itself, erecting a wall that blocks her from her stepdaughter day after day?

It's not the same, she tells herself. Mabel is neither Jake nor Shelby, and regardless, Gigi *was* a villain. Gigi deserved to be ousted from her castle. (But surely every "other woman" tells herself that?) (Then again, the stories David has shared! Like how he would return from work to find Bethany wailing in her crib, her diaper sodden and heavy, while Gigi binged *The Kardashians*. She watched it on her iPad, wearing AirPods to block out her daughter's sobs.)

Mabel focuses on Jake's phone, thumbing the screen to keep it awake. She squints at the jumble of squiggles until they resemble words.

Dear Shelby,

I shouldn't have left that comment on your Facebook page. I shouldn't have taken my private pain and made it public. But Shelby . . . what the fuck?!

When Adam and I first learned about Liam's heart defect, you were the one who kept me from falling off the ledge. You told me that being "different" wasn't something to be afraid of, and that being born with a birth defect made you who you are.

Only now, that conversation feels tainted. The whole time you were comforting me, were you secretly thinking, "Ha-ha, joke's on you! People with birth defects don't deserve special treatment. They're broken. Just look at me!"

Not to be an asshole, but if your cleft lip made you who you are, what's the takeaway? That people with clefts are ugly, inside and out?

I can't even type that without feeling sick. That's not what I believe, obviously. But Shelby, you slept with Adam in my home, in my bed. Everything I thought was true turned out to be false. What am I supposed to do with that?

I thought we were friends, when all along you were having sex with my husband behind my back. I'm an idiot. No argument here. One day maybe I'll wise up, but you will forever be ugly to the bone.

That's how it ends, no loving sign-off or final fuck you.

Mabel reads the email again, her stomach twisting. Shelby hadn't just misquoted Jake—she'd twisted the truth into something unrecognizable.

She has a vague recollection of a professor being outed on social media for using the n-word in class. The professor was fired immediately, and good riddance—at least that's how it seemed at first.

Later, it came out that the word hadn't been used as a slur, but as part of an overview of terms classified as hate speech. And the professor hadn't said the word itself, but the euphemism: "the n-word." A bewildered international student had asked for clarification. *The* n-word? *What* n-word?

After class, the professor explained the term and its ugly history. That was all. The end.

He lost his job anyway. So it goes. But the headline—"Professor Fired for Using Racial Slur"—was a gross misrepresentation of what happened.

As for Shelby? She didn't misquote Jake out of confusion or misunderstanding. She roasted her alive, deliberately, with malicious intent.

Beyond the wide front windows, the streetlight flicks on. In Jake's house, it's dark and shadowy. Mabel hears timid footsteps and knows Jake is watching her, hesitating right outside the living room.

"Do you still like me?" she whispers through the gloom.

"Of course, I still like you!" Mabel says. She sets Jake's phone on the coffee table and pats the sofa. "Come. Sit."

Jake does, sidling over like a crab and tucking her hands beneath her thighs.

"Shelby threw you under the bus," Mabel states.

Jake's breath rushes out of her in a whoosh. "Omigosh. You have no idea how good it feels to hear you say that."

"It's true."

Jake falls back against the sofa and lets her head loll toward Mabel. "You're the only person I've told all this to."

"And now you're going to tell me more," Mabel says. "I want to know every last detail about that crazy bitch."

"Why?"

"Jake. I have a nemesis of my own, or have you forgotten?"

"The woman on GoodNeighbors? WarriorMom?" Jake frowns. "Or do you mean your husband's ex-wife, Gigi?"

"I suppose I have two nemesises," Mabel concedes. "Nemeses? Nemesi? Three, if I add Vanessa. Four if I add Shelby."

"You only now learned about Shelby."

"So? When someone messes with my friend, they're messing with me. You feel the same, right?"

"Um . . . sure?"

"Of course you do! That's why you invited me in and let me rant and rail about stupid Vanessa! *And* Gigi." Mabel gives Jake's knee an encouraging squeeze. "We agree on that, and I sure as hell hope we agree about what needs to happen next."

"Which is?"

Mabel grins. "Payback."

13

WENDELL

Half a block from Jake's house, six-year-old Wendell kneels backward on the sofa in Aunt Evelyn's living room, staring out of the single-pane window before him. His bottom faces the TV, which is broadcasting *Wheel of Fortune.* His forearms rest on the sofa's upholstery-covered frame. With his straight spine and alert expression, he resembles a prairie dog poking its head out of its hole. If a nice lady caught sight of him—the lady with the fat cat, for example, or the lady with the cookies who is friends with the lady with the cat—either of them would see Wendell and melt . . . as long as they only saw the right side of his face.

Wendell has an excellent view of the cat lady's house from his perch. He saw the cookie lady go inside. He saw the cat lady and the cookie lady talk and laugh and drink liquor poured from a bottle. The liquor made them happy, and the ladies laughed more, with bigger, opener mouths.

When Wendell's daddy drank liquor, he didn't laugh. He got mad.

"Your mama didn't want to tell me, but I knew," Aunt Evelyn said not long after Wendell and Delilah arrived. "He'd get drunk and beat on her. She was ashamed of the whole ugly business, so she took too goddam long to ask for help." Aunt Evelyn had shaken her head with tight, angry movements. "She did it, though, didn't she? She got you out of there, and your sister, too."

Because here they are in Colorado—Wendell and Delilah, both. They live here now. Wendell knows this, but it still feels unreal. The purpling sky confuses things, taking Wendell back to that moonless night three months ago.

"Come on, babies," his mom had whispered, hustling them from the house. "Be real quiet and follow me."

"Mom, why?" mumbled Wendell's big sister. "I'm tired."

"I know, sweetie. But we need to go."

Delilah drew up short when they reached the station wagon. She blinked and shook off her mom. "My quartz collection! I need my quartz collection!"

"Baby, I packed them," their mom said. The whites of her eyes were huge. "Get in, get in!"

But the noise had woken their daddy, who raged out like a bull, shotgun in hand. "Don't you leave me!" he'd bellowed. "You leave me, I'll shoot. You know I will!"

There was the crack of gunfire, and Delilah started crying, which made Wendell start crying. His tears were everywhere, hot and thick and red. Then the emergency room, with doctors rushing and fluorescent lights blinking. Wendell on the gurney, flying. His mother's wide eyes, Delilah's sobs, the mask with the tube that plunged Wendell into darkness.

They started across the country the day Wendell was discharged, and this time their escape went better. Wendell's face was a mess, and their mom had a not-insignificant wound on her upper arm, but no one waved a shotgun as they drove away. No one ran after them, cussing and hurling threats.

"Your father's in prison, and that's a good thing, even if it doesn't feel like it," their mom said, catching Wendell's good eye. His bad eye was bandaged shut, and his head was wrapped in gauze. It felt like a bowling ball taped to a Tootsie Pop stick.

"He's not going to hurt us ever again. Even so, we're going to stay with my sister for a while. Doesn't that sound fun?"

On their trip across the country, Delilah made up funny names for the states they drove through, like "Misery" for Missouri and "Ill and Annoyed" for Illinois. That was a good one, because Wendell got car-sick and Delilah got annoyed. The smell of Wendell's barf wafted up from the floor mats for the rest of the trip.

In Kansas, which Delilah called "Can't Stand Us," Delilah begged their mom to let them see the world's largest ball of string, but when they got there, the pavilion was closed. They couldn't even pull into the parking lot.

"I'm sorry, Delilah," their mom said. So many apologies for so many things. "It's just a ball of string, you know. It doesn't do anything." She pulled up a picture on her phone, and there it was, a ginormous ball of string in a wooden building with people in chairs all around it. It did seem kind of dumb after that, like the people in the chairs were expecting the ball of string to burst into flames or perform some kind of miracle.

They arrived in Fort Collins two days later. Aunt Evelyn's one-story ranch house had peeling white paint and a garage door that didn't fully shut. The houses behind hers were equally dumpy. The row of houses across the street, however, could have been dropped out of a fairy tale. It was as if someone had opened a giant picture book in the sky, sending eight perfect gingerbread houses tumbling down.

"That land used to be a horse pasture," Aunt Evelyn grumbled when she saw where Wendell was looking. "I preferred the horses."

Then Aunt Evelyn noticed the maxi pad taped to their mom's upper arm. It was soaked through with blood and had a funny smell.

"It works, okay?" Wendell's mom said defiantly. "And it was cheaper than the bandages at the store."

"You are going to urgent care the minute you've got some food inside you," Aunt Evelyn said. "Good Lord."

The physician's assistant took one look at the infected wound and sent Wendell's mother straight to Poudre Valley Hospital. Five days later, she was dead.

Delilah jerks Wendell back to the moment by smacking his butt. "Turn around and eat."

Wendell rotates his body and slides down onto the sofa cushion. Aunt Evelyn sits in the armchair close to the TV, eating mac and cheese straight from the pot. Wendell's serving waits on the coffee table, in a plastic bowl next to a plastic fork. He uses the fork to spear four noodles. Three make it to his mouth. One falls to the floor. Wendell leans forward and talks to it in his head.

Hi, noodle, he tells it. *You're okay, noodle.*

"Young man, sit up and eat like a normal person," Aunt Evelyn says.

Delilah elbows him to drive the words home. If Aunt Evelyn decides to get rid of them, they don't have anywhere else to go.

"A friend in need is a friend indeed," Aunt Evelyn says, pointing at the TV with a long-handled wooden spoon.

"A friend in need is a friend indeed," says a toothy contestant.

"That's right!" says Pat Sajak.

Aunt Evelyn purses her lips and pushes herself out of the armchair. "You two clean up your mess when you're done."

"Yes ma'am," Delilah says.

"Scrape what you don't eat into the trash and take the garbage bin to the street. Tomorrow is trash day."

"Yes ma'am."

The sky is deep blue when Delilah wheels the bin out of the garage. Wendell admires the way she doesn't let it get away from her as it rattles and bumps down the driveway.

She parks the trash can at the curb and pivots on her heel.

Wendell stays where he is, hypnotized by the pretty houses across the street. A boy lives in the last one, one down from the lady with the cat. Wendell's only seen the boy once, on the day the boy moved in, but Wendell figures he'll come out when school starts. He and Delilah will meet him then.

The sun dips behind the foothills, dipping the pretty houses in gold.

14

JAKE

Do people grow to fit their names, or does our perception of a name change once we get to know the person it belongs to? This is what I'm thinking about the next time I visit the house on Hemlock Avenue.

I already saw Professor Lee, trading the pages I marked up for twenty pages of new material. Now I'm enjoying some well-earned "me time" in Adam and Shelby's claw-foot tub and imagining myself as a "Mabel."

I shake my head. It just doesn't work. Mabel is a Mabel, freckled and rosy and capable of wearing gingham. If I wore gingham, I would resemble a picnic table.

I paddle the water with my foot. To be honest, I'm not enjoying my "me time" as much as I wished I would. It's a workday for the nine-to-fivers, a camp both Adam and Shelby fall into. I saw them leave on the security camera. I've got my phone open to the app, so if they return unexpectedly, I'll see that as well.

It would be too late, of course. A minute's lead wouldn't even allow me to drain the tub.

And there it goes, my mood is dampened. I might as well get out. At any rate, I haven't done my trifling yet.

I flip the drain with my big toe and pour a healthy dollop of Shelby's fancy bubble bath into its swirling maw. I pat myself dry and slip back into my clothes, still thinking about names. When I was pregnant, I thought about names all the time. It's huge, giving a human a name.

When we learned we were having a boy, I put forth "Tobias" as my top choice. Adam lobbied for "Liam." We agreed we'd use both, but argued giddily about which would come first.

"Liam Tobias Swift," Adam said. "It's more dignified."

"We're having a baby, not a statesman," I countered. "Tobias Liam, and we can call him Toby. Toby's a boy to catch frogs with, who won't freak out when they pee on him. Because they will, you know."

"The frogs?"

"Always."

"Is that something he'll want on his résumé? 'Undaunted by frog pee'?"

"He's not going to have a résumé. We're having a baby, not a statesman, remember?"

When we found out about his heart problem, we withdrew our stakes in the name game simultaneously.

"We'll name him Liam," I said, still shell-shocked after the ultrasound.

Adam sat beside me on the sofa. He wouldn't look at my belly, which I couldn't stop cradling. "Tobias is fine," he said. "Or Toby. Whatever you want."

"Liam," I pronounced, praying that if I let Adam win, my selflessness would be rewarded and my little boy would live.

Liam died anyway, and with him, Toby died all over again.

I've gone teary in Adam and Shelby's bathroom, which is unacceptable. This house has been baptized with enough of my tears already. I fold the damp guest towel and return it to the linen closet. Using Shelby's personal towel—I know it's hers from the hint of Very Irresistible—I mop up the water I dropped on the tiles. There's a spiderweb behind the toilet, and I swipe it up as well, a nasty sticky thing with an egg sac in its folds. I take care not to crush the egg sac, but leave it intact on the edge of the towel.

I do nothing juvenile or vile, nothing with toothbrushes and toilets and the like. (I regret the lube. That crossed into pervy, and there won't be a repeat.)

Instead, I rearrange Shelby's perfume bottles, swapping their spots on the vanity. I scatter Q-tips on the floor, nudging them under the sink where they'll grow waterlogged eventually.

The kind of mess that's small, insidious—nothing they can prove. Nothing they'll even notice, necessarily.

I lock up, bound across the backyard with its lovely tall privacy hedges, and retrieve my bike from behind Professor Lee's shrubbery. This is not something I'll tell Mabel about, never ever. Not that I don't appreciate the solidarity she's offering. She volunteered to Facebook-stalk Shelby for me, and I told her to go for it. She's planning to send Shelby a friend request and report back to me this Sunday, at Todd and Lisa's neighborhood party.

I didn't have the heart to tell her that Shelby's posts are dull and that my alter ego, Lola, is keeping tabs on her already.

15

BILLY

The school year starts on a Wednesday, which is dumb. Why not start on a Monday instead of waiting till the middle of the week? Isn't it the whole point of school to attend on *school* days? But Wednesday is finally here, and Billy doesn't bother to hide his excitement. He's been counting down the days all summer.

He flashes his newly minted fifth-grade smile at the office ladies, then pops by the media center to give Mr. Hankins a cheerful hello. Last year, he was Mr. Hankins's student aide. He's eager to take up the position again.

In his primary classroom—he got stuck with rhinoceros-like Ms. Lipowski—he chooses a seat at the back, because the back row is best for watching his classmates and sizing them up. He listens with half an ear as Ms. Lipowski drones through the boring rules and expectations. Blah blah blah, boring boring boring.

There's a new girl in his class, and Billy lets his gaze linger on her. She's not boring. She's tall and hostile and lives in the dumpy ranch house across the street from him. Billy saw her come out with her little brother, and then he trailed behind them on the short walk to school. When they stopped by the playground fence, Billy stopped too. There were lots of kids crowding the sidewalk, so he was able to sidle up close.

The girl placed her hand on her brother's shoulder, coaxing him to turn around. When he did, Billy's stomach flipped. *Wowza. Wow. Za.*

"Wendell, do you remember what the doctor said, about how some people might say mean things about your face?" the new girl asked.

No shit, Billy thought. The right side of Wendell's face was fine, or as fine as a stupid little kid's face could be. The left side? *Woof.*

"If someone does," the girl went on, "do you remember what to say back?"

"That they're the ones who are ugly for saying something ugly," Wendell recited.

"Exactly," said the girl. "Meet me here after school. This is where we'll always meet, and we'll always walk home together. Okay?"

Watching Wendell nod was like watching a dandelion sway in the breeze—a late-summer dandelion the size of a baseball, but with chunks of floaties missing. There was a dent in the kid's skull, and his left eye appeared to be sliding off his face like a greasy egg. His skin was puckered in places and shiny in others. His jaw was off-center, his lower lip drooping and slack.

What the hell happened to him?

"Bethany," Ms. Lipowski says, her sharp tone pulling Billy from his reverie. "*Beth*any."

"Yes?" Bethany squeaks.

"I asked you a question."

"You did?" Bethany's knee jerks and bumps her desk, which makes a grating sound against the floor.

Azaiah fakes a cough into his fist. "She farted," he says. Melón, who's next to him, laughs, as do several others.

"Enough," Ms. Lipowski snaps. She sweeps her eyes over the class. "Thirty-one," she mutters. "Thirty-one ten-year-olds crammed into one room. Can you believe it?"

Agatha and Martha, the twins, shoot up their hands. "We're eleven," they chorus. "Our birthday was August eighteenth."

"Do you want a medal?" Ms. Lipowski inquires.

Agatha and Martha regard one another.

"Is anyone else eleven?" Ms. Lipowski asks. "Is anyone else gunning for a medal, simply for existing?"

Almost everyone grows interested in the tops of their desks. The new girl is the only kid who doesn't seem cowed.

"Well then, let us proceed," Ms. Lipowski says. She gestures at the new girl. "Class, say 'hello' to Delilah, who moved to Fort Collins this summer."

"Hi, Delilah," everyone says.

Delilah scowls.

Ms. Lipowski returns her attention to Bethany. "Bethany—as I was saying—I'd like you to be Delilah's Sweetwater student ambassador."

"Oh," Bethany says faintly.

"Yes, *oh*. Can I assume you're up to the job?"

Bethany nods with big, round eyes.

"During snack break, take Delilah on a tour of the school."

Bethany twists toward Delilah, smiling tentatively and lifting her hand. Delilah ignores her. Ms. Lipowski moves on to the care and handling of math books, and Billy taps the eraser end of his pencil against his desk.

At ten o'clock, while the other kids pull out juice boxes and plastic bags of grapes, Billy watches Delilah rise from her desk and go to the door, waiting for Bethany to join her. Bethany does, but twice her socks slip down, and twice Bethany stops to pull them up, doing a little hop dance. In the real world, an ambassador is someone chosen to represent a group because of how great that someone is. If Bethany is one of Sweetwater Elementary School's finest, Sweetwater Elementary is in trouble.

But Billy has a soft spot for Bethany, who is weak and timid and has never crossed him.

Bethany leads Delilah on the world's most boring tour of the world's most boring school, with Billy shadowing them just out of sight. It isn't hard. The fourth graders are on their way to PE, so there are plenty of jostling bodies. But out of an abundance of caution, Billy grabbed a stack of worksheets from Ms. Lipowski's desk, which he clutches to his chest. *Ms. Lipowski told me to take these to Mr. Davis*, he practices silently. If Bethany or Delilah asks why he's there, that's what he'll say.

The girls pause outside one of the first-grade classrooms, and Delilah waves at someone within. Wendell, Billy assumes. After a moment's hesitation, Bethany smiles and waves too. After that, Delilah loosens up, like maybe she's decided Bethany isn't the worst after all.

By the time they return to Ms. Lipowski's classroom, Bethany's hair is falling out of her headband, and her face is sweaty. Billy scans the room for Ms. Lipowski. She's writing something on the whiteboard and has her back to him, so he approaches her desk and returns the stack of worksheets.

"From Mr. Davis," he says to no one.

He stays there, leaning against the desk and sliding his hands into his pockets. Bethany's sock has drifted past her heel and into her sneaker yet again. Delilah stares at it, and it isn't even her sock.

"There was an accident," Delilah says at last, as if she's been holding in the words. They're pitched low, meant just for Bethany, and Billy has to strain to hear. "That's why my brother's face is like that."

Billy's skin prickles. He bends to tie his shoe.

"Oh no," Bethany says.

"Someone shot him. They thought he was a bear."

"What?!"

Billy is taut and still. *I'm not even here*, he says silently. *I'm not here, and neither are you, so just keep talking.*

"We were out in the woods, searching for quartz."

"What's quartz?"

"A type of rock. A crystal. When I was younger, I had a collection."

From the corner of his eye, Billy sees Delilah shuffle closer to Bethany.

"Someone saw us in the woods and thought we were a bear," she says in a breathy rush. "Maybe it was my fault. Who knows?"

"How would it have been your fault?" Bethany asks.

"I didn't say it *was*. I said *maybe*."

Ms. Lipowski turns from the whiteboard and uses her teacher's voice to say, "Return to your seats, students. Snack time is over."

Billy rises from his crouch and gives Ms. Lipowski a broad smile.

"What did I just say, Billy? Get to your desk," she says. "And Delilah, I'm not sure what your school was like in North Carolina, but at Sweetwater, I expect you to do as you're told."

A volcanic burp erupts from the back of the classroom, followed by a second smaller one, a cheeky peep that earns a swell of laughter. Ms. Lipowski strides off to berate the offender, and Delilah makes a face at her back.

"What crawled up her butt and died?" she mutters. She turns to Billy with the same peeved expression. "Yes?"

Billy feels caught out. "I'm Billy," he says. "I live across the street from you."

"Whoop-de-do," Delilah says.

Billy can't decide whether to be impressed or annoyed by Delilah's disdain. Bethany, on the other hand, is regarding him worshipfully. He rewards her with a grin, and her face grows pinker than ever.

Once everyone is seated, Ms. Lipowski launches into a spiel about respect and consideration and what it means to be a fifth grader. Billy tunes her out and stares at the back of Delilah's head. Why did she make up that story about Wendell and the bear? Whoever shot Wendell did so at close range. No way did they mistake him for a *bear*.

Delilah must feel Billy's eyes boring into her, because she looks over her shoulder and flips him the bird.

16

WENDELL

After Wendell was shot, the doctors kept him in the hospital for forty-eight hours. They dug the shotgun pellets out of the soft flesh of his face, cleaned his wounds, and stitched them shut. They taped something that looked like a popsicle stick to his nose to help the bone heal straight. Finally, they put puffy white cotton on the left side of his face and bound it in place.

"There's quite a lot of swelling, as you can see," the doctor told Wendell's mom. Wendell's mom was concerned, so Wendell tried to reassure her with a smile. Only his smile was out of order, so he gave her a thumbs-up instead. He felt self-conscious in the leaving-the-hospital wheelchair, his legs too short to reach the footrests and his mummy-wrapped head so enormous it kept bobbling around.

"You've got a journey ahead of you," the doctor told Wendell with an uncomfortable chuckle. "But you're tough, aren't you, buddy?"

Delilah stepped forward, narrowing her eyes and practically growling. *Don't you laugh at my brother*, her glare said. *Don't you dare.*

"It's okay," Wendell told her. He nodded, which was a mistake, as it tweaked a muscle on the back of his neck. "I'm okay. Really." Delilah's anger made him just as anxious as his mother's worry. He didn't want to let either of them down.

The doctor told Delilah's mom how to clean Wendell's wounds and change the packing. As he spoke, Delilah grew more and more pissed. It was because of how slowly he talked, exaggerating the shape of each word and especially the three-syllable ones. Delilah, Wendell knew, interpreted the doctor's mannerisms as evidence that he saw them as poor mountain hillbillies, boo hoo hoo.

Wendell wished he could say, "No, Delilah, it's you. You're making him nervous." But he didn't, and the more the doctor spoke, the more he sounded like a kindergarten teacher instructing a student on how much food to give the class bunny.

When Delilah interrupted to say that their mom did, in fact, know the difference between Gatorade and bottled water, the doctor blinked and said, "Ah. All right, then."

"All right, then," Delilah repeated, cocking her head to the side.

"De*li*lah!" their mom exclaimed.

"Bring him back in five to seven days to get the sutures removed," the doctor said when he reclaimed his rhythm. "Then we can start thinking about reconstruction and physical therapy."

Except Wendell, Delilah, and their mom took off on their cross-country road trip instead.

With all that happened next, it was weeks before anyone remembered Wendell's sutures. By then, most had fallen out on their own. Aunt Evelyn took Wendell to a veterinarian who snipped the rest of them off for free, since Aunt Evelyn wasn't sure yet about health insurance and kids and all that. Afterward, she took Wendell and Delilah to Safeway and told Wendell he could pick out whatever kind of breakfast cereal he wanted, even one of the sugary name-brand cereals with cartoon characters splashed all over the box.

Wendell was debating between Franken Berry and Count Chocula when a teenager wearing cowboy boots and dark blue jeans sauntered by. He did a double take when he saw Wendell, then laughed and said, "Monster cereal? Really? Isn't that kind of redundant?"

Delilah kneed the guy in the groin, which made him squeal and sink to his knees, and it became a whole thing.

Wendell's first week at Sweetwater Elementary, though, is going well. Kids stare at him, but so far, no one has called him names.

Wendell's fifth-grade reading buddy is especially cool. He drops down next to Wendell in the hall outside Ms. Merry's class and looks Wendell squarely in the eyes. *I'm not bothered by how you look*, his expression says. *Why would I be?*

"I'm Billy," he says, and there's something familiar about him.

"I'm Wendell," Wendell says. "I think you live across the street from me."

"I do," Billy says. "Your sister's in my class."

He shows Wendell the book he chose. It's a picture book Wendell read when he was three. Wendell's one of those kids who taught himself to read super early, another thing that makes him weird.

"I'm supposed to make you practice reading aloud," Billy says. "Want to give it a try?"

The book is called *Hug*. It's about a baby monkey named Bobo who can't find his mommy.

"No, thank you," Wendell says.

"Too much pressure?" Billy displays his palms. "Because listen, I'm not here to judge."

There are only three words in the entire book: "hug," "Bobo," and "Mommy." Wendell shakes his head.

Billy pulls his eyebrows together. "You think I'll make fun of you," he says. "How you look, how you talk . . . But that's not me. I'm not going to treat you like a freak even if everyone else at school does. Even if everyone in the world does."

Wendell unzips his backpack, pulls out *Artemis Fowl*, and says, "Maybe we can read our own books? I can read mine, and you can read yours?"

Billy gives Wendell an odd look, something shadowy Wendell can't quite grasp. Then he smiles. "Sure," he says, and they read together companionably, a big boy and a little boy side by side in the hallway.

Ten minutes before the class period ends, it starts to rain. Big, fat drops drum on the roof, and a girl named Elsa lifts anxious eyes to the ceiling.

Like Wendell, she's also sitting in the hall. There's a clap of thunder, and she jumps.

"What's the matter?" her reading buddy asks.

"Nothing. Storms. I don't like them," Elsa says.

Thunder rumbles again.

Elsa's lower lip trembles. "Can we go back to Ms. Merry's room?" she asks her buddy. "I don't like them at all."

Later, during afternoon snack break, Wendell finds Elsa and drops down beside her on a beanbag chair. He offers her an Oreo, which she accepts with a tremulous smile.

"Thanks," she says.

"You're welcome," Wendell replies, and then the two of them sit companionably, just two first graders being first graders on a pellet-filled cushion.

By the time school lets out, the rain clouds have dispersed, and the sky is a brilliant blue. Wendell and Delilah are halfway to Aunt Evelyn's house when Wendell hears the slap of sneakers on the damp sidewalk. He turns and sees Billy jogging to catch up with them.

"Billy, hi!" Wendell says.

Delilah shoots Wendell a look. "How do you know Billy?"

Billy grins and holds his knuckles out for Wendell to bump. "Hey, bruh." He acknowledges Delilah with a dip of his head. "Delilah," he says.

Delilah raises her eyebrows. "How do *you* know my brother?"

"I'm his reading buddy," Billy says.

Delilah harrumphs and picks up her pace. Billy keeps up with them with an easy, loping stride.

"That girl in your class," he says to Wendell. "Why was she upset?"

"What girl?" Delilah asks.

"Elsa?" Wendell says. "It was the storm."

"What storm?" Delilah demands, and Wendell knows exactly what she's thinking. She's thinking that when it storms in North Carolina, it *really* storms, with lighting everywhere and thunder that shakes the earth. The rain shower they had this morning? *Pfff.*

"I know, right?" Billy says. "I mean, poor kid, but c'mon. Is she afraid of cotton balls, too?"

Delilah almost smiles, a tiny curve pushing at the corner of her mouth.

Wendell doubts Elsa is scared of cotton balls. Then again, who knows? Most everyone is scared of something. Maybe even Billy. Maybe even *Delilah.*

Not of storms, though. The three of them have that in common. The sun is out, and every puddle they tromp through sends up a glistening spray.

17

BILLY

From the sidewalk, Billy watches Delilah and Wendell go into their house. As soon as they're safely tucked away, he starts walking again, continuing around the block until he's on Seneca, which runs parallel to Sweetwater Lane. The houses on Seneca butt up against the Sweetwater Bungalows, backyard to backyard. On the Sweetwater side, the yards are cheerful and the fences well constructed, whereas on the Seneca side, the yards are choked with weeds and the fences are old and rotted out.

Billy thinks it's funny. Not funny *ha-ha*, but because it shows how two truths can exist side by side, one shiny and the other dull. The shinier truth always wins, because it glitters more.

Like when Wendell said that Elsa was afraid of storms, and Delilah said, "What storm?" Delilah's truth mattered and Elsa's didn't, because Delilah is a fifth grader and Elsa's a puny six-year-old.

When it comes to Billy versus anybody, young or old, Billy's truth is the truth that matters because Billy isn't just a truth-sayer. He is a truth-maker. *Let there be light! And there was light. Let Wendell worship the ground Billy walks on! And Wendell worshipped the ground Billy walked on.*

Billy giggles. He can't get over how loud and wet Wendell's words are, especially when Wendell gets excited. When he's excited, his words become hard-boiled eggs crammed into his mouth and spit out whole.

What a kid, Billy thinks, kicking a stone down the cracked sidewalk.

Ahead of him is his favorite Seneca Street house, the one with the peeling blue shutters. The Santangelos live there, a gray-haired man and a white-haired woman who rarely venture out their front door. There's an abandoned shed in their backyard that Billy has claimed for his own.

He's almost to it when he draws up at the sight of a garter snake sunning itself on the concrete. Snakes come out on days like this, driven from their holes by the rain. This one's a beauty, nearly two feet long. Billy kneels and swiftly grabs it, positioning one hand below the snake's head and the other by its tail. It struggles, and Billy is filled with shuddery excitement. The snake is a coil of muscle, but Billy is stronger, even so.

He hurries with it into the Santangelos' shed. He finds an empty bucket, flips it over with his foot, and shoves the snake beneath it. Wriggly bits try to slip out. Billy pokes them back in. Finally the snake is contained, and the rim of the bucket makes a seal against the floor.

Billy sits down and rests his forearm on top of the bucket, breathing hard. He lifts the bucket for a peek, then slams it down. The snake thrashes. Billy squirms with the thrill of it.

The snake lashes about wildly for many minutes. Then less so. Then not at all.

Billy raps on the bucket. "Hey, snake. You okay in there?"

Nothing.

Billy brings his fist down hard, and the bucket jumps.

Still nothing.

Icy-hot pinpricks ripple beneath Billy's skin. What if the snake is dead? It probably isn't, but can't know for sure unless he lifts the bucket and checks. In the taffy-stretched moment where both outcomes are possible, the snake is both dead and alive.

He eases up the rim of the bucket. If the snake were smart, it would zip out faster than lightning. When it doesn't, a great wonderful wave builds inside Billy.

When the pressure is almost too much, he raises the rim higher.

No sound.

No movement.

Tilting the bucket like a hinge, Billy lifts the rim until it's two-and-a-half inches off the floor.

Five inches.

Six inches, all while keeping the far edge of the bucket pressed to the floor.

Billy lowers his head and sees two flat eyes staring out at him.

"Hey, buddy," Billy whispers.

The snake stays motionless in the bucket's half-moon shadow, and Billy drops the bucket back down. He thinks, *Too bad for you, dumb snake.*

He considers putting a heavy rock on top, but ultimately chooses a medium-heavy one. He centers it on top of the bucket and exits the shed, pulling the door shut behind him.

Dinner that night is frozen chicken pot pie, microwaved and then forgotten about. By the time Billy's mom spoons a serving onto a plate and pushes it to Billy, it's cold and has a blob of congealed grease on top. Billy thinks of the snake, alone and with no dinner. His tongue becomes a piece of overcooked meat, so dry that it glues itself to the top of his mouth.

He doesn't ask to be excused until he's forced down every bite. Then he slips out of the house and sprints down Seneca Street. Time is no longer made of taffy, and Billy no longer wants to be God. He just wants to set the dumb snake free.

Inside the shed, the bucket is overturned. The snake is gone. Billy's shoulders sag, his relief tinged with only a whisper of disappointment.

18

JAKE

I itch to return to the Hemlock house, but it's Saturday and Adam and Shelby haven't left the house all day. I imagine them cuddled up on their pristine white sofa, bingeing some new series. Could I disable their streaming services? Could I call Netflix and Hulu and Apple TV and identify myself as Shelby, then ask to cancel my subscriptions?

I piddle about the house, dealing with the rogue boxes still only partially unpacked. I spend some time on Professor Lee's manuscript. This latest chapter concerns dangerous mushrooms found in Colorado, and reading it makes me hungry for mushroom risotto. Adam used to love my mushroom risotto.

By 1:00 p.m., my brain is mushy. I've been sufficiently productive, so I reward myself by flopping onto my bed, pulling out my phone, and navigating to GoodNeighbors. Every day I do this, happily clicking the heart icon on Mabel's posts and the frowny face on WarriorMom's. It's Lola DuBois who sprinkles these hearts and frowns, not "Jake Nolan," so Mabel doesn't know it's me cheering her on. It pleases her regardless, I hope.

"Oh, Miss Manners, you minx," I say after reading her response to a rant about miller moths.

"I don't know how they get past the window screens, but they do," the ranter complained. "They're everywhere!!!"

To which Mabel replied, "Not for long," throwing in two skull emojis and a butterfly emoji. Then, in all caps, "WINTER IS COMING."

Farther down, Mabel gave baking tips to a woman whose cookies keep flattening into puddles on her baking sheet. "Decrease the amount of sugar, add more flour, and throw in an additional half teaspoon of leavening agent," Miss Manners advised. "And check the expiration date on your baking soda and baking powder!"

Heart, heart, heart; like, like, like. I feel merry, spreading my love.

I continue down the feed and learn that Trish Campus has called her neighbor a big baby for refusing to mow his lawn. Jess Y suggested leaving a box of adult diapers on his front porch with a bow on top, and a handful of others jumped on with ha-has and laughing faces. Wilma Godfrey put an end to that by posting, "Not sure that ableism and equating adult incontinence with laziness is the solution here."

Wilma is the prim and proper schoolmarm of the site. I click on her name, wondering if she'll be hangrily thin or middle-aged heavy? Lululemon or oversized Mickey Mouse attire? Her profile picture is just a green circle with a W in it. *Boo.*

I search for WarriorMom, newly curious. Her profile photo looks like a jellyfish at first glance, but when I enlarge it, I see it's the top of a paddleboard—a blue paddleboard decorated with a purple henna-styled elephant.

My pulse quickens. I've seen that paddleboard before. It came out of the moving van last week. Vanessa's, presumably.

There could be other elephant paddleboards, I tell myself. But a quick Google search suggests otherwise. My research reveals that the board in the photo is a one-of-a-kind specialty design.

Which means that the board in the photo belongs to Vanessa.

WarriorMom is Vanessa.

Holy shit.

An alert tells me that WarriorMom just commented on a post. My adrenaline spikes, and I navigate to the conversation. It starts with a complaint by a man named Curtis Taylor, who was woken up at 2:00 a.m. by fireworks. There's the standard back-and-forth between those who think fireworks are harmless fun and those who don't, followed by a suggestion that Curtis should simply have a face-to-face talk with whoever keeps setting the fireworks off. People *love* suggesting civil face-to-face discourse.

It's usually at this point that the conversation devolves into a decidedly uncivil exchange, and the fireworks debate doesn't disappoint.

DoctorJohn
Knock on the door and talk to your neighbors. It's not that big a deal.

Jess Y
Seriously. Just be a decent human instead of calling the police over a couple of loud bangs.

WarriorMom
Rules are rules, and rules are enforceable. **Curtis Taylor** shouldn't have to confront possibly off-balance individuals engaging in illegal activities.

Then Mabel enters the fray. It's possible I squeal.

Miss Manners
Oh look! It's buzzkill **WarriorMom**! Hi, buzzkill! 👋

WarriorMom
Name-calling isn't a good look, **Miss Manners**. And not everyone wants face-to-face interaction.

Miss Manners
None of your neighbors want to hear from you, is that it?

WarriorMom
On the contrary. When I say something, people listen, because they know it's actually important. What I don't do is force myself onto neighbors who want to be left in peace.

Miss Manners
Silly me. People who want to have casual, friendly interactions should be met with stony silence. That sounds reasonable.

Wilma Godfrey
WarriorMom and **Miss Manners**, please remember that this is a community-building platform. We should all model kindness and respect.

Wilma Godfrey
Curtis Taylor, I'm sorry you experienced such an unpleasant disruption to your day. As someone who has an intolerance to gunpowder, I encourage you to do whatever you need to do to take care of YOU.

I hold my breath. Is that it? Did Wilma shut them down?

After a minute passes with no further activity, I laugh and close out of the app.

My mattress jiggles, accompanied by an asthmatic grunt. Do cats grunt?

"Oh, Lump," I say. I do not want a cat. I certainly don't want this cat, with his greasy, matted fur and unimpressive toilet routine. It's not that he doesn't use the litter box I reluctantly set up for him. He does. But he hasn't sorted his dingleberry problem, and the special haircutting scissors I purchased for trimming my bangs are now reserved for snipping off clumps of soiled butt fur.

"You're disgusting!" I tell him. "I'm sure you don't mean to be, but you are."

The vet, when I took Lump in, couldn't find a microchip that would identify his owners. The chip might have migrated, she told me, or maybe a chip was never implanted.

"But he's definitely a house cat, don't you think?" I asked. "There's got to be someone out there looking for him."

With a sigh, the vet suggested that Lump might have been purposefully abandoned. She told me it happens more than people think, pet owners realizing they no longer want their pets once the novelty wears off.

"They dump them on the side of the road, miles away in an unfamiliar neighborhood," she explained. "Then it's someone else's problem."

"That's terrible!"

She shrugged.

"What am I supposed to do with him?" I floundered.

"You can take him to the humane society. That's always an option." The look she gave me told me what that option meant. "Or you could spread the word on Craigslist and GoodNeighbors? Maybe someone will claim him."

We regarded Lump, and Lump regarded us, sinking low against the metal exam table. He does this when he's anxious, but flattening himself out like a pancake does nothing to increase his cuteness quotient. It just makes him look wide, weird, and deranged.

"And if no one does?" I said bleakly.

The vet rubbed the back of her neck. "Just make sure he stays an indoor kitty for the time being. His blood work suggests a compromised immune system, poor fella. What he really needs is a sense of security."

On the bed, Lump headbutts my thigh and meows. As always, he sounds pissed. But when I graze his cheek with my knuckles, he purrs a rusty purr.

My thoughts return to Mabel's feud with WarriorMom, aka Vanessa. Tomorrow is Todd and Lisa's neighborhood party. Perhaps I'll pull Mabel aside and tell her that her anonymous nemesis is anonymous no longer. Her nemesis is Vanessa.

19

MABEL

Six bungalows down, Mabel soldiers gamely through family game night, although she sucks at all things *Mario Kart* and has yet to figure out the complicated array of buttons on the strange, jabby controllers. But it is a Saturday, for heaven's sake. Mabel wants to be sipping champagne and eating oysters, not drinking Izzes and hurtling off Rainbow Road in a car manned by a gorilla. (Mabel, of course, is the gorilla. Somehow this has become a tradition. Bethany is always Princess Peach, David is always Yoshi, and Mabel is always Donkey Kong.)

When their next-door neighbor knocks on the back door and calls, "Yoo-hoo! Anyone home?" Mabel rises from the sofa so quickly that she jars the coffee table, making everyone's pop bottles tremble.

"*Dad!*" Bethany yelps.

Mabel steps toward the back door. "It's Danielle. I'll see what she needs."

"She did it on purpose," Bethany accuses, pulling her blackberry Izze toward her and tucking it between her thighs.

"Sweetheart, she didn't," David says.

"And she made me skid off the track! Da-a-ad!"

Mabel hurries out the door, pulling it shut behind her and breathing in the cool evening air.

"Heya," Danielle says. Danielle is tiny and blonde, married to an estate lawyer. She's nice, but Mabel feels no spark of friendship toward her. Danielle's favorite topics of conversation are Ozempic and designer handbags. Mabel has no opinions on either and so has little to contribute.

Mabel smiles. "Hi, Danielle. What's up?"

"Can you talk?" Danielle asks. She taps her phone against her opposite palm. "I have something I think you better see. A Silk Stockings thing."

Mabel groans. Danielle's third favorite topic is the Fort Collins social scene, such as it is. Danielle hangs with a crowd of twenty or so women who dubbed themselves the Silk Stockings Society. She's always dashing off to this or that event, saying, "I'm off to a Silk Stockings party at the Jewelry Emporium!" or "I've already told Leroy not to even *peek* at this month's Visa bill. A girl needs her diamonds!"

Mabel finds the Silk Stockings Society problematic for two reasons. One: Like Danielle, Mabel is also a member of the social club, which makes it harder to trash talk it without feeling like a hypocrite. Two: So is Gigi, David's ex. In fact, Mabel is in the Silk Stockings Society *because* of Gigi, in a twisted and dishonorable sort of way.

Mabel has been married to David for three years, but . . . they've been together longer than that. In fact, Mabel kind of fell in love with David when he was still with Gigi. That's the thing.

Five years ago, a friend of Mabel's from the pottery studio told Mabel about the Silk Stockings Society and invited her to become a member. Mabel said yes, because she knew from Facebook that Gigi was a member. When she saw that Gigi had RSVP'd "yes" to an upcoming event, Mabel promptly signed up as well.

It's all terribly complicated, the past she shares with David and Gigi. Mabel knows that her version isn't *the* version, but it's her version nonetheless.

It goes like this:

Gigi and David were married, but they were both unhappy.

David wanted a divorce. So did Gigi. But, Gigi was Gigi, so she dragged things out.

When Mabel fell in love with David, he was living with Bethany (and apart from Gigi) as he waited (and waited and waited) for his divorce to be finalized. To make a long story short, he *didn't* wait (and wait and wait) to fall hard for Mabel, nor Mabel for him. Which is why Mabel said yes to the Silk Stockings opportunity. She wanted to see Gigi with her own two eyes, this woman who both was and wasn't such a huge part of her new life with her new love.

By the time David and Gigi's divorce was final, Mabel and David were together, and since Mabel had inserted herself into Gigi's social sphere, it wasn't altogether surprising that Gigi caught a whiff of their relationship.

Is Mabel proud when she thinks back on all of that? Of course not, but here she is. All roads led to David. She wouldn't have it any other way.

Does Mabel put herself in the same camp as Shelby, the woman who "stole" Jake's ex? Not a pleasant question to consider, but . . . maybe? Mabel didn't construct a false narrative out of Gigi's pain and use it to publicly humiliate her, however. There is that.

Gigi no longer attends the Silk Stockings parties (from Manhattan, that would be quite a commute), but she remains active on the group's Facebook page. If Mabel's neighbor, Danielle, wants to talk to Mabel about "a Silk Stockings thing," there's only one sort of "thing" it can be.

"Let me guess," Mabel says. "Gigi said something about me on Facebook?"

"I'm afraid so," Danielle says. "She's upset you listed yourself as Bethany's mother in the school directory."

"For heaven's sake," Mabel says. "David filled out the forms, not me."

"I believe you. Just, Gigi wasn't pleased."

"Does she think I'm trying to steal Bethany? Because I'm not. I know I'm not her mother, believe me. Although"—Mabel barks a laugh—"if I *were* her mom, I wouldn't let her go out of the house with panty lines bulging under her leggings! Jesus!"

Danielle's eyes widen, and Mabel berates herself for going too far.

Who judges a ten-year-old for having panty lines? At any rate, it's really the leggings that are at fault. What is Bethany supposed to do, wear thongs?

Okay, *no*. Mabel pushes that image away fast.

"Sorry," she tells Danielle. She waves her hand awkwardly through the air.

Danielle taps the screen of her phone and passes it over. "Here," she says, angling her body so she can read along over Mabel's shoulder.

Mabel skims Gigi's post, which, as usual, is self-indulgent and too long. It starts with, "I, as the mother of a Sweetwater fifth grader, care about our children as only a mother can." Farther down, she says, "Parenthood is not to be taken lightly. Mothers, especially, know this. Geographical distance does not—cannot—weaken the love a mother feels for her child."

Oh barf, Mabel thinks. *That love didn't lead you to bring said child to New York with you, did it?*

Gigi helpfully bolded certain sections of the next paragraph, making them jump out at Mabel like spiky black nettles. "But beware, ladies. As many of you already know, there is someone in our group **who is not who she pretends to be**. She walks among us, ready to **steal our husbands** and **tear us from our babies**. Please spread the word: **I am the mother of Bethany Merriweather**. If anyone wants to arrange playdates with my beautiful daughter, you know where to find me."

"For fuck's sake," Mabel grumbles, returning Danielle's phone.

"At least now you can do damage control," Danielle says.

"Damage control? Why?"

Danielle puts her head to one side. "You don't want people reading between the lines and drawing unfortunate conclusions, do you?"

"Why would they? Gigi's crazy," Mabel protests. "You're the one who told me that, Danielle. 'Gigi has crazy eyes, crazy little beady eyes,' that's what you said."

"I did," Danielle admits. "And, she does."

"So why would anyone take her seriously?"

Danielle crinkles her nose. "It's just . . . listen. When a woman feels backed into a corner, when she feels as if her *family* is at stake—"

"If she cared about her family, she wouldn't have treated them like she did!" A flush of heat makes Mabel woozy. "Gigi and David's marriage was over long before David and I met."

She wishes she could tell Danielle about the abuse Gigi heaped on David over the years, how she hit him and yanked at his hair and clawed at him so viciously she drew blood. How she took a hammer to his iPhone when she discovered he'd added a password to keep her out. How she put his laptop behind the wheels of her car and backed over it out of spite.

"I think Gigi sees things differently," Danielle says with a pious air.

Mabel stands frozen as Danielle departs, her indictment hanging in the air. *I think Gigi sees things differently*. Well, duh.

Inside, she finds David alone, watching *The Big Bang Theory*. She kisses his cheek. "Bethany's gone to bed?"

"She's upstairs, but not asleep," David says. "She's playing *Like A Dino!* on my iPad."

Mabel slides in next to David on the sofa and grabs her own iPad, opening it to Facebook. She rubs his neck as she navigates to the Silk Stockings group page. There it is, Gigi's "beware the evil husband stealer" post. Rereading it gives Mabel a churning feeling, a mix of anger, shame, and defensiveness.

Mabel asked Jake why she didn't fight back at the height of the #lipservice kerfuffle by publishing her email to Shelby in its entirety. If the public understood the nuances of Jake's grief—first the loss of her child, then the sting of Adam and Shelby's affair—surely they would have cut her some slack.

Jake laughed ruefully. "It hurt too much. And, it was mine, you know? My son. My pain. Not for public consumption."

"But you could do it now," Mabel pressed. "It's been almost a year. You've healed. Ish. Don't you want to clear your name?"

"Anything I say would just rile people up again," Jake said. She'd given Mabel a funny smile. "I'll let karma do its thing, you know?"

But Mabel is of the opinion that karma works best when given a helping hand. Also, she needs a distraction. Jake was right: Dredging up the past just reopens the wound.

She tucks her legs beneath her and is about to exit the Silk Stockings page when a name jumps out at her. "Our Sunday spotlight shines on new member **Shelby Bryant**, who will be hosting our first ever Panty Party!" a recent post announces. "Shelby brings her charitable spirit to **The Silk Stockings Society** and encourages everyone to attend this fun event, dedicated to collecting feminine hygiene products for those in need!"

My goodness, Mabel thinks. She'd planned to pop over to see if Shelby had accepted her friend request, and she will. But first, this.

She clicks on the "more details" link and learns that Shelby's panty party is a ticketed event, three weeks from today. The money raised will go to Crossroads Safehouse, and all Silk Stockings members are invited to attend. Every guest is encouraged to bring new underwear, tampons, and pads to be donated to the women at the safe house.

"Do you know that eighty-five percent of the homeless women in Fort Collins have fled abusive partners?" Mabel reads. "These women, like all women, need underwear and feminine hygiene products, but all too often, these items don't show up on the needs lists distributed by charitable organizations. So woman up, ladies! Sisters helping sisters!" Then there's a string of emojis: a power fist, a bikini, and five two-girls-dancing emojis, each in a different skin tone.

It's a fantastic idea for an event, though the name doesn't strike quite the right note. "Panty party," Mabel murmurs, trying it out.

"What's that?" says David.

"Hmm?"

"You said 'panty party.' Is that an invitation?"

"Ha-ha, no," she says, flicking away his wandering hand. She admires his quads, so strong beneath his jeans, and reconsiders. She rakes her nails over his inner thighs and grins. "Then again . . ."

He grabs the remote and turns off the TV with gratifying promptness. "Mmm," he says. "That feels good."

She traces the outline of him through his jeans. Fuck, he's hot. Stealth hot. Nerdy hot. Hot for Mabel and Mabel alone. She's just unbuttoned his jeans when a voice makes her freeze.

"Daddy?"

Mabel keeps her gaze down and her hand where it is, silently begging David to send Bethany away. *For once, choose me*, she pleads.

Small feet pad down several steps. "D-daddy? I'm done with screen time. I need you to tuck me in."

David sighs. Mabel drops her hand. Is the hitch in Bethany's voice manufactured? Does it matter?

"Go," Mabel says.

David stands up, keeping his back to his daughter as he zips up his jeans. "Head on back to your room," he tells Bethany. "I'll be right there."

To Mabel, he says, "To be continued?"

"Of course."

When he's gone, Mabel returns to her iPad. She RSVPs "yes" to Shelby's panty party and includes a personal message. "Hi!" she types. "Your panty party, SO FUN. Looking forward to meeting you, Silk Stockings sis!"

She's about to close out of Facebook when her iPad pings. Shelby accepted her friend request. It's done, just like that.

Mabel does a little shimmy. She can't wait for tomorrow, when she'll pull Jake aside at Todd and Lisa's party and share the news.

20

BILLY

On Sunday, Billy transfers baby carrots and cut red peppers from a plastic King Soopers party tray onto a porcelain platter while his mom scoops hummus into a matching bowl. This is the "dish to share" they'll bring to the neighborhood party. Billy's mom considers it her job to make sure there's at least one healthy option at such things.

Once upon a time, she would have shown up with the sealed plastic party tray, not even bothering to pop off the lid with its slapped-on price sticker. But last summer, Billy and his mom went to a potluck in their old neighborhood, and one of the other mothers made a sniffy remark about Billy's mother's vegetable tray.

"Oh dear," tutted the woman, whose name was Louise. She had a son named Zach, a toddler. She ran a disdainful finger over the edge of the plastic plate and said, "Someone needs to learn the fine art of replating."

When Billy's mother raised her eyebrows, Louise misread her reaction.

"I know, I'm terrible," Louise said. She bugged her eyes and lowered her voice. "But it's just so *tacky*. If you know, you know."

Two months later, on the night before Zach's much-anticipated fourth birthday, Billy saw his mom slip into their neighbor's backyard with a lidded plastic container. For three days, the container had sat in their hot garage with the lid partially cracked. The stench was unbearable.

When she reached Louise's outdoor furniture set, Billy's mom—wearing plastic gloves—coated the bottom of the picnic table with the container's contents, wedging chunks into the nooks where the frame met the rippled glass table and smearing the legs with the soupy dregs.

The next morning, Louise spread a plastic tablecloth over the table and set out the party food. Kids and parents arrived. The air rang with happy shrieks and laughter. At noon, Louise clapped her hands and told Zach and his guests to take a seat at the table. "Cake time!" she cried gaily.

The maggots couldn't migrate upward, so they dropped onto the plump, bare thighs of Zach and his friends. When one of the mothers bent down and lifted the plastic tablecloth, a squirming clot fell wetly onto her cheek. The shrieks took on a different tenor.

"So tacky," Billy heard his mother murmur, watching with folded arms from their back porch.

Now Billy's mom replates the dishes she brings to potlucks and barbecues.

Billy's stomach rumbles, but he knows better than to sneak a carrot into his mouth. Meals are for mealtime, no snacking. But the hummus smell tickles its way into his nose and makes his mouth water, and that says something, because . . . hummus! Hummus is not Billy's favorite.

Don't think about food, he tells himself. *Think about something else.*

"Hey, Mom?"

"Yes?"

"Does Dad have our new address?" He knows that his father regularly wires money to his mom's bank account, but it's been a while since Billy's heard from him. He's been wondering if his dad still knows where to find him, should he want to.

Billy's mom scrapes a spoonful of hummus from the plastic container. "Why in the world would I give him our new address?"

Billy reddens. "You know, just in case."

"In case of what?"

"I don't know. An emergency?"

Billy's mother points at Billy with the spoon. "What would he do, in the case of an emergency? Rush to our aid? Has he ever rushed to our aid in all the years since he kicked us out?"

Billy's heart pounds. "No, but—"

"Why are you so concerned with him when I'm right here in front of you? Am I not enough?"

"Mom. You are."

"Then leave it." She bangs the spoon on the porcelain bowl to dislodge the clingy bits.

Billy bows his head. He misses his dad and wishes he could hear his voice. There wouldn't have to be any rushing for aid; just a phone call would be nice. But Billy isn't allowed to call his father. His father has to call him, or rather, his mother. They don't have a landline. Billy's mom's cell phone is the only way his dad can get in touch.

One day, maybe Billy will take the initiative and call his father himself. He'll have to borrow someone's phone, but it's doable. He knows his dad's number by heart. He rehearses it as he arranges the raw vegetables.

"You know, Billy," his mom says, eyeing him critically. "Your attitude isn't the best. I wonder if you should stay home from the party."

If Billy doesn't go to the party, he won't get to eat. "I'm sorry, Mom."

"Listen to me. If at any point your father decides to play a bigger role in your life, he is more than welcome to do so." She tosses the spoon into the sink and stands before him. "He could find a way to pay for extra allergy shots, for example. For your gluten intolerance and your asthma." Her gaze is steely. "Don't you think?"

Billy doesn't have a gluten intolerance or asthma. He doesn't have any of the medical conditions she's assigned to him over the years. "Yes, ma'am."

"I'm the one who takes care of you day after day." She thumps her chest. "*Me.* Do you even care? Do you care about the sacrifices I make for you every single day?"

"Mom. I do."

"Maybe you need a little alone time to think things over."

He can smell meat on the grill from the party house. "I don't care about Dad. He doesn't deserve to know our new address."

His mom purses her lips and looks to the left, in the direction of the food smell. She turns back to Billy. "Come on, then. Let's go."

At the party, there's food everywhere. Hamburgers and baked beans and fruit salad. Plates of cookies and other desserts. Five bags of chips lie open on a green plastic table, including a jumbo bag of Fritos. Billy can't tear his eyes away.

His mom laughs and ruffles his hair. "Go on, silly!" she tells him. The man who lives here, Todd, stands nearby in a flamboyant Hawaiian shirt. He has a big belly and lots of chest hair and holds a tumbler full of something brown. Billy's mom smiles at Todd and says, "Do you remember being that age, when you could eat and eat and never put on an ounce? When you could get away with absolutely anything?"

Billy doesn't have to watch to know that Todd is running his eyes all over her. Men always do.

"Vanessa," Todd says, "you can still get away with absolutely anything."

Billy's mom laughs and gives fat, hairy Todd a teasing shove.

By the time his plate is loaded, Billy's mother has joined a cluster of grown-ups wearing dressy clothes. Billy migrates away from them, wandering into the backyard and sitting on a low stone wall. He drums his feet and eats Frito after Frito. He looks around for Bethany.

He freezes, a Frito halfway to his mouth. The lady from next door, the one whose big fat cat sits in the window and glares out at him, is coming toward him. She wears an "Oh look, a *child*!" expression that makes his heart sink. Billy hates it when adults try to make conversation with kids. What's the point?

"Hi, I'm Jake," the lady says. She takes a seat beside him and throws her thumb over her shoulder, indicating the bungalow between Billy's house and the one they're at. "That's me, there."

"I'm Billy," he says reluctantly, preparing for an onslaught of tedious questions. *How old are you? What do you want to be when you grow up? Do you like fire trucks? Big, shiny FIRE TRUCKS?*

"You're in the fifth grade, right?" she asks. "I've seen you walking back and forth from school. How's it going?"

Billy eyes her warily. "Fine."

"Fifth grade is when I discovered Cheez Whiz," Jake tells him, not that he asked. "Every day for a year, I packed a Cheez Whiz and bologna sandwich for lunch. On white bread." She lifts her eyebrows and grins, as if to say, *There! What do you think of that?*

Billy thinks nothing of that. Then he thinks, *Whoopee, yay for you*, but not in a nice way. He would happily eat Cheez Whiz every day, so it isn't very nice of Jake to go on and on about it, her own Cheez Whiz love affair.

Jake looks at him expectantly. He returns the stare. He doesn't know what game she's playing, only that adults don't babble on to kids like this unless there's a lesson at the end, like "And that is why you never lick a frozen flagpole."

"Who's the paddleboarder, you or your mom?"

"Huh?"

"I saw the board when the movers were here," Jake says. "It's nice."

Heat rushes to Billy's face. Last summer, when his mom came home with that expensive one-of-a-kind board and promised to take him to Horsetooth Reservoir, he believed her. All summer long, he kept thinking, *Maybe today. Maybe today'll be the day!*

"I bet you're good," Jake says.

That's it. Billy's not going to sit around and let her make fun of him. His voice sounds rough when he says, "Well, you're wrong, because guess what? I've never been."

Jake's smile falls away. "Oh," she says. "I'm sorry. I didn't mean to make you feel bad."

"You didn't. I hate paddleboarding."

"Me too, actually."

Billy's ready for her to leave, but she keeps on sitting there. It's super awkward.

Billy tosses a Frito onto the grass and grinds it into bits with his sneaker. "I like sharks," he says gruffly, just to fill the stupid silence. "Do you?"

Jake thinks for a moment, then says, "I mean, yeah. From a distance."

"Most sharks won't bother you."

"Not in Colorado," Jake agrees.

"Not in the ocean, either. Not even great whites, which are the deadliest sharks there are."

"Huh," Jake says. She swings her legs. "I guess that's not so surprising."

"Why do you say that?"

"Statistically, donkeys kill more people every year than sharks."

He gives her a *How dumb do you think I am?* look.

"I'm serious," she says. "So you better watch your ass."

Billy laughs before he can help it.

"Hello," Billy's mother says, appearing above them. She smiles coolly. "I'm Vanessa, Billy's mother."

A funny look crosses Jake's face. "I'm Jake. Nice to meet you."

They trade boring life details, like how Billy's mom is a radiologic technologist, which is a fancy way of saying an MRI tech, which means she's the person who guides patients through the MRI machine when a doctor wants to see the patient's insides.

"Cool," Jake says.

"It's very rewarding work," says Billy's mom. "And you? What do you do?"

"Not a dang thing," Jake says with a shrug. At Billy's mother's confusion, she adds, "I'm temporarily unemployed. I'll figure something out eventually."

"I see," says Billy's mom.

They keep their boring small talk going for another minute, and Billy knows that his mom is doing a mental tally. Both are unmarried, but Jake has neither kids nor a job, so Billy's mom wins.

She places her hand on Billy's shoulder. Like the hair ruffling, this is something she only does around other adults.

"So . . . what were you and Billy talking about?"

"Oh, there's Mabel!" Jake announces. She rises and waves broadly at a woman with springy red curls. "Mabel! Hi!"

This Mabel person is wearing something that looks like a janitor's jumpsuit, only more billowing and printed all over with flowers, as if a forest animal from a Disney movie upchucked all over her. Behind her is

Bethany. Her eyes glom on to Billy, and she gives him a windshield-wiper sort of wave. Billy feels suddenly and weirdly shy and doesn't wave back.

Jake dashes across the yard and pulls Mabel off to the side. They speak excitedly, their conversation punctuated with giggles. Mabel says something that makes Jake squeal, which makes the grown-ups around them turn and stare.

"Those women are making fools of themselves," Billy's mom says. She lifts her plastic cup. "I'm going to get one last refill, and then we'll go. If you want to eat anything else, do it now. This is tonight's dinner."

Billy nods. His mom studies him, then makes an exasperated sound and goes to get more wine.

The moment she's gone, ants rush in. That's what it feels like. Millions of little ants rushing over Billy's body. He searches for Bethany, but she's gone.

He looks upward and is reminded of a time when he was much younger, when his parents were still together. His dad had taken Billy to the grocery store, and at the checkout line, the clerk had given him a red balloon. In the parking lot, the string slipped from Billy's hand. He'd felt himself on the verge of tears, but his dad squatted beside him and said, "Hey, no, it's all right. Let's just watch it, okay?"

He put his arm around Billy and the two of them craned their heads at the sky, the same as Billy's doing now. The balloon went up and up and up, until it was a pinprick, until it turned as white as the blue-white sky and winked out of sight.

21

WENDELL

Happy chatter calls to Wendell, a chorus of voices traveling through the sky and into Aunt Evelyn's kitchen.

"Maybe, if we went over, they'd say, 'Come have a hot dog!'" he says.

"Not a chance," Aunt Evelyn retorts. She wipes the Formica counter with brusque flicks of a rag. "Snobs, all of them. Preppies. What's the new word?" She sniffs. "*Hipsters.* You're better off without them, young man."

Wendell wishes his aunt would use his name instead of calling him "young man" all the time.

"Want to go to the playground?" he asks Delilah, who sits across from him reading a book. "You can practice your handstands. I can time you."

Delilah's look says she knows what Wendell is up to. "Nope. If they don't want us, we don't want them."

"What if they do want us? What if they do, but they just don't know it yet?"

Delilah goes back to her book. Aunt Evelyn shakes her head, pursing her lips.

A man's laugh booms out, and Wendell thinks of his father, who's in jail. His father is in jail and his mother is dead, forever and ever, amen.

He slips off the chair. "I'll go by myself. To the playground. If you want me, that's where I'll be!"

"Don't eat too many hot dogs," Aunt Evelyn says sourly, and Delilah laughs.

Tears prick against Wendell's eyes. Delilah puts her book down on the table, pages splayed like bird wings. She says, "Omigod, c'mere."

"The party people are stupid," she whispers, squeezing him tight.

"I know," he whispers back. His words whistle in the hollow of her neck, because that's how he talks now. He has an "acquired deformity." The shotgun pellet that lodged in his jaw messed with the nerves and muscles that control his tongue. Sometimes he drools a little, and when he speaks, he sounds like a creature from a fairy tale, half beast and half human.

Outside, Wendell strolls along the sidewalk and tries to look friendly so that one of the bungalow people might see him and think, *Why, isn't that the boy who lives on Roxborough Street? That's not so far. How in the world did we forget to invite him to our barbecue?*

A man spreads his arms and sings a song, launching it at Billy's pretty mother. Wendell's seen her going in and out of her house.

"'Jeepers creepers, where'd ya get those peepers?'" the man croons. His shirt is colorful. A gold necklace glints among tufts of chest hair. "'Jeepers creepers, where'd ya get those eyes?'"

Billy's mom tosses back her head and laughs. Her gaze falls briefly on Wendell, or Wendell thinks it does, but the man with the cheerful shirt clasps her hand and spins her so that her skirt flares out.

"For the love of Christ, Todd!" an older woman says. She bats at Todd, but she's smiling. She's not *hitting him* hitting him. "Give Vanessa room to breathe!"

Wendell searches the crowd for Billy. His left peeper doesn't work as well as it used to. The whole left side of Wendell's face doesn't work the way it used to. But his right peeper is fine.

Maybe Billy is out of sight in the backyard, or maybe he went inside to use the bathroom. Maybe he'll come back out through the front door, and when he does, he'll see Wendell on the sidewalk, right smack in front of him.

Hi, Billy! It's me, your reading buddy! Wendell would say. They're pals, Wendell and Billy. Billy would be happy to see his good pal, Wendell. Wendell is sure of it.

Wendell presses his droopy cheek up with one hand and holds his lower lip in place with the other. He practices his smile, just in case.

22

JAKE

For two weeks now, Mabel and I have gotten together almost every day. At 9:00 a.m., after watching the parade of children file past on their way to school, I head up the street to Mabel's house. Her backyard is too steeply inclined for lawn furniture, so she's created a patio at the far end of the driveway. There's a sofa and chairs and a low metal table where we rest our espressos.

It started after Todd and Lisa's party, this ritual of ours, and it's continued ever since. Sometimes Danielle, Mabel's next-door neighbor, joins us, but she doesn't drink coffee—she says her body doesn't do well with caffeine—so her visits are brief, just a quick pop-by and a few friendly words.

It's yet another weekend, and the playground across the street is empty. David is most likely at the gym, and Bethany is no doubt around somewhere. But for the moment, it's Grown-up Land, just me and Mabel.

Mabel's curls are tied back with a red bandana, and she wears matching red capris, a white sleeveless blouse tied at the waist, and gold hoop earrings big enough to encompass a child's fist.

"Look at you, being sporty," Mabel calls as I bike up the driveway. "You must have shaved all of ten seconds from your commute."

"Every second counts," I say, hopping off my bike and flipping down the kickstand. In the bag attached to the frame is Professor Lee's dangerous mushroom chapter, which I'll return to him later today. I also packed a jumbo bag of embroidery thread, which I pull out. "For Bethany. Is she inside?"

"You are so sweet," Mabel says. She lounges on the sofa, her hands around her coffee cup and her toes curled over the edge of the coffee table. Her fingernails and toenails are painted red to match her bandana. "Try the great room."

I enter the house through the back door and spot Bethany in front of the TV. She's watching Saturday-morning cartoons, which look very different from the cartoons I watched as a kid. On the screen, flat-eyed giants careen around and wreak havoc in what might be a medieval Japanese town. It's confusing. Also, the giants are naked but have no genitals.

Then again, Tom and Jerry were equally unencumbered by genitalia. Same for SpongeBob.

So, never mind.

"Knock-knock," I say, rapping Bethany lightly on the head. "I brought you more string."

Bethany twists sideways. "Hi, Jake!" Her eyes drop to the pack of embroidery floss. "Wow, so many colors!"

"Use all you want," I say. I came over yesterday after school let out, watching Bethany for an hour so that Mabel could attend a meeting at the pottery studio. I taught her how to make friendship bracelets, and now she's addicted.

Bethany fishes five skeins of thread out of the crinkly sack and looks to me for approval.

"Solid choices," I say.

"Want me to make you one? If you do, what colors?"

"Of course, and maker's choice," I say. At Bethany's confusion, I add, "You choose for me, whatever you think I'll like."

"Okay," Bethany says, nodding happily.

On the driveway, I settle into a chair and accept the coffee Mabel offers me, poured from a polka-dotted pot into an itsy-bitsy polka-dotted mug.

"Everything you do is so *charming*," I marvel. I run my finger along the mug's shiny glaze. "It's kind of annoying."

"A burden and a curse," Mabel replies. "Here's a thought. I'll teach you how to be charming if you teach me how to get along with Bethany. You make it seem so easy!"

"It is," I say. "She's a good kid." I wait a beat. "Do you remember the first time you came over?"

"Obviously."

"I asked if you and Bethany got along, and you were all, 'Absolutely! We're pretty much besties, don't you know?'"

Mabel gives me a look. "It's possible I was exaggerating."

"Ah."

"I just don't know what I'm supposed to do to make her like me," Mabel complains.

I'm sure it's hard being a stepmother, but it's even harder being a kid. Mabel's forgotten this, I think. Most grown-ups do.

"Nemesis catch-up time?" I propose.

Mabel lights up. "Nemesis catch-up time, yes ma'am. First on the agenda: Shelby and the panty party."

I fake-vomit.

"We have a while. The event isn't until October. But so far, all I've got is to show up and radiate hostility."

"Hmm."

"I'm open to suggestions. Do you have any ideas?"

Yes, as a matter of fact, but mine isn't one I can share with Mabel. This afternoon, after stopping at Professor Lee's, I'll pop in at Adam and Shelby's. They have a baby shower to attend at 5:00 p.m., all the way out in Boulder, so they won't be around to get in my way.

(Actually, they don't have a baby shower to attend at 5:00 p.m. The shower starts at 2:00 p.m., so by the time Adam and Shelby arrive, it should already be over. Adam and Shelby will look like jerks, showing up so late. Of course, they've been showing up late for so many things. Oh well. Maybe, in addition to finding a new hiding spot for the spare key, Adam should have given some thought to changing his computer password after the divorce. A fresh new start and all that. But he didn't, which makes it all too easy to mess around with the events on Adam and Shelby's shared Google Calendar.)

While they're trekking to Boulder and back, I'll snatch a pair or two of Shelby's panties, those lacy thongs she likes so much. I'll drop them off anonymously, on the day of the party. Or maybe I'll mail them to her? I haven't decided.

Mabel's waiting for me to answer. I adopt a pensive expression and cross one ankle over the other. "I think radiating hostility is a solid approach," I say. "I mean, you've got a knack for it."

Mabel's mouth falls open. "What?!"

"Like that, yeah."

She tries to swat me.

I smile and avoid the blow. "Shall we discuss the latest installment in the Mabel–Vanessa wars?" I ask. When I told her at the neighborhood party that Vanessa was WarriorMom, Mabel had *died.*

"I can't believe it," she said, smacking her forehead with her palm. "Except I totally can."

"I know, right?" I said.

"How did you figure it out?" she eventually thought to ask. "I thought you weren't on GoodNeighbors."

"I am. I'm just more of a lurker," I told her, a half-truth. "Just because you don't see any posts from Jake Nolan doesn't mean I'm not there."

Mabel scooches closer and taps on her phone, angling it so I can see. She's navigated to the most recent source of conflict.

"'Friendly dog poop reminder!'" Mabel narrates, reading aloud a post by an elementary school gym teacher. "'In case you didn't know, school is officially in session for all the kiddos in our district. That means that school playgrounds are once again filled with CHILDREN, and these children wear actual SHOES. These children will track actual POOP into our schools if dog owners don't DO THE RIGHT THING and pick up after their fur babies! Just this morning, I picked up ten piles myself. Yuck!'"

"I'm not crazy about the all caps," I say, "but I'm definitely anti-poop-on-playgrounds."

"As am I," Mabel says, talking as she swipes. "But *Vanessa*, being Vanessa . . ." She hands me the phone. "Scroll till you get to the good part."

I skim the comment. After clarifying that she, too, was anti-poop-on-playgrounds, Vanessa, aka WarriorMom, pointed out that it was illegal for Fort Collins residents to walk their dogs on school property, period.

"'Dog owners need to abide by the laws of our city,'" I intone, sternly and without humor. "'There wouldn't be any poop to pick up if dog owners stayed off the playgrounds entirely!'"

"And now, from stage right, enters our heroine, Mabel."

I straighten my spine. "Miss Manners," I announce as if I'm at a fancy ball.

"That's me," Mabel says in a stage whisper.

"'And how does that solve the problem, WarriorMom?'" I read in a mild tone. "'Will making the poop illegal make it disappear?'"

Mabel cackles. "Sing it, sister."

"WarriorMom," I say in my announcer's voice. I then switch to a pinchy, sour persona. "'*Miss Manners*, it's unfortunate—but not surprising—to see that once again you have *entirely* missed the point of my comment. Denying the truth of the poop is a form of gaslighting—'"

"'The truth of the poop!'" Mabel exclaims. "She actually said that!"

"I see that."

She rolls her hand. "Go on."

"'Denying the truth of the poop is a form of gaslighting, so congratulations on adding to the problem instead of contributing to the solution.'"

Mabel bounces. "Read my response."

"'*You're* the problem, WarriorMom,'" I huff. "'Go away.'"

"And she did! 'WarriorMom has left the chat!'" Mabel chortles and slaps her thigh. "All that discussion of poop probably made her have to go."

"Vanessa never poops, silly. She's too law-abiding."

"Ew. That's quite a backlog."

I waggle my eyebrows. "That's no backlog. That's my neighbor."

Mabel's laugh delights me. In this moment, everything delights me. The sun is warm, and my heart is light. It's been so long since I've had a friend like this.

Could this be enough? What would it feel like if I let the rest go? No more waterlogged Q-tips or down-the-drain diamonds, no pilfered panties?

I play with the idea in the back of my mind as Mabel and I move on to different subjects. It might be nice to relinquish my fantasies of revenge.

David returns from the gym, my cue to leave even though he's brought bagels and invites me to stay.

"I can't, but thanks," I say.

"Rain check?" David says.

"Definitely."

"See you tomorrow?" Mabel says.

"You know it," I reply. I swing my leg over my bike and I'm off, muscle memory taking me straight to Hemlock Avenue.

23

JAKE

My crisis of conscience doesn't happen until I'm back at home, panties in hand.

Panties in hand.

Jesus.

Who have I become?

I wad the lot of them in my hand, a poof of lacy cotton, then fling them away.

Lump pounces on them, elated. He separates one pair of panties from the others and bites at them.

And this is how the world ends, I think. *Not with a bang, but a thong.*

I drop my head into my hands as shame carries me back across the years to memories I thought were locked and sealed. My fifth-grade year, and a graduation party to mark the end of elementary school. Then off to Boone for summer vacation, spent with my father in his house in the woods. My father and Carrie and Toby.

I was ten. Toby was three. My stepmother, Carrie, would have been . . . what? In her twenties? Younger than I am now. My God, she was a child.

Toby wasn't potty-trained yet, and my father wasn't pleased.

I was on Carrie's side, and together we cheered Toby on, hoping to shield him from my father's scorn.

"Pee coming! Pee coming!" Toby would announce, his chubby legs pumping as he sprinted for the bathroom. Once there, he'd tug off his shirt, his pants, and each stubborn sock before pushing his toddler-sized briefs to the floor and stepping out of them. He'd furrow his brow as he positioned himself in front of the toilet, and then he'd beam at the sound of success.

"Well done, Toby!" Carrie and I would exclaim. "Yay, Tobes!"

Sometimes, Toby didn't make it to the toilet in time, and a wet spot would bloom on his size three Wranglers. If Carrie and I were the only witnesses, it was okay. Carrie would say, "Run, put on fresh undies, quick-quick-quick."

If my father was there, it was a different story.

"Why, Toby?" he would demand when the wet spot appeared. "Why?" He said it so accusingly that sometimes, just for a moment, I wondered if Toby *had* wet his pants on purpose. Then tears would well in Toby's eyes, and his lower lip would tremble, and I'd remember that of course Toby hadn't wet himself intentionally.

"He's too old to be having accidents," I overheard my father telling Carrie. Toby and I were in the backyard, sitting beneath a great magnolia tree and building a fairy house out of its waxy leaves. We were hidden by the boughs. My father and Carrie didn't see us.

"John, he's three," Carrie said. "He's a little boy."

"You're too soft on him, and I'm too soft on you," my father carried on. I peeked through the leaves and saw him rake his fingers through his hair. "Love is duty. Duty is love. What about that is so hard to understand?"

"I do understand. But John—"

"What's the consequence when he fails? It's a simple question, Carrie. What is Toby's punishment when he wets himself?"

I wrapped my arms around Toby, who burrowed into my chest.

"The books say to keep him on a schedule, and I do," Carrie said. "Every two hours, I make sure he goes to the bathroom—"

"So why the accidents?"

"Toby's pediatrician, Dr. Joyce. You like her, remember?" Carrie's tone was cajoling. "She says it takes longer with boys. We need to be patient."

"I don't need a doctor to tell me how to raise my son," my father countered. "If you can't teach him, I will, and I'll make sure the lesson is learned."

"Like with that dog?" Carrie said. Her tone shifted. "Did that poor dog learn its lesson?"

"That dog didn't belong in our yard."

"That dog was someone's *pet.*"

I tightened my grip on Toby, knowing that Carrie was approaching dangerous territory. If my father owned a gun when he and my mom were married, I never knew it, but by the time he'd set up house with Carrie, he owned three: a handgun locked in the trunk of his car, another he wore holstered in accordance to North Carolina's concealed carry laws, and a shotgun in the coat closet. He used the shotgun to deal with the dog, a rambunctious terrier who had no concept of property lines.

"Don't you pass judgment on me," my father growled.

Toby pushed up so that his mouth was against my ear. "Yellow day, go away," he whispered. A "yellow day" was a yelling day. Toby could read my father's moods as well as the rest of us.

We backed out of our fort unnoticed. Any noise we made was masked by the sound of flesh striking flesh and the fast rise of heated voices.

When we were free from the branches, I scooped Toby up and planted him on my hip.

"Creek?" Toby asked.

I shook my head no. We weren't allowed to go to the creek without first telling a parent. I took Toby into the forest, held him in my lap beneath a sycamore tree, and told him a story that my mom used to tell me. It was about two little girls who fall into a well and land in an enchanted realm, where they're confronted with a series of tests. The good little girl passes the tests with flying colors and returns home with the help of a diamond-studded key, her arms overflowing with ruby apples and bread loaves made of gold.

The bad little girl is rude, selfish, and mean. She's given a firm tongue-lashing and sent home in disgrace, pelted with rotten fruit and blackened crusts of bread. Toby loved the story for the same reason I did, I think. It painted a world where virtue was rewarded and cruelty punished.

By the time I reached the end of the story, the yelling had stopped. Carrie's voice, normal again, wove through the sky and called us to dinner. At the table, I averted my eyes from the pulpy mark on Carrie's cheekbone.

That night, I slipped out of the guest room and tiptoed to Toby's room. He wore a Pull-Up at nighttime. He was allowed. He lay on his tummy with his bum in the air, fluffy and padded. I placed my hand on his back, reassured by its even rise and fall. Only then could I return to bed and fall asleep myself.

And now here I am, with Shelby's panties. Where is the virtue in this?

It's not actually her panties that are the problem. When I stepped into Shelby and Adam's bedroom this afternoon, a light flicked on in the neighboring house. I froze, gluing my eyes to the illuminated window. Was someone watching?

I don't think I was spotted. I don't see how I could have been. I turned on no lights and stuck to the shadows. Still, I made quick work of the job, swiping a handful of fluff from Shelby's underwear drawer and getting out as fast as possible.

When I got home, I found a photo tangled within the silk and lace, a photo of a woman holding a little girl. *Sue Ellen and Shelby, 1997,* someone had written on the back. Shelby is dimpled and adorable, wearing a Pull-Up and nothing else. Her mother, who died when Shelby was young, is fresh-faced and sweet.

I didn't mean to take the photo. I certainly don't want it. I tell myself it's no big deal. If Shelby cared about it, she wouldn't have left it there for anyone to take.

I tilt the photo and study it. I look away, distraught.

This is not the prize I wanted.

24

BILLY

In the last week of September, Ms. Lipowski gives a pop quiz in math. Billy gets the highest grade. Bethany gets the lowest: a sixty-eight. Billy knows because he's the one who passes back the quizzes. Ms. Lipowski picks him because he's the best.

Bethany turns her quiz over fast on her desk and blink-blink-blinks, which she does a lot, and which is too bad because it makes her look like a mouse.

"It's okay," Billy whispers. "It's just one grade on one stupid quiz."

"What did you get?" Bethany asks.

He shows her his paper. Her eyes go round.

"A ninety-*eight*?"

He shrugs. "I have a math brain. So does my dad."

After school, when he's on his way home, he stops and helps a little baby kindergartner tie his shoes because the kindergartner is too little and dumb to do it right.

"Now it'll never come undone," Billy says, after tightening the double knot.

The kindergartner looks at Billy the way Bethany did, like Billy can do anything. It feels good being good, sometimes.

When he reaches his house, he digs around for his key before realizing he doesn't need to. His mom's home early. This means she's done taking images of people's insides for the day and can focus on her own life, which, as usual, involves sitting at the kitchen table and typing away on her iPad.

He grins and raps on the windowpane. She looks up from her iPad, and he waves.

"Hi, Mom," he says when she lets him in. "Guess what?"

"What?" she says, already sliding back into her chair and pulling her iPad closer. A peek over her shoulder tells Billy she's on that GoodNeighbors site. She's always on that GoodNeighbors site.

"I got a ninety-eight on my math quiz."

"What happened to the other two points?" his mom says, but she's not really paying attention.

Billy steps closer. "It was the highest grade in the whole class."

"Oh?"

He leans forward and reads the comment she just posted. It says, "Thank you, Judgy McJudgerson, for explaining why only Perfect People like you should get to decide who puts their trash cans where."

He fishes the quiz out of his backpack and puts it in front of the screen. "I got an A-plus, see? A ninety-eight is still an A-plus."

His mom bats the quiz away. "I'm in the middle of something, Billy."

"Okay. Yeah. But . . . can I tell Dad?"

She looks at him. "Tell him what, Billy? What exactly do you want to tell 'Dad'?" She says it in a mocking way, as if Billy's father is something Billy should have outgrown, like Santa Claus.

"About my quiz, and being the best kid in the whole fifth . . ."

His mother lays her iPad on the table. Billy's words trickle off.

"Why?" she says. "Are you more concerned with his approval than with mine?"

"I'm sorry, Mom. Forget it."

His mother cocks her head. Billy feels his heartbeat in his throat. Finally, she flutters her fingers and says, "Go away, Billy. Just leave, all right?"

She doesn't make him dinner.

She doesn't speak to him for the rest of the night.

The next morning, when it's time for Billy to leave for school, he hovers at the front door. "Well . . . bye," he says.

"Bye," she says as if he's a stranger.

"About my quiz," he starts. His plan is to explain that he doesn't care about his dad knowing. It was just a dumb idea that landed in his brain and then flew away. Only his mouth goes dry, because of how she's looking at him.

"Do you know what would be amazing?" his mother says. "If you could get through one day without showing off. Just one day." Her eyes are dark, flat pools. "You're not special, Billy. You're just not."

Outside, his blood fizzes and thrums. He kicks the dirt next to the sidewalk. He kicks the metal fence post bordering the school field. Then he draws up short, fists at his sides, and breathes in and out like a bull until his vision clears.

He is calm. He is controlled.

In the media center, as he makes his rounds as Mr. Hankins's aide, he thinks about how pointless everything is. The second graders he's monitoring are making "interest boards." Copies of *National Geographic* are pushed back and forth over smooth tables. Fingers fumble with scissors and glue sticks, and it's just. So. Pointless.

One boy has garlic breath. His mom probably made spaghetti for dinner last night, probably with garlic bread, which is unhealthy, nothing but empty carbs.

"Your breath stinks," Billy whispers.

"Huh?" the boy says.

"That's why no one wants to sit by you."

"I don't stink," the boy says uncertainly.

Billy gives him a pitying smile and squeezes his shoulder. *It's okay, kid. You've got this.* Then he reconsiders, and makes sure the kid sees him reconsider. "Sure," he says. "And Santa Claus is real and your mommy and daddy love you very much." He points at a clump of glue on the boy's interest board. "Oops. Messy!"

Billy straightens books and picks up scraps of paper and pencil nubs.

One girl, her name is Gracie, tries to navigate her scissors around a koala bear, but her hair gets in the way. Waist-length princess curls that catch the light. How long did Gracie's mother spend fixing Gracie's hair this morning? Did they share happy mommy-daughter time in front of the TV, Gracie watching *Dora the Explorer* while her mommy brushed those silky blonde strands?

Gracie's mom probably used that tangle-remover spray and a "no owies" brush. Gracie has probably never had an owie, ever.

Billy ducks behind a bookshelf, watching Gracie frown and try again. Once more, her hair falls in her way.

She's such a show-off, and not just with her glossy, curly hair. She wears light-up sneakers and hair bows larger than Billy's hand. Her backpack is pink and puffy and decorated with all sorts of dangly crap: a pom-pom, a small squishy SpongeBob, and a pair of AirPods in a purple clip-on carrying case. She's seven years old and has a pair of AirPods! Every morning, she prances into school, holding her mommy's hand, swinging it back and forth like life is one big party.

It's not, Billy could tell her. *And Gracie? By the way? Your mom might say she loves you, and maybe she does, sometimes. But I guarantee you that at other times, she hates your guts. Okay, Princess Gracie?*

Sometimes Billy is his mother's best silly Billy billy goat in the whole wide world. Sometimes she pulls him onto the sofa and cuddles him, and even if there's too much cuddling, Billy doesn't squirm.

Other times, Billy is a bad billy goat. Once his mother made him drink sour milk, almost half a gallon, because he didn't shut the refrigerator door all the way. Another time, she put rat poison in his SpaghettiOs and didn't tell him until he'd eaten every last bite. When he ran for the bathroom, clammy with fear, she laughed and called him back.

"Your face!" she said. "Why would I poison you, silly Billy?" She raised her eyebrows. "And if I did, why would I tell you?"

Gracie cries out in distress. In one hand is her cutout koala, minus its right rear leg. In her other hand are the scissors, the pink plastic handles too big for her thumb and forefinger.

Billy ambles over. "What's wrong, Gracie?"

"I ripped my koala," she says. "He's ruined!"

Billy drops to one knee so he's at Gracie's eye level. "You can fix it. I'll help you."

Gracie looks unsure.

"Glue the koala bear to your poster, then glue the paw to the koala bear."

"It's not a *poster*. It's an *interest board*," Gracie says sulkily. But she leans forward and pushes the ripped-off piece of paper in place. Her hair falls in her way, and she flings the scissors down.

"You know what I'd do? I'd just cut it off," Billy tells her.

"My *hair*?"

"Yeah. You can glue it back afterward, like the koala." It thrills him how reasonable he sounds.

"You can't glue hair."

"Sure you can. That's how wigs work, and extensions."

Gracie frowns.

"Hey, you do you," Billy says, flashing his palms and standing up. "Just don't cry when everyone else's posters are better than yours." He thunks his head. "Interest board. My bad."

He moves to a boy who's using too much glue to paste cutout cars on his piece of poster board. "Dude, that looks awesome," he says. "You've made interest boards before. I can tell."

Seconds later, Billy hears sawing sounds and a soft grunt, followed by the swish of blades finding purchase. Then, music to his ears, a torrent of great, heaving sobs.

"Gracie, what have you done?" Mr. Hankins exclaims.

The next day, Gracie shows up with her hair cropped short. She walks unevenly, as if she isn't used to her new lightness.

"I like your haircut," Billy says as she hangs her backpack on its hook.

Gracie's lower lip trembles. "I hate it, and I hate *you*!"

Billy touches his chest. "Me? What did I do?"

He's covered this territory already, with Mr. Hankins and with Principal Vasquez. That part had been as fun as the rest.

"Gracie seems to think it was your idea, Billy," Principal Vasquez said yesterday, after Gracie's parents were called and Gracie was led away, a blubbering mess. "Did you suggest she cut her hair?"

"No," Billy replied, quirking his eyebrows to convey just the right mix of concern and confusion. "Why would I . . . ?"

Principal Vasquez filled her cheeks with air and then puffed it out. "Of course," she said. "Kids . . . well, they're *kids*, aren't they? They don't always show the best judgment."

In the hall, Gracie's hand goes to her hair, which is no longer there. Her eyes well with tears, and something strange happens. Billy's throat tightens, and he's possessed with the urge to hug her.

These things I do, I do for you, he thinks, because she's broken now. So is he. They're both broken, but maybe two broken things could feel their way to wholeness?

"Go away," Gracie says when he steps toward her. "You're mean!"

His body loosens. "Yeah? And you're not special," he replies. "You never were."

25

MABEL

David is off on a business trip. He left today, which is Friday, and will be gone through Monday, September 29. Mabel will be in charge of Bethany for four full days and is determined to make it work.

"After all, if you want the goose, you have to take the goslings," she tells Jake, who sits beside her on the makeshift patio. "Isn't that what they say?"

"Who's 'they'?" Jake asks. The air is cool. Soon they'll have to hold coffee hour inside.

"The ganders?" Mabel says. "Or maybe the other geese."

"Maybe the goslings' therapist," Jake suggests. "Maybe the ganders' therapist?"

Danielle's screen door gives a bang, and Danielle struts over in skinny jeans, a tight top, and pink UGGs. "Do you love them?" she asks, sticking out one leg and propping her foot on her heel. "I got them on eBay, new with tags, but at half the original purchase price. I'm *obsessed*."

The discussion moves to the approaching sweater weather, and talk of goslings, geese, and ganders falls to the wayside.

When school lets out, Mabel greets Bethany with homemade iced oatmeal cookies.

"I don't like oatmeal cookies," Bethany says mulishly, going to the pantry and retrieving a box of Cheez-Its.

"Oh? I thought you did." Mabel says. She regroups. "How about a game of Uno?" She taps the card deck, prepped and ready.

"That's a game Daddy and I play," Bethany says. *In what world would I want to play Uno with you?* her expression says.

Mabel asks Bethany if she wants to watch a movie. Bethany does not. Movies are boring. She asks if Bethany wants to go on a walk. Bethany does not. Walks are boring. Forcing herself to remain upbeat, Mabel mentions the friendship bracelet Bethany made for Jake, a lovely chevron of navy blue, white, and periwinkle. Perhaps Bethany can make a similar one for Mabel?

Bethany cannot. Her fingers are too tired.

In desperation, Mabel offers to take Bethany to the pottery studio, where once a week, she teaches senior citizens how to make bowls and ashtrays. (It's astonishing how many seniors want to make ashtrays.)

"Really?" Bethany says, perking up. "Can I make a pot?"

With your weary, weary fingers? Mabel refrains from saying. "Absolutely! You can make anything you want, except an ashtray. Actually, strike that. You can totally make an ashtray if that's where the spirit leads you."

Bethany looks at her funny. "I don't smoke."

"Right. Excellent lifestyle decision." Mabel claps. "Put some grubby clothes on and we'll get going."

"Cool," Bethany says with an actual smile.

Mabel smiles back. When Bethany gives her even the smallest taste of approval, everything feels possible.

Five minutes later, Bethany clatters downstairs in leggings and an old shirt of David's. "Can we see if Jake wants to come?"

"Abso-frickin-lutely," Mabel says. "We'll swing by her house on our way."

At first, Jake declines, but Bethany wears her down, making praying hands and saying, "Please? Please, please, please?"

Well done, Mabel thinks approvingly. All week, Jake's been a little off. Nothing major, just distracted. Moody.

On the drive to the pottery studio, Mabel remarks on the sign she saw in Vanessa's front yard. It reads, Is This Your Poop? PICK IT UP!

"How long has it been there?" Mabel inquires. "Is it handprinted? Did Vanessa make it herself?"

"It appeared yesterday," Jake says. "Maybe she made it herself, but she could have just as easily bought it online or at Ace Hardware. There are a lot of poop-themed yard signs in circulation these days. 'I don't poop in your yard. Don't let your dog poop in mine!' That sort of thing."

"But Vanessa isn't against the pooping, necessarily," Mabel points out. "What matters to her is that the poop gets picked up."

"I'm pretty sure she's against the pooping."

"No, no, I don't think so. According to the sign, I can poop in her yard all I want, as long as I leave no trace. Or . . . ooh, I have a better idea!" Mabel throws Jake a glance. "Let's make some poops!"

"Excuse me?"

"Out of clay, silly. The proof is in the poop, remember? If it's not actually poop, I can leave it wherever I want."

"I think it was 'the truth is in the poop.'"

"You two are weird," Bethany interjects, leaning forward from the back of the car. "Can I make some poops, too?"

At the studio, the three of them make an impressive collection of clay poops using the "pinch pot" technique Mabel teaches them. Mabel even coaxes a laugh out of Jake by reminding her, repeatedly, to pinch off her poops.

When the poops are dry, Mabel will bisque fire them. After that, she'll bring Jake and Bethany back to the studio to glaze them.

"We'll have to pick the perfect brown," she tells them.

"Ew!" Bethany says with a giggle. She points at the biggest and most realistic of her clay poops. "I'm going to give this one to Daddy. Do you think he'll like it?"

"Oh, Bethany," Mabel says. "He will be so proud."

26

MABEL

On Saturday, Mabel and Bethany invite Jake over for lunch. They eat on the front porch, chatting about this and that, and when they can return to the pottery studio and glaze their poops.

"How about tomorrow?" Mabel suggests.

"Yeah!" Bethany says.

Mabel turns to Jake. "Does that work for you?"

"Hmm?"

Mabel snaps her fingers in front of Jake's face. "What's going on with you, lady? You in there?"

"Hey, look! It's Delilah!" Bethany exclaims, rising and pointing at the school playground. "Can I go say 'hi'?"

"Who's Delilah?"

Bethany gestures toward a tall girl crossing the playground with a younger boy. "My friend, and that's her brother." Bethany waves and calls out, "Hi, Delilah! Hi, Wendell!"

The kids don't hear. They're too busy trying to climb the red slide that shoots out from the play structure. The girl, Delilah, purposefully loses her footing each time and slides back to the beginning, making Wendell, the little boy, double over with laughter.

"Where do they live?" Mabel asks.

Bethany points toward Jake's end of the street. "Down there."

"The ranch house at the intersection of Sweetwater and Roxborough," Jake clarifies. "I see them walking to school every day." She glances at Bethany. "The little boy, Wendell, what happened to his poor face?"

"He got shot," Bethany says.

"He got *shot*?" Mabel says.

"It was an accident."

"Sheesh," Mabel exclaims. "But yes, you have my permission to join them."

Bethany shifts her weight from foot to foot. "Actually, could we all go? And Mabel, could you bring cookies?"

Mabel looks at Jake, who shrugs.

"Sure," Mabel says. "I'll grab them now."

On the playground, Bethany makes a beeline for Delilah and Wendell while Mabel and Jake spread out a picnic blanket. Bethany drags her friends to the grown-ups, and introductions are made and cookies passed around. Mabel tries to hide her wince when she sees Wendell's face up close. Her heart hurts for him. She wishes she could wrap him up in a hug.

"Let's swing," Delilah says, and Bethany nods eagerly. Mabel feels a wash of affection for her awkward, needy stepdaughter.

After the kids run off, Mabel says, "So, what gives?"

"Huh?"

She nudges Jake with her knee. "Something's on your mind. All week, you've been barely there. Want to talk about it?"

Jake looks surprised. "Oh. Ah. Hmm." She hesitates, then gestures with her chin at the swing set. "Has Bethany told you what the deal is with those two?"

"What do you mean?"

"How they ended up here. Why they're living with their aunt." Jake bobs her head. "I *think* she's their aunt. She's not the friendliest."

"All I know is what Bethany's told me," Mabel says, "which is that their father is incarcerated and their mother is dead. She died not long after she and the kids got here."

"That's terrible! What happened?"

"She went to the hospital with an infection and never came back."

"Poor kids," Jake says. "Will the aunt get Wendell the reconstructive surgeries he needs?"

"He needs reconstructive surgeries?"

"Well, yeah. I mean . . . his face."

"Oh," Mabel says. "Now that you say that, it makes sense. As for the aunt . . ." She shrugs. "I have no clue."

"I know about facial abnormalities because of my work with Miles of Smiles," Jake says. She frowns. "Should I talk to their aunt? Or should I just stay out of it?"

The kids wander over for more cookies, and Jake's question goes unanswered. Mabel's question, too, has gone unanswered, Mabel realizes. Jake breezed right past it. Was that Jake's way of suggesting that her problems, whatever they might be, aren't Mabel's business?

Mabel tosses the Ziploc bag of cookies to Bethany, who brings her hands together and catches it in a half squat.

"Sweet," says Delilah approvingly.

The three kids settle in on a nearby patch of grass, where in between bites of cookies, they pass a rock back and forth and occasionally erupt into laughter. Mabel assumes it's some sort of game, but the point of it is either very subtle or nonexistent.

"Hey, I was thinking," says Mabel, who isn't interested in staying out of Jake's business.

Jake grows wary. It's subtle, but Mabel notes the slight tensing of her facial muscles.

"Oh yeah?" she says.

"Yeah, about poops."

"Back to that old fixation."

"We'll give some to Vanessa, obviously—"

"I don't think that's a good idea."

"And, since we made so many, I'm thinking we should deliver some to Shelby and Adam as well. As a gift!"

"Mabel? No."

"Oh, Jake, it's not like you to be stingy," Mabel chides. She taps her lower lip. "There's a term for someone who's stingy with poop. Now, what is it?"

Jake rolls her eyes.

"Anal retentive!" Mabel says. She points at Jake. "You, my friend, are being anally retentive. Why? No one knows."

"I do, actually," Jake says. "I know why."

"By all means, share."

"Because I've kicked the hornet's nest enough."

"What are you talking about? You haven't kicked the hornet's nest at all, not since the whole original brouhaha." Mabel looks at Jake more closely. "Unless . . . have you?"

"What? No. Just, no more hornet's nest kicking, end of story."

"Even if the hornets deserve it?"

"Doesn't matter, they'll still sting you."

"So?"

"*So?*" Jake repeats. "Mabel. Have you ever been stung by a hornet?"

Mabel hasn't, not that she recalls. She considers lying, but Wendell gets in before her.

"I have," he says, and Mabel and Jake both swivel their heads to see him sitting a foot or so behind them. He has abandoned Bethany and Delilah and the rock game and is plucking pieces of grass and stacking them into a pile.

"Been stung by a hornet," he adds. "It hurts."

Jake's laughter bursts out of her. "Exactly! Thank you, Wendell!"

Mabel's heart lifts. This is the Jake she's been missing these past few days. "Fine," she says. "You win. I surrender."

"Good," Jake says. "So no poopy deliveries? To anyone?"

Mabel throws back her head and groans. "It physically pains me to see you turn into such a goody-goody."

"Since we're on the subject . . . I think you should nix the panty party. Be the bigger woman and all that."

"No!"

Jake winces. "Yes?"

"Jake. You are *killing* me. You are literally sucking the joy from life, right here, right now."

Jake pats Mabel's thigh. "I know. It's a lot. But I believe in you, Mabel."

Mabel pulls out her phone, opens it to the camera app, and passes it to Wendell. "Take a picture for us, will you? To commemorate this day of sadness?"

"You are the biggest drama queen I've ever met," Jake marvels. "Don't you think, Wendell? That Mabel's a drama queen?"

Mabel slings her arm over Jake's shoulders. "Say 'poopy'!"

When Wendell hands back the phone, Jake and Mabel take a look at the image and say, "Awww!" Jake's cheeks are sun-kissed, and Mabel's curls are a wind-tossed halo around her face. Both are smiling.

"Thank you, Wendell," Mabel says. "You are a rock star!"

"Yes, Wendell. Thank you," says Jake.

Mabel opens Facebook and posts the photo immediately, she's that pleased with how cute she looks. (And Jake, too! Jake is *very* cute.) She puts away her phone, checks to make sure Wendell has returned to his grass-pulling, and leans toward Jake.

"No anonymous poop deliveries, for real?" she asks.

"For real."

"She's in Bora-Bora, if that changes things. Shelby, not Vanessa."

Jake looks pained, but not surprised.

"With Adam," Mabel goes on, watching Jake's face. "Shelby's in Bora-Bora with Adam."

Jake presses her lips into a line, and Mabel's sure of it. Jake knew about Bora-Bora already, which means that Jake has her own means of keeping tabs on Shelby.

"Hypothetically, someone could make a poop delivery with zero fear of being caught," Mabel says. "It could be an anonymous donation. I could monitor Shelby's Facebook page and report back on how they're received."

Jake shakes her head. "Mabel, you are very clever, and should you ever launch a newsletter, I'll be the first to subscribe. But I'm taking a break from social media."

"What? Why?"

Jake shrugs.

"Let me get this straight," Mabel says. "No more WarriorMom updates *or* Shelby gossip? Good Lord, woman, what will we discuss?"

"Oh gosh, I don't know," Jake says. "Football?"

Mabel shoves Jake's shoulder. "Ha! You kidder."

"That's me."

"And a party pooper, if I'm being honest. A huge, huge party pooper."

"You can't stop talking about poop, can you?"

"I can't," Mabel acknowledges. She looks pointedly at Jake. "Just know I'm on your side, 'kay?"

"And I'm on yours," Jake says. She gives Mabel a quick, hard hug.

27

JAKE

I leave Mabel and the kids at the playground to soak in the last of the sun, hurrying home with my head down and my hands in my pockets. I don't stay in my house for long. I just grab the photo and go, wheeling my bike from the garage and pushing off before I can talk myself out of it.

The photo I accidentally stole, the one of Shelby and her mom, has become the rotting albatross around my neck, the invisible blood on my hands, the heart of a dead man beating like a drum beneath my bed.

I have to return it or I'll go mad. Because what if it was a picture of Toby? Of Liam? Of anyone loved and lost?

I pump hard. The blood pulsing through my quads is real, my ragged breaths a welcome distraction. I maintain my feverish pace all the way to Mountain Avenue, braking only when I approach Professor Lee's driveway.

I don't announce myself or pay him a visit, not today. I swing my leg over the frame of my bike, balance on one pedal, and hop off my bike as it glides to a stop. I stash it behind a scrub of bushes and throw a glance at the neighboring houses, especially Mrs. Abernathy's, whose second-floor windows are flush with the windows in Adam and Shelby's bedroom.

She didn't see me, that last time. *I* might have seen *her*, but *she* didn't see *me*. If she did, she'd have said something, if not to me then to Shelby or, God forbid, Adam. And had she said something to Shelby—or God forbid, Adam—they would have said something to someone.

I would know, is the point.

The 5:00 p.m. sun is at its blinding worst. Any squinting neighbor would be hard-pressed to make out anything. I dash across the backyard of the Hemlock house, ducking into the shadowed area beneath the eaves. I insert my key into the back door, then pause. Something doesn't feel right. *This* doesn't feel right.

Of course it doesn't. Breaking and entering probably shouldn't. Still, I pause and take stock. There's no action at Mrs. Abernathy's house, and, as expected, Adam and Shelby's house is cloaked in vacant silence. I know from Facebook that the Bora-Bora trip Mabel mentioned is a long one. They won't be back till the end of the week.

Something registers, and I see it now, the difference that triggered my alarm. In the eaves above the door is a vast spiderweb, able to spread freely since Adam and Shelby aren't around to knock it down with a broom. It's just a spiderweb, intricate and fine and casting shadows that weren't here before. I huff a breath of relief. A spiderweb! I was letting guilt and paranoia get the best of me.

I twist the key, push open the door, and make quick work of my self-assigned task. *Done*, I think after returning the photo to Shelby's underwear drawer. The photo was here, then gone, now back again, with no one the wiser.

I jog down the stairs and through the house to the back door, feeling pleased with myself and morally righteous.

My hand is on the doorknob—twisting it, even—when I change my mind. I guess I'm not that good after all. I spin on my heel, plant myself on the TV room sofa, and fart long and loud into the cushion.

Better. My twisty stomach's not so twisty anymore.

I rearrange the magazines on the coffee table. There's a stack of RSVPs for Shelby's stupid panty party; it seems she sent out physical invitations as well as her Facebook e-vite. Fancy, fancy. I riffle through the cards and slide several beneath the couch. It probably won't matter. She's had her head count and caterer instructions done for weeks, I imagine. But the thought of Shelby finding herself off by a dozen or so guests pleases me.

I'm carefree as I bike home, and I make swirling loops on the wide, empty streets. As I approach my neighborhood, the elementary school playground appears gilded. At first, the little boy standing beneath the stop sign is unrecognizable. The shadows shift, and I slow down.

"Wendell, hi," I say, dropping a foot to the sidewalk.

The streetlight flickers on, illuminating Wendell's scars. He points at my house, and I turn to see Lump illuminated in the window.

"I like your cat," he says. "He's pretty."

Lump looks a lot better than he did, that's for sure. A bath and a good brushing did wonders.

"Thanks," I say. "Would you like to meet him?"

Wendell smiles and nods. "Yes, please. When?"

"Um . . . right now, if you want?"

A screen door squeaks open across the street. Delilah calls for her little brother, and Wendell's face falls. Right now won't work, I deduce.

"Or whenever," I say. "Just knock on my door, anytime."

Wendell glances over his shoulder, then beckons furtively. I move toward him, straddling my bike. He puts his hand on the back of my neck and pulls me close.

"I agree with what you said on the playground, about how you shouldn't kick hornets," he says.

"Oh," I say dumbly.

"Once a hornet got trapped under my shirt and stung me three times," he goes on. His breath is hot on my face and smells of maple syrup, and I have the uncanny sensation of having lived this moment before.

"Honeybees die after they sting you," he goes on. "But hornets just keep stinging."

There's the pound of sneakers, and Delilah joins Wendell under the streetlight. "You're not supposed to be out here by yourself," she scolds. She shoots daggers at me with her eyes and grabs Wendell's wrist. "Come on."

Wendell waves goodbye as Delilah drags him off. He does so in the little-kid way of opening and closing his hand like a sock puppet, or a mouth.

28

JAKE

I dismount from my bike at the top of my driveway and go to the back door, thinking of entering the house here and opening the garage from the mudroom. But the back door is locked, and while I have Shelby and Adam's key, I forgot my own.

My front door is locked, too. I retrace my steps and peer through the kitchen window. There are my keys, sitting placidly on the granite island.

Lump spots me from within and waddles over. He opens his mouth and mews, and I don't need to hear him to know what he's trying to communicate. It's dinnertime, so what's the deal? I shouldn't be outside. I should be inside, with him, doing that delicious magic with the tuna.

Unlike Adam, I don't keep a spare key under a pot or hidden beneath a rock. I could call a locksmith, but that seems like a lot of trouble. All too easily, I can imagine Lisa and Todd stepping out of their house to watch. "Oh, locked yourself out, did you?" they'd say. "That's no good."

Can I get in through the garage? The remote control lives in my car, and my car is parked in the garage, so no luck there. There's a second door built into the rear wall. It opens onto a slim stretch of grass on the side of the house. I've used it maybe once . . . but perhaps I left it unlocked?

I go around the house and try the handle. No luck. At the bottom, however, there's a cat door. One of the workers talked me into adding it when the house was being constructed.

"All the bungalows have pet doors," he said.

"So it's peer pressure," I replied.

He laughed and carved an opening, from which hangs a heavy rubber flap. If I lie on my back, maybe I can reach through the cat door and grab the handle?

My head barely fits through the opening. I ease out and try a different position, sticking my arm through the cat door and grasping about. Nope. My fingertips graze only air.

I fish a stick from the window well and feed it through the cat door. I'm now able to whack the handle, but I can't disengage the lock.

Hmm. What I need is a piece of string.

A piece of string—of course! Back I go to my bike, where I grab a length of purple embroidery thread from the tangle of discards in my bike bag. I tie a loop on the end of the stick, lie back down, and angle my tool into position. It takes half a dozen attempts, but at last, the loop catches, and the lock releases with a click.

As I scooch backward, I hear raised voices from Billy and Vanessa's bungalow, only several yards away. Their kitchen window is cracked open, allowing me to make out the rise and flow of their conversation. I hear "selfish" and "lazy" and "tits?" "Shits?"

Vanessa's voice is strident. Billy's is lower, pleading. I sit up. Through a gap in the blinds, I see slices of both of them. Billy almost matches his mom in height, but his cowering posture makes him look like a much younger child.

I crane forward and listen.

"Then you're an idiot," Vanessa says acidly.

"Mom," Billy implores, holding up his hands as if to ward off a blow.

I rise before thinking. A branch snaps beneath my foot, and I freeze.

Vanessa and Billy freeze, too, their heads whipping toward the window. Vanessa jerks open the blinds, and there she is, her expression poisonous in the harsh light.

I step sideways into the shadows. Her gaze stills, and the muscles around her eyes tighten. *Shit, shit, shit.*

Vanessa stays at the window for a long moment. Her lips are the color of cranberries. She'd be lovely if she weren't so ugly. At last, she turns away, and my breath rushes out. I slip into my garage and lock the door behind me.

"I did it!" I tell Lump when I join him in the kitchen. I'm whispering for no good reason. "Aren't you so proud?"

He meows and twines around my ankles. He likes me, but he likes his tuna more.

29

BILLY

Billy's mom spends Saturday hate-scrolling GoodNeighbors, while Billy tries to work up the courage to join Bethany and Delilah on the playground across the street. He never does, but he enjoys watching them.

His mother is back at it on Sunday, leaving Billy to his own devices as she scrolls through GoodNeighbors and watches a series called *Selling Sunset* on the television that lives in a wooden entertainment center with doors that shut. When the television isn't being used, the entertainment center's doors stay shut and the TV stays off. When Billy is a grown-up and pays the bills himself, he can watch TV whenever he wants. Until then, tough titties.

Billy knows better than to interrupt his mom. The thing is, he's hungry. When Billy grows up and pays the bills, he can buy his own groceries and eat whatever he wants, whenever he wants. Until then? Tough titties.

But he's a growing boy. People are always saying so. He's a growing boy, and growing boys need to eat, but his mom is a grown-up lady and doesn't always remember that. She skips right over breakfast and right over lunch, which means that Billy skips breakfast and lunch alongside her. That's the way meals work in their house.

By the time Sunday evening rolls around, Billy is so famished, he could faint. He's had nothing to eat all day. He stands politely at the end of the sofa. Eventually, he clears his throat.

"Miss Manners is up my ass again," his mother informs him. She says "Miss Manners" like it's a bad smell, and she offers no explanation because none is necessary. Miss Manners is practically family in Billy and his mother's world, assuming—as Billy's mother does—that family members are more likely to be scorned than supported.

"Some idiot left two hundred dollars in his truck," his mom explains. She focuses on her iPad, her lips curving slightly. "It got stolen. Of course. The truck wasn't even locked! *I* said, 'Who leaves two hundred dollars in their unlocked vehicle? Maybe take a moment to think, next time, before encouraging thieves to ransack our neighborhood.'"

"It happened in our neighborhood?" Billy asks, scouring his memory for driveways with trucks.

"That's *so* not the point," Billy's mom says. "Jesus, Billy. Everyone agreed with me. Everyone with a brain. But Miss Manners, she leaves a comment saying, 'I'm so sorry that happened to you, Richard.' Then, to me, she says, 'Richard was giving everyone a heads-up so they could be careful. No need to victim blame him.'"

"Does Richard live in Miss Manners's neighborhood?"

"How should I know? She just wanted to slap me down so that I'd look like the asshole."

Billy's stomach rumbles. He flattens his palm against it.

"I pointed out that I wasn't victim blaming, just stating the obvious: The world isn't all rainbows and sunshine fairies. If you leave money out for the taking—or your propane tank, or a bowl of Halloween candy corn—guess what? Someone's going to take it."

Billy is so hungry that even candy corn sounds good, and he hates candy corn. "Should I set the table for dinner?" he asks as politely as he can.

Billy's mother types furiously. The furrow between her eyebrows tells him she's returned to her own world, where he doesn't exist.

He goes to the kitchen, eases open the pantry door, and reaches for the Choco Milk, which is a powder you stir into milk to give it vitamins.

Milk is healthy, so a glass of milk might be okay, he reasons. When he draws the canister out, a box of Triscuits topples from the shelf.

"Billy?" his mom calls.

"I bumped the counter and my backpack fell! Sorry!"

Triscuits are made of only three ingredients: whole wheat, oil, and salt. An individual cracker is twenty calories, which isn't terrible, Billy's mom says. Still, he can't just plunge his hand in and grab a handful, because that would spread germs. Billy is positively crawling with germs. All boys are. Anyway, the Triscuits, like everything else, have to be portioned out by his mother.

But there they are, the whole box of them staring at Billy from the floor. He squats and carefully picks at the cardboard flap until it springs free. He plucks at the cellophane bag, which crinkles.

"Don't make me come in there," his mom warns.

Billy releases the bag and hits his head with his clenched fist. *Stupid, stupid, stupid.*

He sits on the floor and breathes shallowly. He tries not to think about the Triscuits.

If he waits long enough, maybe his mom will get sucked back into *Selling Sunset.* The *Selling Sunset* ladies have boob jobs and bright white teeth. One of them has a fake blonde ponytail she clips on for special occasions, a clump of hair so long it hangs below her ass. Billy's mom doesn't know why any man would be attracted to any one of those tramps, but if their idiot boyfriends fall for their idiot games, then tough titties for them.

Billy once saw a show where a kid got home from school and fixed himself a big bowl of ice cream, squirting chocolate syrup from a bottle over the whole thing. The boy's TV mom took one look and said, "Wow, honey, would you like some ice cream with your chocolate sauce?"

Both of them laughed, and the kid got to eat his ice cream.

Television shows are so fake.

He extends one leg and uses his foot to draw the Triscuit box closer. He opens the cellophane bag millimeter by rustling millimeter, coaxes a single cracker out of the bag, and, fast as a rabbit, puts it in his mouth. His tastebuds go *pop pop pop.*

"Billy?" his mother says, terrifyingly close.

"Mom!" he cries. Wet Triscuit hits his chin.

She stands above him, and her eyes are the bad eyes, the flat, black, *you're in trouble now* eyes. "You know Triscuits are off-limits except for special occasions."

"I know. I just—"

"You just what?" She kneels and picks up the box of crackers, folding the cellophane bag with quick, sharp movements. "Please, Billy, explain, because I don't get it."

"Mom, I was just hungry. I'm sorry."

"The weekend's almost over. All I want to do is relax and watch my show. Is that so much to ask?" She exhales. "You know the rules, Billy. I know you do. But you think . . . what?" She raises the pitch of her voice. "'Oh, they don't matter! Mom's just dumb! I don't have to follow her dumb rules if I don't want to!'"

Billy tries to think of a way to fix things. His thoughts bump into one another and get stuck.

"I really thought we'd be happier here," his mom says. "God, I'm an idiot. Do you love me at all, Billy?"

He scrambles to his feet. "Mom! Yes!"

"You ruined the whole day," she murmurs, more to herself than to him. "I was going to order pizza. We were going to have a movie night, just you and me, with popcorn for dessert. It was going to be so much fun." She returns the Triscuits to the shelf. "Oh well."

"We can have a movie night," Billy pleads. "I'll be good."

"I wanted to reward you for getting the highest grade on your math quiz. Can you imagine?"

"*Mom*," he begs. Tears burn in his eyes.

A triumphant smile ghosts across his mother's face. Or not. Maybe it doesn't.

Then Billy is in her arms, and she's holding him close.

"Oh, Billy," she says. "What were you thinking, you silly boy?"

He lets her rock him.

When she's done, she pushes him to arm's length and checks her watch. “If I order the pizza now, it’ll be here in forty-five minutes. Do you think you can wait till then?”

Billy nods. His shame is heavy and complicated, like the back of his mother’s paddle brush against his thighs.

“Good boy,” his mother says. “I’m going to finish watching my show. I need you to let me have this time to myself.”

“I understand. I will.”

“I love you, but you wear me out.”

He takes a small step toward her.

She puts out her palm. “No, Billy. When I’m ready to see you, I’ll let you know.”

30

MABEL

When Mabel was Bethany's age, she presented her mother with a hypothetical question: If there was a life-or-death situation, and her mother could save either Mabel or Mabel's father, but not both, whom would she save?

Mabel's mother had tilted her head and touched her full lower lip, contemplative. She wore Elizabeth Arden lipstick in honeysuckle, a pale, shimmery nude. Her fingernails were a complementary shade of mauve.

"Your father has been alive longer than you have, so I would save you," Mabel's mother said at last. She patted Mabel's hand. "That would be the fair thing to do."

Mabel had felt stripped bare, as if every last stitch of her clothing had fallen to the floor, including her underwear. Her mother's answer wasn't cruel, exactly—and what had Mabel expected? Had she thought her mother would draw her hand to her heart and say, "I'd save *you*, darling! Good heavens! Don't you ever die, my darling girl. If you do, I'll jump into the grave with you!"

Still, her mother's words were a slap. Her mother would save Mabel not out of a great upwelling of maternal love, but because it would be fair.

Twenty years later, while impatiently awaiting David's return from his business trip, Mabel reflects on her mother's response with greater understanding. David, if faced with the same dilemma, would pick Bethany over Mabel in a heartbeat. He's a parent. That's what parents do. But he'd miss Mabel more.

This is what Mabel is thinking about on Monday afternoon as she scrubs at the sticky purple spots on the kitchen floor. Sticky purple *ice-pop* spots, to be exact.

Who craves ice pops once summer has come and gone? Bethany.

Who, just this afternoon, insisted on offering ice pops to Delilah and Wendell after school? Bethany.

And yet, who's the one on her knees like a red-knuckled wash lady, rubbing a wet dishcloth over the floor in endless, angry circles?

It's not Bethany, that's for sure.

She struggles to make friends, that's the thing. Bethany, not Mabel. For as long as Mabel has known her, Bethany has neither hosted nor attended a single sleepover. She's never been invited to someone's house after school, and though she is invited to the occasional birthday party, they're always the "whole class" sort of parties where Bethany and twenty-five other kids take over Chipper's Lanes for bowling, laser tag, and more. Even then, Bethany stands dumbly at the refreshment table and refuses to join in the fun.

But now Delilah's in the picture. Odd, strange Delilah, who seems to genuinely like Bethany. So when Bethany arrived home from school with Delilah and Wendell in tow, Mabel beamed. "Hi, guys," she said. "Come on in!"

When Bethany requested ice pops for the three of them, Mabel said, "Sure, sure, have all the ice pops you want. Just eat them on the porch, please."

Delilah and Wendell filed mutely to the porch—they really are such strange children, especially Delilah—and Bethany flung open the freezer.

"We're out of lime," she complained.

"Then pick a different flavor," Mabel suggested.

"But lime's my favorite!"

"Well, as you said, we're out of lime," Mabel replied. Then, pointedly, "Your friends are waiting on the front porch. It's rude to ignore them."

Bethany huffed and pulled three grape ice pops from the damp cardboard box. One fell and burst free of its plastic wrapper, purple ice skittering across the floor.

"Oh no!" Bethany cried.

"It's fine. Just grab another," Mabel said. She probably should have made Bethany stay and clean up the mess, but her nerves were frazzled. She knew she was close to snapping at her stepdaughter, which she didn't want to do.

She hears the whir of the garage door opening and sits back on her heels, dishrag in hand.

"David!" she exclaims when the top portion of his body appears in her line of vision. "Hi!"

"Honey?" David says. He lopes over and gazes down at her. "Why are you on the floor?"

Mabel feels a stab of embarrassed self-awareness. Did she deliberately wait to clean up Bethany's mess until she knew David would be returning? Why yes, she did.

"Oh, you know," she says. "Just a small ice-pop disaster."

A cloud crosses David's face. "Bethany?"

Mabel smiles like the good sport she wants to be.

David holds his hand out for the rag. "I'll take it from here. You shouldn't be doing this, baby."

Damn straight, she thinks. But really, shouldn't David make *Bethany* clean up the spill? (If David and Bethany's lives were at stake, and Mabel could only save one . . .)

"You know what would help me the most?" she says, rising and brushing herself off.

David pushes back one of her curls. "A shoulder massage?"

Oh, David, she thinks. She says, "That would be lovely. I will definitely take you up on that. But . . . do you think you could take care of dinner? I am so excited to see you, and I'm *so* excited to hug you and kiss you and hear all about your trip, but—"

"Go," David says. "I've got this."

She heads to the pottery studio, where she gathers the ceramic poops she made with Jake and Bethany on Friday.

Friday, wow. Was it just three days ago? It feels as if eons have passed! But yes, on Friday, they made the poops. On Saturday, their little threesome had cookies on the playground with Delilah and Wendell, and yesterday, Mabel took Jake and Bethany back to the studio to glaze their creations.

Jake seemed happier, as if a weight had been lifted from her shoulders. When Mabel inquired about her change in mood, Jake smiled and shrugged.

With the poops clinking pleasantly in a cardboard box, Mabel returns to Sweetwater Lane and parks a little way up from Jake's house, on the opposite side of the street. In Vanessa's yard, she arranges six poops around the Is This Your Poop? sign, stealthy as a cat.

No, not a cat. Mabel is the Easter bunny, distributing poops instead of eggs. They resemble swirly dollops of soft serve, glazed in the perfect shade of brown.

Mabel retreats from Vanessa's yard, fizzy with wicked delight. She wants to dash over to Jake's, rap on her door, and crow about what she's done. She wants tequila and high fives and the wild, intoxicated laughter she remembers from being a kid, where once you start it's nearly impossible to stop.

But Jake asked Mabel not to leave the poop statues in Vanessa's yard. Jake might even be under the impression that Mabel agreed with her request.

No, Mabel decides, she won't bound up Jake's steps and share her daring mischief. Jake has chosen (for the moment) to distance herself from all things petty, so Mabel will respect her wishes. Mabel will wait her out.

Back at home, she calls Bethany into the garage and passes over the biggest of all the remaining poops. It's the size of a kitten and just as cute. "It's the one you made for your dad," she says in a low voice. "Want to give it to him now?"

Bethany squeals. "It's so awesome!" she whisper-yells. "I love it!"

"As you should. It's magnificent!"

Bethany turns pink, and Mabel's heart squeezes. If only things could always be this easy.

In the TV room, Bethany presents the poop to David, who oohs and ahs appreciatively.

"You made this?" he says. "All by yourself?"

"I did!" Bethany says. "I made that entire poop all by myself!"

"It just goes to show," Mabel says philosophically.

"Does it?" David says. His smile is broad, and Mabel's heart contracts. This is all he's ever wanted, for the three of them to be happy. "I shouldn't ask, but what does it show, exactly?"

Mabel joins him on the sofa. "Oh, you know, that sometimes shit happens."

"Mabel!" Bethany says.

"But the things that matter most," Mabel continues, "like family and laughing and being with the people you love?" She grabs a giggling Bethany and pulls her onto the sofa, too. "You've got to *make* that shit happen, know what I mean?"

She kisses the top of Bethany's head the same way that David so often does. It's scary. She doesn't want to be rebuffed. "And we do. Right, Bethany?"

Bethany drops onto the sofa, elbowing both parents until she's settled between them.

"Right," she proclaims.

31

BILLY

Storm clouds roll in wet and heavy over the neighborhood. Billy isn't daunted. He likes storms. Anyway, things have been good for Billy these past couple of days.

Sure, the weekend was bad—especially Sunday with the Triscuits and the scolding and the bad-Billy shame. But after the shame, the night did a 180 and turned awesome, complete with pizza and a full belly and a movie Billy got to pick himself.

He chose *Deadpool*, one of the early ones. He and his mom sat side by side and shared a bag of microwave popcorn, and when his mom laughed at Ryan Reynolds's antics, warmth spread through Billy. He was a star, lit from within. No, his mom was the star, shining her starlight on him. People always think of the sun when they think of stars that give off heat, but even the iciest of stars gives comfort if you press up close.

His mom's good mood has remained steady, and so the storm doesn't matter. It may be dismal outside, but inside, as Billy gets ready for school, everything is cozy and safe.

From downstairs, his mother gasps. "Billy?" she cries. "Billy, come here!"

Billy grabs his backpack and jogs downstairs. "I'm coming, Mom!"

He finds her in the office, standing before the wide window with her fingertips grazing the sill. She's staring at something in the yard.

"Are you okay?" he says. He hurries to her side. "What's wrong?"

She points, and Billy's eyes follow along until he sees what she sees: Dog shit, heaping towers of dog shit, all around the sign she erected that says, Is This Your Poop? PICK IT UP!

The owner of the dog in question did not obey Billy's mother's command. On the contrary, the owner of the dog—dogs?—gave Billy's mother a huge "up yours" by coaxing them not only to shit repeatedly and prodigiously, but to do so with such precision that Billy is struck dumb. It seems almost unreal.

"Whoever did that, they did it on purpose," his mother says, blinking in a strange, juddering way. It's as if something inside of her wants to get out, using her eye sockets as an exit. She strides to the kitchen in her click-clack shoes, grabs a plastic bag from the cupboard beneath the sink, and thrusts it at him. "Scoop them up, every last one. Now!"

Billy jumps to obey. And then, okay, he realizes that it *is* unreal. The shit. Using the plastic bag as a glove, he picks up the first enormous turd and understands. The shit in their yard, every last precarious tower of it, is fake. Does that make things better? Or worse?

When he reenters the house, he holds the bag against his body to keep the fake turds from clinking. He heads straight for the mudroom, hoping to make it to the garage with his mother none the wiser.

The bag rips, and the statues of shit tumble to the floor. It happens in slow motion; that's how it feels. Some bounce. Some break. One dolloped tip pops free and rolls like a deranged pinball toward Billy's mother, who traps it with the toe of her glossy red pump.

She inhales, sucking all the oxygen from the room.

Her eyes shoot toward Billy, who throws up his hands.

"Mom," he babbles. "I didn't . . . I swear . . ."

She bends and grabs the ball of fake shit. "I know that, Billy," she snaps. "Obviously." She paces, squeezing the ball between her palm and her thumb until it breaks into fragments. "It was someone from Good-Neighbors. It had to be. In *fact* . . ."

She paces and thinks, thinks and paces. She grinds the pottery fragments into a fine brown powder.

She stops and says, grimly, "I think it's your friend."

"What? *Who?*"

She jerks her head at the bungalow next to theirs. "Jake, I think her name is? The one you got so chummy with at the neighborhood party?"

"Mom," Billy protests. He backs away from her, but slowly. Cautiously.

"I think she has it out for us. I think that's uncool."

"Me too!" Billy hastens to assure her. "But . . . why would she?"

The soft white light of the kitchen is flattened by a flash of lightning. Thunder booms.

"I've sensed her lurking about," his mother says. "Or if not Jake, then some other nosy neighbor."

"That's creepy."

"It is, isn't it? But do you know what, Billy?"

"What?"

"In the end, busybodies get what they deserve. They always do."

Billy doesn't ask what busybodies deserve. He just nods and says, "I know. But Mom? She's not my friend."

"No?"

"Mom, no. I hate her!"

The rain finally starts, the sound of it a thrumming assault. Across the street, wind whips around the swing set and tangles the chains.

Billy's mom walks forward and places her hands on Billy's shoulders. At first, they lie there like dead weight, her index fingers cold against his neck. Then she presses her thumbs into the hollows below his collarbone, rubbing and tracing circles, while her fingers slide to his upper back. It feels. So. Good.

She massages his shoulders, and a great velvet snake glides through him, smoothing him and soothing him until his head droops forward.

She digs in harder with her thumbs.

He jerks upright.

"Shh," she murmurs. "You're fine."

What she's doing hurts, but he forces his muscles to unclench. He doesn't protest.

"Good boy," she murmurs. "My good, good boy."

32

WENDELL

Wendell sits at his desk and stares out the window at the rain, which is coming down in sheets. Aunt Evelyn had to drive him and Delilah to school this morning, the storm is that bad.

"Don't expect limo service often," she warned as they filed from the house into the connected garage. "When it snows—and it will, believe me—you two are walking, even if it's twelve inches deep. But I can't send you out in rain like this."

She lifted her face to the pinging, dinging roof. Wendell did the same. It was like being in a drum, or an old-fashioned metal lunch box full of toy soldiers being shaken all to bits.

"*Wen*dell," Ms. Merry says in a tone that suggests she's called his name more than once. She taps the whiteboard with the marker. "Eyes up here, please."

Wendell's eyes obey, but his thoughts stay on the rain. The rain, and also his dad, because his dad loved storms. "Now that is pure glory," his father would say when the skies opened up. He'd stand on the covered porch of their old house with his hands on Wendell's shoulders. "Breathe deep, son. Breathe that clean air in."

Does it rain in prison?

Don't be dumb, Wendell says in his head. Of course it doesn't rain in prison.

It rains outside of prison, though.

Do prisons have windows?

Wendell glances at Elsa, who keeps throwing anxious looks at the classroom windows. Maybe Elsa's afraid of storms for the same reason that Wendell used to be afraid of his dad: Because they're unpredictable. Sometimes Wendell's father was nice. Sometimes he watched rainstorms with Wendell and told him to breathe in deep. But other times, he yelled and stomped and hit Wendell's mom if she did something wrong. Sometimes he hit Delilah and Wendell, too.

"When I was your age, my father whipped me every time I misbehaved," Wendell's father told Wendell once, after striking him with the back of his hand. "And I misbehaved a lot. I was a bad kid."

Wendell's cheek was on fire, but he tried not to show it. He tried to hold his father's gaze.

"But you're not bad, Wendell," his father said. Now that the hitting was over, his eyes had gone mournful, and he was dabbing antibiotic ointment on Wendell's cheek. "You're a good boy. Just, sometimes you make mistakes. When you do, it's my job to correct you. I don't enjoy it, but it has to be done. Do you understand?"

Wendell hadn't understood, no. Also, his father did enjoy it. Wendell saw it in a certain little smile that curled around his lips.

When Wendell thinks of that man, the one with the certain smile, he's glad his father is in prison. He wishes, for Elsa's sake, that the bad weather could be thrown in there with him.

But storms can't be locked up. Neither can fear or love.

Wendell sighs. Sometimes he misses his sad-eyed father, even though he knows he isn't supposed to.

33

JAKE

After two days of rain, the morning sun is a welcome gift. It's warm enough on Thursday that I open the front room windows, prompting Lump to hop onto the wide windowsill and sniff hungrily at the autumn air. For a cat who didn't fare well in the great outdoors, he sure seems interested in giving it another go.

"Not on my life," I tell him, scratching behind his ears. "Your immune system is compromised. I've got to keep you safe."

Lump looks at me reproachfully, but I don't back down. Lump gets to spend all day eating and sleeping and stretching and purring, and at the end of the day, not a single person asks what he's accomplished.

Speaking of getting things accomplished, I need to spend some time on Professor Lee's manuscript. But first things first. It's time for my morning espresso.

I find Mabel reclining on her outdoor sofa, laptop on her thighs. When she spots me, she slams it shut.

"Vanessa or Shelby?" I ask.

She feigns ignorance for all of two seconds, then laughs, caught out. "Both, and Vanessa is having a moment, let me tell you."

I hold up my hand. "Nope. I'm on a break, remember?"

"Okay, let me rephrase," Mabel says. "Vanessa is having a veritable meltdown, but I will *not* tell you all the gory details, even if you beg."

"Oh, really? Even if I beg?"

She grins. "Fine. If you beg, I'll relent."

I sweep Mabel's feet off the sofa and sit down. "I'm here for the coffee, not the tea." I spot a small, insulated espresso cup and lift it. "For me?"

"Yes ma'am, and I made pumpkin muffins." She slides a cookie tin my way. "Even Bethany said they were good. Oh, and she asked if I'd make cookies for her. She said, 'Mabel dearest, would you please make those delicious chocolate chip cookies, the ones with the salt on top?'" Mabel touches her fingertips to her temples and explodes them outwards. "This, from Bethany, who supposedly *hates* my baking."

"And?"

"And I said yes! Duh! I expect my Mother of the Year tiara will arrive any day."

I smile, although I feel a pang. I'd like to win mom of the year, but my baby is in the ground, cold and alone.

Stop it, I tell myself.

Across the street, the midmorning bell rings, and kids tumble onto the playground like jelly beans. I search for Wendell as we chat, but the first graders must have recess at a different time.

Back home, I delve into edits on Professor Lee's book, though I make little progress. I can't stop yawning. He did warn me that this chapter would be dry, but promised the next one would make up for it.

"I plan to do a deep dive on ethnobotany," he told me with wide eyes. "Do you know what that is?"

"I do not," I said.

"It's the study of how plants are used by different cultures. It encompasses many things, but I'm particularly interested in plant-based medicine. Ointments and potions and the like."

"Like what witches cook up in their cauldrons?"

"Not just witches. Shamans as well, and Eastern medicine practitioners. Healers from all walks of life, myself included."

"So you're still dosing Cindy Pawford," I commented.

"Oh, yes," Professor Lee said. "Not that it does much good!"

At 3:05 p.m., the afternoon bell rings, and I gratefully put down my pencil. I move to the porch, drop into a chair, and enjoy the exodus across the way. The first kids out the door are loud and raucous, with mouths stretched wide and flailing limbs. They would run you over and not think twice.

The second wave is more controlled. Pairs of girls file to the playground, where they'll swing until their parents arrive. Other kids dash toward the field with footballs and soccer balls. Still others file toward the buses, the crosswalk, and the carpool line. Cheerful voices rise and fall, and I feel nostalgic for handprint turkeys and cartons of chocolate milk.

I spot Wendell on a strip of grass between the playground and the road. He leans against the diamond mesh fence, waiting as Delilah and Bethany conduct an animated conversation.

From behind me comes a thump and a twang—and then an alarmed meow. I twist to see Lump clinging to the window screen. His claws poke through the steel mesh, and his heavy body hangs suspended in midair.

"Lump!" I chide. "What are you doing, you goofball?"

Lump rips one paw free, only to bat at the air and reanchor himself on the screen. He yowls, his tail whipping back and forth.

I scramble out of my chair and hurry inside, where I grab Lump beneath his rib cage and try to hoist him free. He's as docile as a bag of flour, but a bag of flour with claws. Each time I unhook one paw from the screen, he readheres himself with another.

I finally wrench him from the window screen, at which point he decides he's no longer a bag of flour but a Tasmanian devil. With a great thrust, he explodes from my arms and bolts through the open door.

"Lump, no!"

I rush after him, gasping sharply when I spot him trotting across the carpool-busy street, his massive belly swaying. A truck rounds the curve. Lump freezes. He turns and takes great, bounding leaps in front of a red convertible that's approaching from the opposite direction.

Brakes squeal, and I fling my arm up over my eyes.

"Is that your cat?" demands the lady driving the convertible.

"Sorry!" I cry.

"We have leash laws for a reason!" she yells as she speeds away. "And yes, they apply to cats!"

Lump is on the opposite side of the street, skulking between the curb and the asphalt. But he's scared. As soon as I get close enough to grab him, he flattens his ears and dashes beneath a Range Rover idling in the pickup lane.

"Lump!" I implore. I wave to get the driver's attention. "Excuse me, sorry, but my cat's under your car!"

The man drums his fingers in time with his country music, which I can hear through his rolled-up windows. He follows the cars ahead of him as they creep forward, stop, and creep forward again.

I squat and slap my thighs. "Lump!" I coax. "C'mere, Lump!"

A crowd of kids forms on the sidewalk, Bethany, Delilah, and Wendell among them. Wendell's face creases with concern, and Delilah steps forward and wraps her arms around him.

Billy elbows past the others and joins me in the middle of the street.

"It's my cat," I say, gesturing at the Range Rover.

Billy drops to his hands and knees and peers beneath. The driver, who has caught on that something interesting is happening, rolls down his window.

"Your cat's under there?" he says. "Not the best idea."

Yes, thanks, I tell him with a tight smile.

Billy fishes around in the shadows while I chew on my lower lip, aware that I'm basically letting a fifth grader play in traffic. "Billy, please. It's fine."

"Not if your cat's under there," says the driver of the Range Rover. He leans out the window. "Though I guess a kid's even worse, huh?"

Billy crawls backward from beneath the car, Lump clutched to his chest. When he stands, everyone claps.

"Yay, Billy!" Wendell cries, thrusting a fist into the air. To the others, he says, "That's my reading buddy! Guess what, guys? That's my reading buddy!"

Billy keeps a firm grip on Lump, who tries to scale his torso.

"Billy, you are a hero," I say when he passes him over. "Thank you."

"No problem," he says, his cheeks pink with pleasure.

I carry Lump across the street, up the porch stairs, and back into the house, kicking the door shut behind me. "You dum-dum," I say. I nuzzle his head with my nose. "Why are you such a dum-dum, dum-dum?"

There's a rap on the door, followed by the *bzzzz* of the doorbell. I deposit Lump on the sofa and return to the entryway, cracking the door to see Bethany, Delilah, and Wendell standing just outside.

"Hi, Jake," Bethany says. She's nervous, but I can tell she's proud to be the one who knows me best. "Can Wendell meet your cat?"

"Of course, yes," I say, waving them in. "Make yourselves comfortable."

I gesture at the sofa, where Lump is placidly grooming himself. He's decided that he prefers being clean, I think. Or maybe it's easier to stay on top of things now that he's not homeless. "His name's Lump."

Wendell holds out his fingers for Lump to sniff. Lump pushes his head against Wendell's hand, and Wendell laughs.

"He wants you to pet him and praise him and tell him how brave he is," I tell him. I pivot toward the back of the house. "Do you guys want a snack? I have chips, Cheez-Its, M&M's . . ."

"Yes, please," Wendell says.

"We're not staying," Delilah says. "Pet the cat, Wendell."

"I am," Wendell says, running his hand along Lump's back.

"Maybe just a drink?" I say. "Does everyone like Coke?"

I go to the kitchen and return with provisions. Delilah opens her Coke only after seeing Wendell and Bethany enjoying theirs. Soon a box of Cheez-Its is making the rounds as well, and I feel absurdly pleased with how my impromptu tea party is unfolding.

"So," I say, sitting down and clasping my hands in my lap. Wendell and Lump take up the middle of the sofa, with Bethany and me on either side of them. Delilah leans against the wall. "Did you guys have a good day at school?"

Three heads swivel my way, and I realize that yes, I really did just trot out the most boring question in the universe.

"Mmm-hmm," Wendell says politely.

"Not really," Delilah says.

"If I'm going to be real, Billy rescuing your cat was the best part," Bethany says.

"Oh, barf," Delilah says. "Bethany? Do *not*."

A flush rises on Bethany's face. "What? What did I do?"

"If I have to hear how *wonderful* Billy is one more time, I'm going to stick a piece of duct tape over your mouth and smoosh it down so hard that when you rip it off, it rips off all your facial hair."

"I don't have facial hair!" Bethany protests.

"You do, Bethany. We all do. Everyone who has a face has facial hair." Delilah turns to me. "Bethany isn't petting your cat. You wanna know why?"

"Um, sure?"

"Because Bethany doesn't like cats."

"I do so!" says Bethany.

"*Bethany* likes Billy."

Bethany turns scarlet. "Delilah!"

"Oh, please," Delilah says. "You do, and you know it."

"I just think he's nice," Bethany says. "And smart. And he saved Jake's cat. That doesn't mean I have a crush on him."

Delilah snorts.

I turn to her. "You don't like Billy, Delilah?"

"He's creepy," she states. "There's something off about him, which Bethany would realize if she wasn't simping over him all the time."

"Nuh-uh!"

Delilah ticks off examples. "He eats lunch by himself, he has snack break by himself, he hangs out by himself during recess—"

"Maybe he's shy," I suggest.

"Billy? No, he's broken inside, I'm telling you."

"I like him," Wendell offers. "He's my reading buddy."

Delilah pushes off from the wall. "Come on, Wendell, let's go. Aunt Evelyn will be wondering where we are."

"Aw, man," Wendell says under his breath. He lowers his face to Lump's and touches noses with him. "Bye, Lump! See you soon!"

"*Now*," Delilah says.

He scrambles off the sofa, and Bethany follows suit. I escort all three to the door.

"Speaking of your aunt," I say, touching Delilah's shoulder.

Delilah looks at my fingers on her arm, then at me. She steps backward and out of my reach.

"Never mind." If I decide to broach the subject of Wendell's scars, I'll approach Evelyn on my own.

I watch from the porch as the kids clatter down the front stairs. Before they part ways at the sidewalk, I say, "Hey, Bethany?"

She turns back, as do Delilah and Wendell.

"I think Billy's a good kid," I say.

"See?" crows Bethany. She jabs Delilah. "Told you!"

Delilah rolls her eyes.

"He's a little awkward," I say, "but he's got a big heart."

34

MABEL

Mabel continues to monitor Shelby's Facebook page, even though Jake asked her to let it go. Even though, in truth, it's becoming a little boring, as is the overinflated drama on GoodNeighbors. So many people working themselves into a lather over such silly, silly things.

But it's become such a habit that it's hard to simply let it go. Not to mention that Shelby is still in Bora-Bora, living it up and documenting every moment of her perfect life, the life she stole from Jake.

That's not fair. Shelby didn't "steal" anything from Jake any more than Mabel stole anything from Gigi. But the way Shelby gloats about it gets under Mabel's skin. (Or is it that Shelby "stole" Adam and got away with it, while Mabel "stole" David and still carries lingering shame about having done so, despite her conviction that David, Bethany, and even Gigi are happier now than they were before Mabel's . . . interference?)

But.

Shelby.

"A week in paradise with the perfect man!" Shelby boasted when she and Adam arrived on the island. Every day since, she's graced the world with an abundance of aspirational photos. Shelby in a white bikini. Shelby in a blue bikini. Shelby in sundresses and drawstring linen pants.

Today's photo shows Shelby in an adorable lime-green sweatshirt that Mabel finds herself coveting, dammit. She uses Google Images to search for the brand, but comes up dry.

According to Shelby's timeline, she and Adam will depart the island tomorrow, which is Friday, which will put them back in Fort Collins by Saturday morning. To Mabel, this seems crazy. Shelby's panty party is on Sunday, the very next day! Will Shelby show up bleary-eyed and exhausted, or is she the sort of person who looks fresh as a daisy whether coming or going, the sort of person who laughs and says cheerfully, "Jet lag? Me?"

Mabel feels for Jake. She really does.

Bethany arrives home from school later than usual, flushed and excited. Mabel puts away her laptop and switches gears. Today is Mabel–Bethany bonding day, with cookies!

As Mabel helps Bethany assemble the dough, Bethany bubbles over with stories of "Billy this" and "Billy that."

"Billy, Vanessa's son?" Mabel asks.

"He was *so* brave crawling under the car, don't you think?"

"Totally," Mabel says.

She instructs Bethany on how long to microwave the butter, taking care not to melt it entirely but rather soften it into a glistening yellow blob. She also teaches her to spoon the flour into the measuring cup instead of dragging it through the canister. Finally, she tells Bethany the trick for baking in Colorado's high altitude: Reduce the quantity of both brown and white sugar while slightly increasing the amount of baking soda.

When the dough is ready, Mabel retrieves three bags of chocolate chips from the pantry: milk chocolate, semisweet chocolate, and dark chocolate.

"The different flavors keep your tongue from getting bored," Mabel explains.

"Oh," Bethany says. "Cool."

Mabel tells Bethany that it's best to let cookie dough rest in the fridge for several hours, but that they can skip that step if they choose. They *could* bake one tray of cookies right now if they want to. Do they want to?

They do. Mabel guides Bethany in spooning out equal portions of dough onto the cookie tray, flattening them slightly before crumbling flakes of sea salt on top.

She pops the tray into the oven, and soon the kitchen smells sweet and buttery. Mabel catches Bethany glancing at her, then looking away, then glancing at her all over again.

"What's up, buttercup?" Mabel prompts.

"I have a question," Bethany confesses. "It's kind of embarrassing."

"Shoot."

"Do you think a boy who's nice to animals is, like, a boy who would be good to go out with?"

Mabel is surprised. She teased Bethany about Billy at the beginning of the school year, didn't she? She teased Bethany about having a crush on Billy, and Bethany ended up shoving her chair from the table and fleeing to her bedroom.

This time, Mabel will do better.

"Go out with, as in go to a movie with?"

Bethany looks horrified. "No! Not a *movie*!"

"Sorry, sorry," Mabel says, understanding belatedly that "going out with" must be the current way of designating elementary school romances. When Mabel was in the fifth grade, the term was "go with." "Go where?" her dad would ask. It drove Mabel batty.

"I think being nice to animals is a good sign, one hundred percent," Mabel says.

Bethany nods vehemently. "Me, too! But Delilah doesn't. Delilah doesn't agree *at all*."

"Does it matter what Delilah thinks?"

"I mean, she's my best friend."

"You can be best friends with someone and not agree with them about every little thing," Mabel suggests.

"You can?"

"Sure."

Bethany searches Mabel's expression. "Do you and Jake disagree about stuff?"

"Good heavens, yes! That's what keeps things interesting." She can see Bethany isn't convinced. Delilah has a big personality. A big, scowling personality, while Bethany is timid and meek. It's probably hard for her to hold her own at times.

"You get to choose what you share and what you don't, you know."

"I guess," Bethany says uncertainly. "What if she's right, though? And I'm wrong?"

"What if you're right and *she's* wrong?"

Bethany looks baffled. Mabel doesn't blame her. She tells Bethany to go watch TV, and that she'll call her when the cookies are done. Then she turns her attention to the memory Bethany's query triggered.

The night before David's first wedding, Gigi's brother pulled David aside and urged him not to go through with it. David confessed this to Mabel sheepishly, probably looking back at the past and considering the same conundrum Bethany is facing in the present. Everyone always says, "Listen to your gut," but what if your gut has been fooled, at least temporarily?

According to David, Gigi's brother warned him straight up that Gigi was bad news. "She's my sister. I shouldn't be saying this. But she's mean, David," Gigi's brother told him. "She'll eat you alive."

He was right, as it turned out.

The timer dings, scattering Mabel's musings like dust bunnies.

"Bethany! Cookies!" Mabel calls. She slides the cookie tray from the oven, holds it above the granite countertop, and releases it. Bethany, who's materialized beside her, startles at the bang.

"Dropping them like that makes the texture better," Mabel says. "Now you know all my secrets."

"Can I have one?" Bethany asks, eyeing the cookies as they deflate.

"They need to cook for two more minutes, which they'll do by sitting on the tray."

She leans against the island and considers her stepdaughter. She considers David and Gigi, David and herself. "Do you know what I did with your dad when I first realized how much I liked him?"

Bethany looks nervous. "No, what?"

"I wooed him with cookies. Every time I baked a batch, I put a couple in a brown paper lunch sack for him, along with a handwritten note."

"What did the note say?"

"Different things. Whatever I felt like writing. But basically just, 'Hey, I made cookies and thought you might like some.'"

Bethany's eyes go to the still-warm cookies.

"You can have one now," Mabel says. "I'll join you."

The next morning, Mabel puts four cookies into a brown paper lunch sack for David, folds the top down, and plants a lipstick kiss on the front. She puts four more cookies in a second sack and leaves it on the counter, positioning it haphazardly on a stack of junk mail. Then she busies herself in a different part of the house as Bethany packs her lunch.

"Bye, Mabel!" Bethany calls at a quarter past eight.

"Bye!" Mabel calls back. "Have a great day!"

When she returns to the kitchen, the junk mail is still there, but the sack of cookies is gone.

35

BILLY

Billy knows things about his classmates. Secret, private things, like how Shandra keeps a scrap of a battered baby blankie in her backpack, which she sniffs for comfort on the sly. How the twins, Agatha and Martha, suck juice from each other's fingers when they bring blueberries for snack break. Once, when Martha got a paper cut, Agatha put Martha's finger in her mouth and sucked off the blood.

Stephanie rolls her earwax into little balls, which she smushes onto the underside of her desk. Marco, who sits behind Bethany, picks his nose and flicks the boogers into Bethany's hair. Azaiah gets after-school tutoring because he's a bad reader, way below grade level, and Melón, Azaiah's best friend, feels invisible even though he's the fattest kid in the class. Melón burps and makes farting sounds because it's better to be annoying than ignored.

Billy doesn't have ESP or anything. He's simply curious and observant, and not the least bit squeamish. If he's walking along a trail and comes upon a large, flat rock, for example, he'll toe it with his sneaker and flip it over. That's who Billy is, a boy who flips over rocks to reveal the squirming things beneath.

On Friday, Billy watches Marco flick his boogers into Bethany's hair and feels anger coil in his belly. Any other day, he'd watch impassively. If he responded at all, it would be to yawn. (In the fifth grade, boogers never stop coming.)

Today, Billy rises from his seat, strolls past Marco's desk, and jabs an unfolded staple into Marco's neck.

"Ow!" Marco exclaims, his hand slapping the spot where he was pricked. "What *was* that, bruh?"

Billy lets the staple fall to the ground. He turns and says, "Dude, I don't know what you're talking about."

"You . . . stung me," Marco says.

"I *stung* you?" Billy repeats.

Marco looks around for support. Melón and Azaiah shrug.

"Maybe it was a bee," suggests Agatha.

"Are you allergic?" asks Martha. "Bee allergies are really dangerous!" Martha is the older of the twins by two minutes and likes to mother other kids.

"It hurts," Marco whines.

Ms. Lipowski sighs. "Marco, go to the nurse if you really think you must. Otherwise, please stop disrupting the class."

Yeah, Marco, Billy says silently. He continues to the front of the room, where he plucks a tissue he doesn't need from the box on Ms. Lipowski's desk. He smiles at Bethany as he returns to his seat. She turns bright red and smiles back.

During snack break, he eats the cookies she gave him, which he found on his desk when he arrived that morning. They were inside a brown paper lunch sack, along with a letter in a sealed envelope decorated with hearts and rainbows and smiley faces. Billy eats the cookies, but he has yet to read the letter. So much hangs in the balance, like a slithery thing that will or won't escape.

He opens the envelope at the end of snack break. He can't wait a moment longer. He pulls out Bethany's letter and reads it under his desk. Then he reads it again. Then he sits there, shocked, because . . . Bethany likes him? That's what she claims, and he has the letter to prove it. Not that he would!

This is between him and Bethany. It's their secret. Billy has lived his entire life convinced that secrets are shameful, but now he revisits that belief, because this kind of private feels good. This secret is intoxicating. He folds the letter, puts it back in the envelope, and slides the envelope into his pocket, where it beats like a second heart.

Ms. Lipowski flashes the lights to say, "Fun time is over, boys and girls. Put away your things and let's get back to business."

Billy can't get back to business. No way!

Ms. Lipowski calls to him as he slips into the hall. "Excuse me, Billy," she says. "You need the bathroom pass in order to go to the bathroom. You can't go to the bathroom without the pass!"

Fuck you, he thinks joyfully. Poor Ms. Lipowski, the rhinoceros. What do rhinoceroses know about anything?

In the boys' bathroom, in the stall with the janky lock (Billy knows it's janky because he locked a kindergartner in here once), he unfolds Bethany's letter and reads it again.

> Dear Billy,
>
> Here are some cookies I made. I hope you like them! Also, I'm glad you rescued Jake's cat. You are a real-life hero!!!
>
> Love,
> Bethany
>
> PS The flakes on top aren't sugar. They're salt. Now you know all my secrets.
>
> PPS I think you are very nice. Now you really know all my secrets!

Billy stares at the letter until it goes swimmy. He thinks of tiny fluttering eyelashes, a raindrop running slowly down a window.

When school lets out, he follows Bethany into the brisk October air. He waits until she parts ways with Delilah, then calls her name and jogs toward her with jangling nerves.

"Can I walk with you?" he asks.

"Um, sure?" Bethany says.

Billy's chest swells. His nerves don't disappear, but they diminish. "Let's take the long way," he suggests.

"What's the long way?"

"I'll show you. Come on."

They follow the crosswalk to the other side of the street, then head east along Sweetwater Lane instead of west, which is the direction they'd normally go. At the intersection of Shields and Sweetwater, Billy takes a left.

"Oh," Bethany says, and Billy sees that she understands. The "long way" means tracing out a square. By taking another left after this one, and one more after that, they'll end up back on Sweetwater Lane.

Neither of them speaks as they walk along Shields. There's too much noise from traffic. When they turn left on Seneca, the traffic noise fades. No one is outside tending the yards of these falling-down houses. The crumbling sidewalk stretches ahead of them, weeds and tufts of grass sprouting from cracks.

"I never go this way," Bethany says. "My stepmom wouldn't like it."

"How come?"

"I don't know. I'm supposed to come straight home."

"Why?"

Bethany shrugs.

"Is she waiting for you? Will she be worried if you're not home on time?"

"Ha. No."

"Why do you say it like that? Does she *not* get worried?"

"Maybe she gets worried. I don't know."

The conversation isn't going anywhere, and Billy's sure it's his fault. He needs to ask better questions. "Do you like her, your stepmom?"

Bethany kicks a stone, which bounces along the sidewalk and hits another stone. "Sometimes I do. Not always."

Billy scours his memory. "She wore that flowered thing, at the neighborhood party."

"A romper," Bethany says.

"A *romper*," he repeats, pulling a face that makes Bethany laugh. Her cheeks are pink, and so is the tip of her nose.

They pass the house with the blue shutters, where the old people live. Billy jerks his chin at it. "Do you know the Santangelos?"

Bethany shakes her head.

"I mow their lawn for them," Billy says. Bethany looks impressed, so he adds, "This winter, when it snows, I'll shovel their driveway."

"Do they pay you?"

"They want to, but I don't let them," he says. "They're like, 'Here's twenty dollars. Take it, please!' But I'm like, 'Nah, that's okay.'"

"Wow," Bethany says. "That's so nice."

Yep, that's me, he thinks. He tries out the idea of mowing the lawn for the Santangelos for real. It wouldn't be so hard.

He points at the falling-down shed. "I clean their shed for them, too. They said I can use it whenever I want."

"Cool."

"And guess what I found?"

"What?"

"A snake."

Bethany's eyes widen. "In the shed? You found a snake in their shed?"

"Don't worry. I took care of it." At her expression, he laughs. "Not like *that*! I mean, it was my pet, for a while. I fed it grass and stuff."

"Snakes eat grass?"

"This one did. But something happened to it, so . . ." He decides to change the subject. "The shed is my personal clubhouse, basically. It's private, so it's a good place to chill out." He's struck by inspiration. "You can share it, if you want."

"Oh," Bethany says. A line forms between her eyebrows.

"Or not. It doesn't matter."

He plays it cool, planting one foot in front of the next until they reach Roxborough, the short street that completes the loop around the neighborhood. Too soon, they're back on Sweetwater Lane, the elementary school hazy in the distance.

"Here's your house," Bethany says when they're in front of Billy's bungalow. She swivels her head to the house where Delilah lives, but Delilah's nowhere to be seen. She swivels her head in the opposite direction, toward her house at the opposite end of the street. She laughs. "Only now I have to walk all the way back."

"I'll walk with you," Billy says, realizing what an idiot he is.

She laughs again. "Then *you'd* have to walk back."

He feels the onslaught of buzzing bees. They want to sting him. They want to sting everybody. Stupid, stupid, stupid!

"Well, thanks for walking me home. Although really, *I* walked *you* home," Bethany says.

Billy stands there.

She shoves his shoulder. She could be a moth. That's how gentle she is. "I'm teasing!"

Billy wrenches himself back. "I know. *Ha!* I'm such an idiot."

"Don't say that. You're not," she says. "Anyway . . . bye!"

He watches her walk away, swallowing repeatedly. A foreign thought pokes at the edge of his consciousness. What if, one day, he *doesn't* swallow the furious stings that come for him? He imagines hundreds of buzzing bumblebees punching through his skin and flying away, and how light he would feel with them gone.

36

JAKE

On Saturday, I return from coffee with Mabel to find Billy sitting cross-legged on the sidewalk in front of our houses. He glances up and says, "Hi, Jake."

"Hi," I say. "What are you doing?"

"Watching an ant colony. Wanna see?"

I go and squat beside him. Before us, a steady line of ants march from the grass to the sidewalk and from the sidewalk to the grass.

"They're pavement ants," Billy says.

"I guess so."

"That's the name of the species," Billy clarifies. He points at the stream of bodies. "See how many there are? There are probably ten thousand workers in this colony alone."

"Why are they going back and forth like that?"

"They're delivering food."

"Pizza?"

Billy gives me a look that says grown-ups shouldn't try to be funny. "They're delivering pollen or seeds, or maybe crumbs from something someone dropped. Worker ants find the food and recruit their nestmates to collect it and take it to the nest. They show the way by smearing pheromones along the path with their stingers."

I sit down, stretching out my legs and leaning back on my palms. The sidewalk is cool, but the sun is warm. "How do you know so much about ants?"

"Nature shows," Billy says. "My dad and I like to watch them."

"Nice," I say. I hesitate. "Where *is* your dad? What's up with that?"

Billy shrugs. "He sees me whenever he can."

"Where does he live? What does he do for work?"

"He's an engineer."

"Here in town?"

"Arizona. That's where I used to live."

"Oh. Cool."

We're quiet for a bit.

"He has a motorcycle," Billy offers, taking a stick and using it to help a wandering ant find its way.

"Yeah?"

"He's going to teach me to ride it. I'll probably learn fast, because I'm a quick learner. That's what people say, that I'm smart like him."

I nod.

"At school, I have the highest grade of all the fifth graders," he goes on. "Every week, the smartest kid gets to be Best Boy and be the first to line up for recess, and every week, it's me. I'm always Best Boy. Hey, can I use your phone?"

"My phone?"

"To call my dad," Billy says. "I call him every Saturday. Usually, I use my mom's phone, but she's not home. He'll be waiting to hear my math grades and if I got Best Boy again. So can I?"

I falter, unsure of the etiquette in this situation. Is it okay to let a kid I only slightly know use my cell phone to call a man I don't know in the slightest?

"And I want to tell him about rescuing your cat," Billy throws in.

He *did* rescue my cat, that's true. Although, now I feel like he's playing me.

He smiles hopefully. "Please?"

"What would your mom say? Would she care?"

Billy scrunches his brow. "He's my dad," he says.

I unlock my phone and hand it over. Billy punches in a string of digits. He hovers his thumb over the call button and glances up at me.

I shake my head. I'm staying right here.

Billy launches the call and lifts the phone to his ear. After several seconds he says, "Oh, hi, Dad." He twists sideways. "It's me, Billy. I guess you're not there? I wanted to tell you about my math quiz. I got the best grade in the whole class, and it's not the first time, either. I pretty much always get the best grade." He ducks his head and drops his voice. "Also, I have a girlfriend. She's really nice, and . . . yeah. Her name's Bethany."

Oh, my heart. I have to stop myself from clasping my hand to my chest. Does Mabel know about this?

Good God. Does Vanessa?

Billy says goodbye and hands me my phone, flushed and happy.

"He wasn't home?" I ask.

"I left a message. It's all good."

37

JAKE

I owe Professor Lee a visit. This is the next "to-do" item on my afternoon agenda. I decide to drive to my old neighborhood instead of bike, in the hopes that parking my easily recognizable car in the professor's driveway will force me to keep on the straight and narrow. *You may not go to the Hemlock house*, I tell myself. *It's not an option. Got it?*

I suspect Adam and Shelby are in an airplane somewhere, or an airport lounge awaiting the next leg of their journey home, but I'm not positive. If I were a better woman, that uncertainty alone would nullify the temptation to pay their house one last visit. (One last visit on top of the one last visit I already paid, that is.)

I'm not that woman. I am sorely tempted to drop in yet again.

I pull into Professor Lee's driveway in my bright yellow Beetle, then stop the car, shift into first, and yank up the emergency break the way my father taught me. Boone was a different world, I suppose, with its gravel roads and bearded men in pickup trucks. I was way too young for the driving lessons he gave me, and yet my ease around standard transmissions might be the one legacy from him that isn't laced with pain.

"Jake! Come in," Professor Lee says. He sees the marked-up pages I'm holding, and his round face crinkles in a smile. "What did you think of the chapter? Are you more well-versed on powdery mildew now than you were before?"

He ushers me into the sitting room, which smells musty. He doesn't smell musty, though. He smells fine, despite Shelby's remark to the contrary. "He's so *old*," she'd complained, wrinkling her nose. "He has old man smell."

You're *old*, I tell Shelby in my head. You *have old man smell.*

"Yes, I know more about powdery mildew than I ever thought possible," I tell Professor Lee.

"The knowledge might come in handy one day," he says. "You never know."

"You never know," I concur.

He keeps talking while he putters around in the kitchen making tea. "I told you that the next chapter, on ethnobotany, will make for more interesting reading, yes?"

"You did. I pray to God you're right."

He shuffles into the sitting room with two cups of tea, the cups rattling against the saucers like chattering teeth. "Here you go, my dear."

He expounds on ethnobotany and how it's shaped society, regaling me with stories of witch doctors and shamans, Appalachian medicine men, and wise women across the globe.

"You have to be careful, of course, but there are endless uses for the plants that grow all around us," he says. He lifts the teacup by its delicate handle. "This tea we're drinking? I plucked, steamed, and dried the leaves myself."

I take a sip and swish it in my mouth. I detect notes of dirt, possibly motes of dirt. "What's in it?"

"Lavender flower. It supports relaxation, digestive health, and mental health."

Professor Lee's cat wanders in on sly paws. When she jumps into the professor's lap, he startles, and his teacup slips from his fingers. It hits the edge of the coffee table and shatters, tea and porcelain flying apart.

"Oh, oh, oh," he says, more distressed than he should be. He pats Cindy Pawford and says, "I'm sorry, Cindy. You took me by surprise!"

I'm up and out of my chair, gathering the broken shards. "It's fine," I tell the professor when he protests. "You take care of Cindy. I'll take care of this."

I take the shards to the kitchen, which is a mishmash of yellows and oranges and hasn't seen an update in decades. I hunt for the trash can and find it beneath the sink. I toss in the broken crockery and move on, searching for a dishrag. Then my body stops of its own accord. I pivot and return to the trash can. I pull it out from beneath the counter and examine the contents in full light.

I feel fuzzy around the edges.

"Is everything all right?" Professor Lee calls.

I scoop something from the trash can and return to the sitting room.

"What is this?" I ask, unfurling my fingers to reveal a damp rectangle of gauze.

"Why, that's a tea bag."

"Right," I say, because I know that. What I don't know is how this tea bag, this specific handcrafted tea bag, ended up in Professor Lee's house. "Did you . . . did Shelby . . . did you get it from Shelby and Adam?"

"Shelby and Adam?" Professor Lee blinks. "I haven't seen either one of them in ages." His tone grows conspiratorial. "You know, Jake, you were a much better neighbor than they are. I shouldn't say it, but I do wish they were the ones who moved and you were the one who stayed."

"Thank you, Professor Lee. That's very kind." The tea bag is clammy in my palm. "Did this come from them? A gift, maybe, when they stopped drinking tea?"

He looks bewildered. "Did they stop drinking tea? They were so fond of it, Shelby in particular."

I gauge the bag's familiar heft. "Was she the one who gave you these?"

"No, no. I prepare my tea myself, Jake, as I was saying. I have quite a range of loose-leaf varieties. You can add flowers, seeds—"

"What about the tea bags themselves?"

"The sachets?"

"Sure. Yes. Shelby used to make sachets like this. Did she make them and give them to you?"

Professor Lee furrows his brow. "Why would Shelby make her own sachets? No, Jake, I'm quite sure she didn't. The tea she came to me for was medicinal. Potent. There are certain phytochemicals you can't play around with, even if they come from your own backyard."

I can't make sense of what he's saying. "You gave Shelby tea? She came to you for tea?"

"For quite a while, yes." He taps his temple. "She suffered from headaches that were quite debilitating." He shrugs. "She wanted to try a natural remedy, and I was happy to help. That said, I certainly never gave her a canister of loose leaves. I put measured portions in individual sachets like that one."

"So *you* made the sachets," I state.

"Yes, of course."

"And the tea."

"Yes, and the tea. Jake, you've gone pale. Won't you sit down?"

I shake my head, and the movement makes me wobble. "I'm fine, just lightheaded. I need to get some food in my belly, that's all."

"I can help with that!" He puts his hands on the arms of his chair and prepares to push himself up. Cindy Pawford glowers from her tilted position in his lap.

"Professor Lee, please, it's time for me to get going anyway," I say. I take my teacup and saucer into the kitchen and deposit them on the counter, along with the sachet I claimed from the trash.

Back in the sitting room, I pick up a stack of papers. "Is this the new batch?"

"It is, yes. Jake, are you sure I can't offer you a snack?"

"Positive, but thank you." When I reach the front door, I turn around. "What kind of tea did you make for Shelby, if you don't mind my asking?"

His face brightens and he jabs a curved finger at the pages clutched to my chest. "Pennyroyal, a fascinating plant. Read the pages—you'll see!"

38

JAKE

I make it less than a block before dizziness blurs my vision and I have to pull over. My brain is sodden with tea, so much tea, which I drank gallons of during my pregnancy and which I've associated with Liam's death ever since.

I never considered it a *cause* of Liam's death. Why would I?

I roll down my windows, kill the engine, and press the back of my head against the headrest. I close my eyes and go to my twenty-week ultrasound, the day everything fell apart.

When the receptionist called my name, I squeezed Adam's hand and grinned. "Let's do this thing!" I said.

We were ushered to a small room, where I was instructed to pull up my shirt and wiggle my jeans past my hips so that Ludy, the technician, could squirt warm gel onto my belly. For thirty thrilling minutes, Ludy pointed out various features and jotted down measurements and notes.

"Here's Baby's heart, and here's Baby's head," Ludy said. "And, oh! Baby's moving! He's a live wire, isn't he?"

She pointed out our baby's spine, neck, and rib cage, all the while entering notes into a tablet. Every few seconds, she said, "Excellent" or "All of this is perfectly normal" in a pleasant, upbeat tone.

When her manner changed, I didn't immediately notice. As much as I loved seeing my unborn son, I really needed to pee. I'd been instructed to drink thirty-two ounces of water before the appointment, and like a good girl, I followed those orders exactly. Halfway through the ultrasound, the pressure on my bladder made me see stars. What if I peed all over the examination table? Had other women done that, or would I be the first?

When it hit home that Ludy was no longer murmuring encouraging affirmations, I said, "Everything okay?"

I said it jokily. Casually. *Earth to Ludy!*

A mask of neutrality slid over her features, and my heart stopped. I pushed up onto one elbow. "Ludy? What's wrong?"

"I'm not qualified to speak to that," Ludy said carefully. She packed away the probe and handed me a tissue to wipe off my stomach. "Let's get you cleaned up. Your provider will be able to answer all your questions."

"Questions about what?" I asked. My pulse beat in sick thuds at the base of my throat. "What's going on?"

Ludy escorted us through the radiology and imaging center and deposited us at the midwifery wing. In a new exam room, a practitioner named Skye studied the ultrasound image. She lowered it with a sigh and told Adam and me there was a problem. My pregnancy was now "high risk."

"Why?" I said. "What does that mean?"

"You'll need to see Dr. Russo," Skye said. "He's the most experienced obstetrician when it comes to this sort of thing."

"What sort of thing?" Adam asked.

"He'll know what to do?" I pleaded.

Like Ludy, Skye was no longer capable of looking me in the eye. "I understand this is frustrating, but Dr. Russo will be able to answer all your questions."

"Nobody's even told us what's wrong," Adam said, frustration making him terse. "Can you at least tell us what we're dealing with?"

Skye hesitated, then said, "It's his heart. I'm sorry, but I can't say more than that."

"When can I see Dr. Russo?" I asked.

"Tomorrow, if we're lucky. Definitely by next week."

"Next *week*?"

"You'll be in good hands, I promise," Skye said. "Until then, try not to worry."

Two days later, we learned that Liam had a congenital heart condition. "It's not great news," Dr. Russo said, "but there's plenty of room for hope."

He explained that as soon as Liam was born, he would undergo surgery to correct the abnormality. Until then, a team of doctors would monitor his development closely. The goal was to get him out of there—the "there" being me—as soon as possible, because once Liam had the surgery, he would be fine.

Or, not *fine*. He'd need a lot of care. But he'd be alive, and one day he'd be fine, and that was all that mattered.

"Right, Mom?" said a neonatologist whose name I no longer remember. I saw so many, my days filled with appointment after appointment. At first, Adam went with me. As the cloud of doom above us became routine, he started bowing out. There really were so many appointments, and Adam had a job. His patients needed him, some of them infants not all that different from Liam.

"The doctors are doing all that can be done," Adam assured me. "At this point, it's just a waiting game. You're okay going to these visits on your own, aren't you?"

Liam lived within my uterus for three more months, during which time I met with a rotating crew of doctors, nurses, and ultrasound technicians. Some were compassionate. Others were brusque. At my final ultrasound—not that I knew then that it would be the last—the technician was of the brusque variety. When her wand stilled on my abdomen, fear clenched at the base of my spine.

"Just tell me," I begged the woman. "Please don't leave me alone in this room while you go find the doctor."

The ultrasound technician turned to leave. I clutched her arm.

"*Please*," I implored.

For a moment, she studied the floor. Then she lifted her head and met my gaze. "There's no fetal heartbeat," she said. "I'm very sorry."

Induction was scheduled for three days later. Until then, Liam's body, his corpse, remained inside me, sloshing around in the amniotic fluid. "Postmortem fetal movement" was what they called those continuing nudges of skull and knees and elbows. It was as if he were still alive.

On the day of Liam's delivery, an awful, sanctimonious nurse told me not to expect a normal-looking infant. The exact date of "the baby's" death was unknown, she explained. "The baby" might have died four days ago, or eleven days ago, or at any time in between. It was possible that "the baby" had deteriorated in the womb.

"He won't have rosy cheeks and the perfect skin of a newborn," the nurse warned.

"His name is Liam," I said through a teary, furious haze.

The nurse regarded me primly, then turned on her heel and departed, leaving Adam and me alone in the room marked with the falling leaf.

"Jake, I need you to manage your expectations," Adam said.

I stared up at him from the hospital bed, my watermelon belly ripe with false promise. What "expectations" were left? What was he talking about?

He rose and went to the window. He said, "I don't . . . I can't . . ."

I sank into the pillow. I didn't have the energy to coax it out of him, whatever it was.

"Don't expect me to hold him," he said gruffly. "I don't think I can."

I'd thought I was all cried out, but hot tears spilled and ran down my cheeks. I hated Adam then.

Do I hate him still?

A succession of thuds wrenches me out of my thoughts. I sit up fast, knocking my knees against the panel beneath the steering wheel.

"What the hell?" Adam says. He's here, just outside my yellow Beetle, his fist aloft from banging the roof. He circles the car and sticks his head through the driver's-side window. His fury is palpable.

"Why are you here?" he demands.

I recoil. "I'm just . . . it's not—"

He slaps the roof, and I jump. My heart is a rabbit trying to escape.

"Professor Lee!" I cry. "Omigod, Adam, relax. I was just visiting Professor Lee!"

"And the other times?"

"What other times?"

"You were at our house, Jake," he growls. "Tell me why."

39

JAKE

My hand flutters from my chest to my lap. Ridiculously, I wonder what I look like. How long have I been zoning out? Is my hair flat from leaning against the headrest? How much does he know?

"Adam? Let's talk like adults, okay?"

"Sure, Jake," Adam says. His fingers curl around the base of the window. "Let's."

An idea presents itself to me, an insanity-fueled idea that billows over me like the parachute my kindergarten gym teacher brought out on rainy days. "One, two, three—up!" he'd say, and the parachute would leap up like a muffin top as everyone lifted the silky fabric over our heads. One kid would run beneath, and then, "One, two, three—down!" Everyone squatted, and the kid in the center would be lifted out of time, captured for a moment in a vibrant, swaying bubble.

I loved that bubble world, where everything floated and anything seemed possible.

What if, right this second, I put aside everything and pulled Adam into that bubble with me? We could talk, just the two of us. We could have a real conversation, unbarbed and unarmed.

I lift Professor Lee's manuscript from the passenger seat. "I'm not sure what you're talking about," I start, "but I wasn't at your house." I show him the pages. "I was visiting Professor Lee, like I do every week."

"Is that so?"

"Yes, Adam, it is. Why would I be at your house?"

He snorts, and it hurts my feelings.

"It's *me*," I say. "The same old me as always. Can't we just be normal with each other again?"

In the parachute game, the bubble deflated slowly.

On Mountain Avenue, one prick makes the whole thing burst.

"I installed a monitoring system," he tells me. "I have video. Not only were you at our house, but I have footage of you taking out a key and going inside. *Inside our house*, Jake. So no, the two of us being 'normal' with each other is not on the table."

Fear sweat breaks out beneath my arms and on the nape of my neck.

"Shelby doesn't know," Adam goes on. "It would only upset her, and you've upset her enough already." He leans forward and squeezes the window frame. "How many times did you break in? Did you think I wouldn't notice? Misplaced documents, my toothbrush turned upside down, a blonde hair in the drawer where I keep my boxers?"

I didn't do that. I went through Shelby's underwear drawer—I suppose a hair of mine could have found its way there—but I never opened Adam's!

"What did you think would happen?" he goes on. "Did you think I'd scratch my head and blame it on a fucking leprechaun?"

"I was returning her photo," I say in a guttural voice.

"What?"

Nope, not going to happen. I lock my jaw.

"I have no idea what you just said," Adam says. "Want to run that by me again?"

I fumble for my keys. Where are my fucking keys?

"At least you didn't take anything, or I'd have no choice but to show the footage to Shelby *and* the police." He leans closer, eyes bulging. "Unless you did. Did you, Jake? Did you steal anything, or did you just creep around our house like a stalker?"

I find them, but my fingers are shaking. Never in my life have I wanted a push-button ignition as much as I do right now.

"The police? I don't know what they'd do. Arrest you, maybe. But Shelby, she would post that footage on every social media account she has. How would that go over, do you think?"

The engine revs to life.

"I'm trying to *protect* you, you psychotic bitch!" Adam calls as I peel away. "I mean it, Jake, don't play with fire. If you do, you're going to get burned!"

40

JAKE

At home, I slosh tequila into a glass and doctor it with lemonade, not to make it taste good but to make it easy to chug. Which I do, grimacing. I still see Adam's flushed face and his hands white-knuckling the Beetle's window frame, so I down another.

I installed a monitoring system. I have video.

I down one more, and that's the end of the bottle. "Fan-fucking-tastic," I mutter.

I have some vodka somewhere. Don't I? I stumble and bang my hip bone against the granite island.

Shelby would post that footage on every social media account she has.

Vodka. Right. I find it in the freezer, clever me, and take a pull straight from the bottle. I need to keep reality dull until I can face it again.

"Please, please, please," I whisper. What am I begging for, and from whom? Beats me. I drink so that I don't cry. My throat is thick and painful; I drink and drink to force the pain down.

The house is oppressive. I need air. I stand on the front porch, gripping my glass with one hand and the wooden railing with the other. It's evening now, which is impossible, but whatever. Life marches on. It's

Saturday evening, the sky is violet-blue, and the full moon is enormous as it crests the horizon.

I sway and drop into one of my porch chairs. Maybe I'll sleep here, just me and the encroaching darkness. I set down my glass, close my eyes, and drift, imagining myself as a feather, an exhale, a collection of atoms dispersing into the night.

There's the sound of breaking glass. My eyes fly open.

"Sorry, Mom!" I hear Billy exclaim. "It was an accident!"

"God*damn*it, Billy," comes the next voice. "I told you not to touch it, and what did you do? You touched it!"

No. Not tonight. I lean forward and cradle my head in my hands, but their voices come at me like poisoned arrows. Vanessa, yelling at Billy. Billy pleading and contrite, his tone as familiar to me as the headache gathering force at the front of my skull.

It's Carrie, all the times my father lashed out at her and she tried to appease him. It's Toby, when he wet his pants and didn't want to be whipped. It's me, sniveling through the years and reminding myself of all my failures.

If I'd stood up to Adam this afternoon, instead of grinding through the gears to get the hell out of there.

If I'd stood up to Shelby at the height of the scandal, instead of hiding away in that cramped and shitty apartment.

If I'd stood up to my father all those years ago at the creek, instead of allowing myself to be dragged back to the house, his grip painful on my wrist.

Vanessa's voice rises. I hear "worthless" and "wish you'd never been born," followed by a yelp.

A cold sweat lays its fingers on the back of my neck, part alcohol, part violent and disorganized grief. For two decades, Toby's death has clung to me. For two decades, I've carried the weight of self-loathing, because to let go of my guilt would be like letting go of him.

But I got it wrong, didn't I? By convincing myself I was powerless, I became powerless. What a fucking idiot.

It's time to shed that idiocy and act.

I stride down the porch steps and onto the sidewalk. *Don't do this*, a tiny voice says. I give zero fucks about that tiny voice.

My pulse is fast and whippy as I mount Vanessa's front steps, and my reflection in the windowpane startles me. For the first time in a long time, I seem more woman than girl.

I ring the doorbell. The voices inside fall abruptly silent.

I ring the bell again, and there's the clack of angry heels.

"Yes?" Vanessa says, yanking open the door.

I run my palms down the front of my jeans. I realize belatedly that my plan is missing teeth.

Vanessa lifts her eyebrows. Behind her, I glimpse a narrow hall and, farther back, a halo of yellow light. Is that where Billy is? The yelp I heard—did Vanessa hit him?

"I heard yelling. I wanted to make sure everything was okay," I say. Am I still drunk? Maybe. I don't know. But Vanessa isn't fuzzy. Vanessa is all sharp angles.

"Everything's fine," she says.

I try to peer past her.

She moves to block my view.

"Where's Billy? Is he all right?"

Her features harden. "I'm not sure how Billy's welfare is your concern," she says. "That said, he's fine."

"Can I see him?"

Vanessa folds her arms across her chest, her red nails stark against her white blouse. "Why, Jake? Are you going from door-to-door, asking how everyone is?"

"Just you. And Billy. Like I said, I heard yelling." I hold myself taller. "We're neighbors. Neighbors look out for one another."

Vanessa twists her mouth. "You call it 'looking out for one another.' I call it interfering." She inclines her head. "Tell me, Jake, do you like interfering in my private business? Have you interfered in other ways?"

I try to remember that I'm here as Billy's ally, not to aggravate Vanessa further. But Vanessa is such a fucking bitch. "Nope," I say, "but it wouldn't surprise me if someone else has. You would benefit from some well-intentioned interference, Vanessa."

"Someone left multiple piles of shit in my yard," Vanessa says. "Is that the kind of interference you think I'd benefit from?"

Holy cow, so Mabel went through with it, I think. A vision of ceramic poops pops into my head, arranged like a miniature Stonehenge. Or Poophenge?

My lips twitch.

"You think that's funny, leaving shit in someone's yard?"

"No, of course not." Yes, very. Well done, Mabel. "But it wasn't actual shit and you know it."

Vanessa's eyes narrow. "You bitch."

"Wait. No. *I* didn't—"

"You've been coming at me on GoodNeighbors, haven't you? You think it's funny?"

"Vanessa. None of that is here nor there." I hear my words as if they dropped out of the sky on little balloons. *None of that is here nor there?*

"I could sue," Vanessa says. "Defamation of character, slander, trespassing. Would a judge find the placement of lewd and offensive statues on someone's property funny, do you think?"

I crane sideways. "Billy?"

Vanessa steps forward. "Billy is *my* son. You have no business being here, and I'd like you to leave."

My heart is galloping, and the old shame is back. "I heard yelling. I need to know that Billy is safe."

"From who? From *me*?"

My body pulls downward, stones in my gut.

"He's doing a whole lot better than your son, Jake. I can tell you that." Vanessa's eyes bore into mine, watching for the jolt of recognition. "Yes, I know who you are, and yes, I've done my research. Frozen peas on your breasts, was that it? But then your baby died. Tragic."

I hate this woman. I hate her and want to hurt her.

"I've kept *my* child alive," she says. "Granted, that's a low bar for measuring success, but you can't say the same, can you?"

I move my neck slightly, loosening the muscles. "My son died, yes. But not from bad parenting. Whereas Billy . . . well, talk about tragic. Because it's not his fault, is it?"

"What isn't his fault?"

"You wonder why people mock you on GoodNeighbors?" I say. "Because there's so much to mock. You're vicious, you're petty, and you're a terrible mother. Literally the worst."

"If I'm such a terrible mother, how did I raise such a great kid?" Vanessa asks. "Billy gets straight As. He's a superior athlete, and he's the most popular boy in his class."

I laugh. "Is he?"

Spots of color rise on her face. "I don't know why you're so invested in tearing down a ten-year-old, but yes, he is. He's well liked by everyone."

Warning bells sound in my head. I ignore them. "Sorry to break it to you, but Billy's classmates think he's weird. 'Creepy' is the word they use."

"You don't know that. How could you know that?"

"*I'm* well liked," I say, "at least by the kids in the neighborhood. I'm talking about Bethany and Delilah, who happen to be in Billy's class, and also Delilah's little brother, Wendell. Do you know them?"

Vanessa's eyes are dark, flat seeds. If I got in there with my thumbnails, I could gouge them out.

"They were at my house this afternoon, complaining about him," I go on, even though their visit was actually several days ago and only Delilah bore Billy a grudge. Bethany was smitten. Even Wendell said he was nice.

"They said there's something 'off' about him. That he's broken inside, no doubt because his mother yells at him every second of the day. Honestly, Vanessa, it's heartbreaking."

I back away, feeling for each next step with my feet. "He's the kid. You're the parent. Do better."

41

BILLY

Something cold blossoms at the base of Billy's brain, a shivering whiteness that illuminates everything for one blinding instant. No one likes him. Everyone thinks he's weird. Creepy. Broken.

Delilah thinks so, and Bethany, and even Wendell with his dented head and slippery egg smile. They see the real him, as much as he's convinced himself that they don't. They laugh and point behind his back.

In his mind's eye, he sees a moth in a flame. He smells the stench of charred wings.

The front door slams, and Billy darts for the basement stairs, knowing he has to make himself scarce. He heard everything Jake said, and if his mother rounds the corner and spots him, she'll know he did. Either the shame will kill him, or she will.

Jake, the traitor.

Bethany, even worse. Billy wants to slice her into little pieces and stab daggers into her soft parts.

"Billy?" his mother calls.

He powers on his PlayStation. "I'm in the basement!" he calls, taking pains to steady his voice. *There's nothing going on here*, he needs his tone to convey. *Was that Jake at the door? Were the two of you arguing? Hell if I know.*

He plays his video game sloppily at first, but then with laser-sharp efficiency, mowing down his enemies in a blaze of bullets. It takes a while, but the roaring in his ears subsides, replaced by staccato gunfire and the agonies of phony death.

When his mother calls down that it's time to come upstairs, he says, "I'm in the middle of *Final Fantasy*. Can I play a little longer?"

"And skip dinner?" his mother says.

What dinner? he wants to retort. He heard her up there, stomping around and taking out her mood on everything but the pots and pans. She ended up in the TV room, banging around in the cabinets beneath the bookshelves before dropping onto the sofa and falling quiet. This, Billy knows from experience, means she'd pulled out their old photo albums, flipping through pictures of better days and wondering why Billy was such a creepy, broken, failure of a son.

After the silence came crying, which made Billy angry. What does she have to cry about?

"I'm not hungry," he calls.

"Fine," she says. "I'm going to bed. Turn off the lights when you come up."

On the screen, shots flare and bodies spasm and fall. Billy rests the controller in his lap and lets his eyes glaze over, knowing the system will play on without him.

Bethany *did* like him. He saw it in her eyes when he walked her home—or when she walked him home. Whatever.

So what changed?

Bethany and Delilah went to Jake's house with stupid egg-smile Wendell. They went to Jake's house and complained about Billy. Why?

Maybe Bethany told Delilah about the letter she gave him, and Delilah disapproved? Or maybe Delilah caught Bethany looking at Billy in that private way that makes Billy warm. Maybe Delilah couldn't stand Billy stealing even an ounce of Bethany's affection.

Jealous bitch.

But maybe Delilah wouldn't mind sharing Bethany with Billy, if Billy weren't so weird. Could he be normal if he applied himself? What parts of him, exactly, needed to be fixed? If Billy lay flat and still on one of the MRI machines his mother feeds people into—he got to see one once when she took him with her to work—what would the images reveal?

No, he thinks. Some kids are damaged on the outside, like Wendell. You don't need an MRI to see that. With other kids, maybe their lungs are damaged, or their spleens or some other internal organ, and an MRI would say, "Yep, there it is, that black spot there."

Billy's damage is invisible. Even if someone were to peel back his skin, there'd be nothing to see.

His shame grows claws and sharp, nipping fangs. It's unfair for Delilah and Bethany to hate him when there's nothing he can do to be better. He digs his fingernails into his palms and imagines it's Bethany's heart he's squeezing, harder and harder until it bursts and blood splurts everywhere.

He thinks about how to punish her. He could share the love letter she wrote him, for starters. He could read it out loud in front of the class, or print copies and pass them around to everybody in the whole school, including the teachers. Bethany would want to die.

Delilah needs punishing, too, and her punishment needs to be worse than Bethany's. She needs to really suffer.

What's the best way to make Delilah suffer?

"Ha," Billy grunts, because that's easy. The best way to hurt Delilah is to hurt her little brother. He mimes cocking a rifle and catching Wendell in its crosshairs. *Kapow.*

Upstairs, all is quiet. Billy rises from the sofa and goes to the storage area, pulling the door shut behind him. It's pitch black. He feels low and dirty for wanting to be here.

He fumbles his way to the furnace, which emits a low hum. He sinks to his knees and pats along the wall until he finds what he's searching for. There, between metal and drywall. He retrieves the plastic lighter and flicks it to life.

His mom can't lock him in here, not without installing a dead bolt on the outside of the storage room door. But Billy has spent hours and hours in other basements. An impulse stronger than logic drove him to take safety measures, just in case.

The flame illuminates a water bottle and a box of saltines, but Billy wants neither food nor water. What Billy wants is *not* to want. Not to be. He releases the striker, and the flame goes out. *Poof.*

He could set the house on fire, he supposes. The concrete walls and floor won't give much, but the corner of the room is stacked with broken-down cardboard boxes. They would burn. His clothes would burn too, and his flesh. His hair and fingernails and skin.

He settles in with his back against the wall. With his hand propped on his bent knee, he flicks the lighter.

He lets the flame go out.

He flicks the lighter.

He lets the flame go out.

He flicks the lighter and holds his palm over the flame until he can't stand it anymore. He suppresses a cry and releases the striker.

His thoughts drift to the shelves in the garage, where there's a can of lighter fluid. He begins to form a plan.

42

MABEL

It's Sunday, the day of Shelby's panty party. At last! But now that it's here, Mabel's on the fence about whether she'll actually go. Isn't the whole idea rather silly? Not the party itself (good cause, etcetera, etcetera), but Mabel's superspy revenge agenda. She's not going to switch out the flower arrangements for ceramic poops. She's not going to throw a public stink and take Shelby to task. What would she even say?

More and more, Mabel's been wondering if Jake is onto something with her suggestion to pull back from petty spitball fights, which is what Mabel's online squabbles basically are. Is Mabel in elementary school? No, she is not, but Bethany is. So is Billy, Bethany's crush.

It is adorable, Bethany with a crush.

Maybe instead of provoking Billy's mother, Mabel should . . . ?

Well, Mabel certainly doesn't see herself becoming friends with Vanessa. But if nothing else, she could put more effort into minding her own business.

Shelby, though. Mabel wants to see Shelby in person at least once, just like she wanted to see Gigi all those years ago. Curiosity, cats, blah blah blah.

She doesn't have to decide this instant. The luncheon isn't till 11:00 a.m.

David and Bethany are having brunch at La Creperie, so Mabel pours a mug of coffee and carries it into the front room. Where is Jake? She has yet to show up for coffee hour. Mabel takes a seat on the sofa, which looks out over the sidewalk. If Jake shows up, she'll see her. She swipes the screen of her phone and opens GoodNeighbors.

At the top of her feed is a complaint about one neighbor defecating in another neighbor's front yard. Mabel does a double take. *Holy shit (literally)!* she thinks. *Did Vanessa repurpose my ceramic poops?*

She's been looking for a mention of the ceramic poops ever since she deposited them, hoping for affirmation that her smear campaign hit its mark. Today, alas, is not that day. The defecation complaint came from Phil H., who explained that the problem has been going on for weeks. Initially, Phil thought the culprit was a dog. On closer inspection, he rejected this hypothesis. "I know human feces when I see it," he griped.

Loads of people jumped in to respond. There was outrage, there was sympathy, there was a resounding appeal for Phil to consider that he might be dealing with a raccoon poop situation, a possibility that branched off and generated its own energetic debate.

Phil H

But is raccoon poop voluminous? What I've got going on is extremely large and seems inordinately so for an animal of a raccoon's typical size.

KattyCate

How big are we talking?

Doctor John

Raccoon poop is much blacker than human waste. If it's black, it's raccoon.

Jess Y

Racoons are random poopers, though. Sounds like **Phil H** is dealing with a repeat offender.

Cassidy Hartman

Put on some plastic gloves and go through it. If it's full of seeds, it's raccoon poop. Problem solved!

Jess Y

Humans eat seeds too . . .

Mabel moves on, skimming posts about stolen bikes, hawks catching garter snakes, and garter snakes catching mice. Soon Mabel reaches the obligatory post about a cat, although this is not an ordinary post about a cat. The subject line reads, "To the person who ran over my kitten on Plum Street last night and left her there, SHAME ON YOU!"

The woman who made the post is named Kimmi, and she woke up to find her kitten dead on the road outside her house. Poor kitty!

Kimmi argued that whoever hit her kitten should have stopped, collected the kitten's body, and gone door-to-door until they found the owner. This gives Mabel pause. She can't quite imagine herself doing that. Still, poor kitty.

The comment section is full of condolences, with lots of "I lost my fur baby, too, and I've never recovered" sorts of posts. Some neighbors took Kimmi to task, pointing out that if Kimmi hadn't let her kitten go outside in the first place, the kitten would still be alive. One man threw down the accusation that Kimmi, based on a review of her posts, had a habit of "losing" pets. Perhaps Kimmi shouldn't be responsible for another creature's life if she's not able to take care of it?

Then WarriorMom entered the fray.

Uh-oh, Mabel thinks, wiggling with anticipation. *Here. We. Go.*

WarriorMom

Kimmi, not only do I agree with those who suggest you take in no new pets only to "lose" them and subject them to a terrible death, but your entire post is absurd. What did you expect the driver to do? Stop and pick up a possibly diseased corpse? I wouldn't pick up a dead cat from the road. Keep your animals inside where they belong!

Jess Y
WarriorMom, maybe the kitten wasn't dead yet. Have you thought of that?

WarriorMom
So the driver should do what? Poke it with a stick?

Tyrone March
You can determine a heartbeat with your hand

WarriorMom
Why would anyone touch someone's dead cat because the owner was too selfish to take care of it? **Kimmi**, you killed your kitten. Grow up and own it.

Kimmi
WarriorMom, just stop. I lost my baby, have some respect!

Jess Y
Kimmi, don't let **WarriorMom** get you down.

Isaac Vernon
What Jess said! **WarriorMom** will be a glassbowl no matter what you do or say.

Melissa Carter
Is there a way we could lock her in *her* house? All in favor, sign below!

Over one hundred people upvoted Melissa's post. As Mabel watches, the number continues to rise.

Mabel realizes she's breathing fast and is appalled. This excitement, this slick adrenaline . . . is this what Shelby's supporters experienced at the height of the #lipservice scandal, when everyone piled on Jake?

Mabel clicks out of GoodNeighbors.

She opens Facebook and goes to Shelby's page. "Oh, nuh-uh," she says. A photo shows a tanned and ecstatic Shelby displaying her left ring finger, with Adam hugging her from behind.

"Adam asked me to marry him—and I SAID YES!!!" reads Shelby's post. "That beautiful man. Talk about paradise!!!!"

Mabel learns that on their final day in Bora-Bora, Adam took Shelby for one last walk along the beach, where Shelby oh-so-amazingly stumbled upon "a real-life message in a bottle."

"You guys, I was freaking," Shelby wrote. "I was all, 'Adam, omigod! Adam!' He played it so cool. He was like, 'Should we pull the message out? Should we read it?' I was like, 'Obviously! Maybe it's from a pirate!' So I opened it, and . . ."

There's a picture of an unrolled scroll, with the edges made to look old and weathered. Written on the scroll are the words, *Shelby, will you marry me?*

Next is a close-up of Shelby's ring finger, the diamond on her engagement ring huge and glittering. "Talk about treasure!" reads the caption. "And, obvs, I said, 'Shell yeah!'"

Mabel exits out of Facebook, clicks on her messaging app, and pulls up Jake's name. News like this cannot be ignored.

She closes her eyes. No Vanessa updates, no Shelby updates. She promised.

She tosses her phone away from her, exiling it to the opposite end of the sofa. She won't text Jake. Fine. But she's going to that panty party. Shelby has enjoyed too much paradise of late. The devil in Mabel thinks it's time to raise some hell.

43

MABEL

Her red curls behave beautifully, her makeup looks fabulous, and her outfit is to die for: A white pussy-bow silk blouse with buttoned cuffs tucked into a herringbone skirt. She wiggles her feet into black patent Mary Janes with a double strap and stands before her full-length mirror.

Mabel gives her reflection a once-over, then nods. She's battle-ready.

The luncheon is at the Fort Collins Country Club, a venue that tries hard but comes up short when compared to the country club Mabel's parents belong to in Atlanta. On any other day, this would be a mark in the club's favor. Mabel loves Fort Collins's lack of pretension. Today, as she strides into the wide entryway decorated with streamers, she dismisses the club as tacky. *Shelby* is tacky.

After accepting a glass of champagne from a round-faced young woman, Mabel moves into a large dining area filled with chattering women. She's jittery, her fizzing adrenaline a sign that she needs to slow down and assess the situation. She can do that. She's happy to do that. No problem!

She downs her champagne and trades her empty flute for a full one, all the while rehearsing her extremely legitimate reasons for being here.

Shelby slept with Jake's husband while Jake and Adam were married, engaging not in a one-night stand with Adam, but a long and secret affair. (Of course, Mabel slept with David when David and Gigi were married. Mabel and David's affair was equally long and secret—and thrilling.)

Shelby never acted the slightest bit ashamed of what she did. She moved in with Adam only weeks after Jake moved out! (Then again, Mabel never apologized for loving David. Why would she?)

Unlike Shelby, Mabel waited for eons to move in with David. (Although, fine, the extended timeline was David's request, with Bethany in mind.)

Okay, Mabel thinks. *Okay, sure, but . . .*

Women brush past her, a flock of high-heeled flamingos. She teeters. If she's going to keep on chugging champagne like this—she's on her third glass now? When did that happen?—she really should eat some food.

She abandons her half-full glass, setting it on a caterer's tray and walking away. (*Happy?* she asks the invisible hall monitor hovering behind her shoulder. *This is me, making good choices!*)

Now, which of her good choices had she been extolling? Oh, yes. Her good choice not to move in with David until after David and Gigi's divorce was finalized, which, thanks to Gigi, took *for-ev-er.*

Fucking Gigi.

What. A. Mess.

But why is Mabel dwelling on Gigi? Mabel is *not* here because of Gigi, and her increasingly labored rationalizations of why she and Shelby are in no way alike do not stem from anything like guilt.

At any rate, Shelby is a stone-cold bitch. Ha! *Gotcha there, Shelbs!* It's Mabel's duty to stand up to Shelby on behalf of poor, beaten-down Jake. That, friends, is why Mabel is here today.

Only poor, beaten-down Jake isn't so poor and beaten-down anymore, and she doesn't want Mabel fighting Shelby on her behalf. She said so loud and clear.

There's a feathery touch on Mabel's arm, and Mabel turns to see her next-door neighbor, Danielle.

"Mabel, hi," Danielle says. "Oh my God, you look"—she flares her hands—"phe*nom*enal. *Love* the fit."

"Thanks," Mabel says, blinking at the polished brunette at Danielle's side. Her pulse jumps erratically, and she thinks, *No, no, no, not like this.*

"Mabel, this is Shelby, our amazing hostess," Danielle exclaims. "Shelby was dying to meet you, so I said, 'Come on! I'll introduce you!'"

Shelby extends her hand. Her fingers are slender and elegant, her nails the same shade of mauve Mabel's mother wears.

Mabel takes Shelby's hand. She has a horrible feeling her palm is sweaty.

"It's so nice to meet you," Shelby says, tightening her right hand around Mabel's and layering her left hand on top. Her new diamond is as big as a Malamute's cuspid and just as sharp. If she isn't careful, she's going to put someone's eye out.

"Thank you for coming," Shelby goes on, oozing sincerity. "We women have to support each other, don't we?"

"Sure," Mabel says, tugging free her hand. Oh Lord, it's slippery. *Do not wipe it on your skirt*, she tells herself. *Don't you do it.*

Servers are bringing out salads, and women are finding their seats and sitting down. Mabel snags a cloth napkin and wipes her hand. Her palm is no longer damp, but now she's holding a damn napkin.

Shelby smiles. "Those of us who are more fortunate have a duty to help those who are struggling. It's just so important. If Danielle found herself in a housing-challenged situation, I would do anything to help."

"Aw," Danielle says. "And me for you!"

Mabel puts the odds of either of them finding themselves "housing challenged" at a million to one.

"Shall we sit?" Danielle proposes.

"Actually, I'm going to pop to the bathroom," says Mabel. She doesn't know what's going on here, but senses that something is up. Not with Danielle, but Shelby. But why? How? She steps away only to be jerked back. Shelby's elegant hand is a vise around Mabel's forearm.

"Go on, we'll catch up," she tells Danielle. She scrunches her nose. "I need two more ticks with your neighbor, 'kay?"

Danielle flutters her fingers and swishes away.

Neighbor, Mabel thinks, scrambling to put the pieces together. Or maybe she says it out loud, because Shelby says, "Well, sure. Danielle lives on Sweetwater Lane, same as you."

There's a hard knock in Mabel's chest. Around them is a buzz of chatter, but to Mabel, it feels like she and Shelby are the only women in the room.

"Yeah," Shelby says, infusing her voice with false sympathy. "I don't know what your plan is, Mabel, but you're not going to do it, 'kay?"

"My *plan*?" Mabel says. "What plan?"

"You're Jake's new bestie. I saw it on Facebook."

Mabel frowns, because Jake doesn't have Facebook. She used to, but not anymore, because of Shelby.

Ohhh. The picture Wendell took of Mabel and Jake grinning like fools on the playground. Had Mabel referred to Jake as her new best friend? With multiple two-girls-dancing emojis?

"Your husband is David Merriweather, who used to be married to the gallerist Gigi Merriweather," Shelby goes on. "I'm so impressed with her commitment to lifting up hungry artists."

Mabel looks at Shelby askance, because Gigi has always promoted her gallery as a space where "high culture meets luxury, with a focus on established luminaries."

"The point is that I *know* Gigi," Shelby says. "Personally. Isn't that a hoot?"

"Small world."

"Indeed. But you, you're a pretty big hypocrite, huh?"

Mabel needs out of this room. It's so hot, and someone is wearing hazmat levels of Flowerbomb.

"I reached out to Gigi after you RSVP'd to my fundraiser. She was *very* generous with her time." She cocks her head. "She told me about the private detective she hired when David asked for a divorce."

Mabel's pulse roars, and she finds herself high above, looking down from the ceiling. Everything the detective collected—and he had a fancy camera; he collected quite a lot—became a bargaining chip. The settlement Gigi was awarded could buy lifetime avocado toast for every artist in the nation.

"Gigi said you don't like talking about it. I get it."

Mabel feels dizzy, just as she did when David told her about the revenge-porn clause he insisted on including in the divorce agreement. "It's there to serve as a reminder," he said the one and only time they ever talked about it.

"Of what?"

"That she can't . . . you know." David had bowed his head and mumbled the rest. "Do anything with the images, not if she accepts the settlement."

Shelby isn't giving Mabel a reminder. She's issuing a warning.

"It must have been such a shock, learning about all those photos." She studies Mabel. "So many of them, and all so . . ." She gives the tiniest hitch of her shoulders. "Explicit? That's really the only way to describe them."

Mabel wants to call Shelby out on what is surely a bluff. Gigi would never. Gigi knows better.

Gigi is Gigi, Mabel thinks, as spots flicker and pulse in front of her eyes.

"Excuse me," she hears Shelby say. "Excuse me, sir?" There's a haze of white and black, a server hurrying forward. "Could you take my friend outside? I'm afraid she's going to faint."

44

JAKE

Needle-sharp pricks wake me, the tap of Lump's claws on my spongy cheek. He's gentle, or tries to be, and any other day I would find it endearing, his clumsy way of saying, "Get up, lady! Get up and face the day!"

Not today. I'm hungover and exhausted after a night of fitful tossing that offered nothing resembling rest. In my dreams, I was late for an appointment. My car had no brakes. I was back in the Hemlock house, and a brusque technician kept ringing the doorbell. He was there to fix the HVAC system, and asked if I could lead him to the furnace.

In the dream, I gazed at the man dumbly.

"Why don't we have a look?" he suggested, and then he was my father, wearing a thick flannel shirt and steel-toe boots. He chased me from room to room, cornering me at last in the basement. "Found you!" he cried with a wolf's slippery smile.

Lump bats at my cheek.

"Lump, *no*," I snap.

He shrinks away.

"I'm sorry," I say. I hinge forward, trying to coax him back. "Come here. It's okay."

Lump jumps off the bed and scuttles out of the room. I fall back against my pillow, gutted. Because of Lump, because of everything, beginning with Adam's ambush and ending with my drunken confrontation with Vanessa.

I groan. My motivation might have been pure—I heard yelling; I was concerned—but I lost any claim to moral high ground when I told Vanessa that her ten-year-old son was unpopular, creepy, and weird.

Did the alcohol play a role? Sure, but I chose to swig that tequila, just as I chose to chase it down with vodka. Adam's tirade likewise played a role, but his accusations weren't false. I *did* do everything he said—and more. I am a self-loathing, psychotic bitch.

Last night, I pushed that loathing out of me and onto the closest target. I mocked a little boy just to hurt that little boy's mother.

I roll over and check the time. Jesus, it's past noon. I've slept for nearly twelve hours.

I wash down four Advil with a tall glass of water. I splash more water on my face and drag my damp hands through my hair, finger-combing it until it's semipresentable. Then I tug on jeans and a sweatshirt, feed Lump, and hurry out of the house.

I need Mabel. Mabel will make things better.

She opens the door looking fancier than I've ever seen her, as if she's just returned from church. Thinking of church makes me think of sins. Thinking of sins makes me think of everything, everything: falling leaves and tiny coffins, lives snuffed out before they began.

"Jake?" Mabel says.

Her concern undoes me, and though I did not come here for this—and neither expected it nor wanted it—I burst into tears.

"Oh, honey!" Mabel says, opening her arms. Her blouse is silky, and I say something incoherent about not wanting to mess it up. She makes a *pfff* sound and hugs me tight, then ushers me into her house, down the hall, and into the great room, where she pulls me down beside her on the sofa.

"Jake, my sweet friend, are you okay? What's going on?"

A waterfall of words, tears, and emotions cascades out of me. All of it leads to Liam, all of it is connected to Toby. My story is as tangled as the sycamore roots that stretched their gnarled fingers along the bed of the creek I played in as a child, and I'm sure Mabel can't make heads or tails of what I'm telling her.

Eventually, I weave Vanessa into my confession, though not Adam or Shelby or my visits to the Hemlock house. (God, no!) When I tell her about Vanessa's jab that Liam died on my watch, Mabel takes me by the shoulders and holds me.

"Jake, no," she says. She waits until I meet her gaze. "Your son being stillborn wasn't anyone's fault."

"It might have been. Who knows?"

"*I* do," she insists. "That was nature. A bad roll of the genetic dice. It wasn't something you could have prevented."

"Maybe not with Liam, but—"

"No 'buts,'" Mabel says. "No one died on your watch, Jake. Okay?"

The pain in my throat is insane, a wad of mucus and grief too large for such a constricted space. I push the words out like gravel, building upon the scant history I shared with Mabel the day we met.

"I told you, remember?" I say. "About Carrie, who made me sleep in the guest room?"

"And the little soaps shaped like seashells! Yes, but what does Carrie have to do with Liam?"

I start and stop and start again.

Mabel's eyes widen when she realizes it's no longer Liam I'm talking about, but another little boy entirely. "Wait. You have a brother?"

I squeeze shut my eyes, but fresh tears leak through. "He's dead. He died when he was four."

My voice cracks, gravelly and raw, and my shoulders heave as more sobs rip through me. "Omigod," I say, choking out a snot-thick laugh. "This is crazy. I'm crazy. Mabel, I'm s-so so sorry!"

"Don't say that. You have nothing to be sorry about." She rises from the sofa and returns with a box of Kleenex. I blow my nose.

"You don't have to tell me if you don't want to," Mabel says.

"I know."

"But if you do, you can. I'm right here."

I use another Kleenex to wipe my nose, then crumple it into a ball.

"Okay, well, Carrie wasn't my favorite, not at first," I tell her. "That part, you know. But after she had Toby—that was my little brother—she got better, or I maybe I did. We got along really well after he came along, because we both loved him so much."

Mabel grabs my hands and squeezes them, snotty Kleenex and all.

"My father, on the other hand, was an asshole." I make a scoffing sound. "I say 'was.' If he's still alive, I'm sure he still is."

"You don't know?"

"Nope, and I have no interest in finding out."

I tell her that he always had a temper, but things didn't get *bad* bad until the summer I was eleven.

"Your daddy's been having some anger issues," Carrie said in a hushed voice, after pulling me aside. "It's nothing to worry about, but I don't want Toby around him when he's in one of his moods, or you either. If you see that he's getting riled up, just grab Toby and go, okay?"

Carrie had a lot more bruises that summer. So did I. Sharing these details and watching Mabel try to mask her dismay made me realize that maybe things had been *bad* bad already.

And then, one day, my father told Carrie to go to the store and get him some cigarettes. He had to have his Marlboros, and he had to have them then.

"Sure, hon," Carrie said. She gestured for me and Toby to go to the car. "Jake, Toby, you two come with me. You can each get a pack of gum."

"They're fine right where they are," my father said, and though I had my back to him and couldn't see his expression, a knot formed in my belly.

"Just Toby, then," Carrie said. "You and Jake can go fishing without a four-year-old slowing you down." She shot me an anxious smile. "What do you think, Jake? Want to go fishing with your daddy?"

No, I didn't—but yes, if that's what Carrie thought best. Toby was only four, but I was eleven, practically an adult. I could handle my father much better than he could.

"I said they're fine right where they are," my father repeated. He belched. "Don't you trust me to take care of my own damn kids?"

"Of course I do, John," Carrie said, her placating manner an obvious giveaway. There were undercurrents at play I couldn't define: Maybe there'd been a dispute that morning, or maybe my father had started drinking earlier than usual. I didn't know what the source of the tension was, but I knew it was there, and I knew Carrie needed my help.

I took Toby's hand. "I could take Toby to the creek if you want."

"That is a terrific idea," Carrie said, shooting me a look that said, *Thank you, you are an angel.* "Jake can look after Toby, and John, you can kick back and relax. I know you didn't get a good night's sleep. Maybe you can take a nap!"

"Thank you, Miss Thing, for telling me how to manage my time," my father said. "Are you going to get me those Marlboros or what?"

"I'm going right now," Carrie said. "Jake, take Toby to the creek. Toby, do whatever Jake says, okay, baby?"

I didn't need to be told twice. I hustled Toby into the woods and down to the creek, where I launched into the story of Toby and the Well. I took my time and embellished it, knowing that going to the store would take thirty minutes even if Carrie was quick.

Ten minutes before she was due back, my father tromped through the forest and found me and Toby at the creek. He planted his hands on his hips and said, "Jake, I need you back at the house. There's some wood that needs stacking."

"Oh," I said stupidly. Toby and I were sitting on an outcropping of rocks. *Little boy, little boy, my branches are heavy and my apples will rot,* I'd cried moments earlier. *Please, little boy, won't you help?*

"Get off your butt, girl," my father said.

I stood, grabbing Toby's hand and pulling him up with me.

"We'll come back later," I promised him.

"And finish the story?"

"And finish the story."

"Did I say I needed both of you?" my father asked. "I did not. Toby, you wait here. You'd rather play at the creek than stack wood, wouldn't you?"

"He's okay with coming," I said. "Aren't you, Toby?"

"He's *okay* with staying," my father said. "I swear, you and Carrie are always babying that boy. If you don't quit babying him, he'll never grow up." He caught Toby's eye. "You're a big boy. You can take care of yourself for a coupla minutes, can't you?"

Toby looked at me, a fatal mistake. My heart drummed fast inside my rib cage.

"That's it," my father said roughly. He jabbed a finger at Toby. "Your sister doesn't tell you what to do. *I* do." He jabbed that same finger at me. "Same goes for you. The quicker you start, the quicker you'll be done."

"Yes, Daddy," I said. "It's just that Toby's not supposed to be out here alone. He's too little."

"If he's too *little*, it's because you made him so. Now get a move on—or do I need to come over there and make you?"

On Mabel's sofa, tears course down my cheeks. I'm not sobbing anymore. I'm just sad, because Toby *was* too little to play in the creek by himself, just as he was too little to know how little he was. He knew that four-year-olds weren't supposed to die, probably, but he didn't know that sometimes they did.

"I squeezed his hand three times, for 'I' and 'love' and 'you,'" I tell Mabel. "Then I took off my necklace and put it around his neck, because the key was what the little boy used at the bottom of the well, when he was ready to come back up."

I see Toby face down in the creek, his fine hair thin and pliant as seaweed. The leather cord of the necklace pulled taut, the key glinting darkly in the tangle of submerged branches.

"Shh," Mabel soothes. She rubs circles on my back.

The creek was barely deep enough to wade in, but the algae-covered stones were as slippery as glass. Toby, left to play on his own, must have slipped on those glassy stones. He smacked his head, which knocked him out, which led to him drawing water into his lungs instead of air. He drowned in a creek that was half a foot deep.

As the EMTs loaded Toby's body onto the stretcher, one of the search-and-rescue officers shook his head and said something to his colleague. I was huddling with Carrie and heard every word.

"The current would have pushed him to safety, if not for that leather cord. It caught on that tree branch, see? Poor kid would be alive right now if not for that damn cord."

"Oh, Jake," Mabel says.

"It was my fault."

"It wasn't."

It was, and I know it. But there's more I need to explain.

"The thing is, I became helpless after that. In all the ways. Because if I was helpless, I didn't have to make choices." I search Mabel's eyes. "I failed my little brother, and so I told myself, 'Okay, you did that. That's who you are, a person who failed your little brother, because you're helpless.' And being 'helpless' meant I didn't have to act."

I exhale. "But last night, I did. I marched over and confronted Vanessa, and I thought I was being so big, so brave, so grown-up. I thought I was breaking the pattern, you know? But when Vanessa lashed out at me, all of those goals fell away, and I lashed right back at her. And at Billy! Who's ten! Vanessa and I were like two kids slinging mud at each other on the playground."

I lean back against the sofa and swing my head toward her. "I don't know if I'm ever going to get a handle on this adulting business, if I'm being honest."

Mabel tugs at the high collar of her blouse. "Oh, Jake," she says. The poise she's shown falls away, and her face fills with what looks for a moment like dread. "You and me both."

45

MABEL

"Oh shit," Jake says. Her gaze travels again over Mabel's outfit, and Mabel sees the moment when the awareness hits her. "I thought maybe you'd gone to church, but today was the day of the panty party, wasn't it?"

Mabel fidgets. "Well, yes, but in the end, I decided it wasn't worth the bother."

"But you're all dressed up," Jake says. She gestures with her hand. "You did your hair, your makeup, the whole shebang . . . you look gorgeous, by the way . . ."

"Thank you?"

"And after all that, you decided not to go? Why do I feel like I'm missing something?"

Oh, I don't know, because I'm choosing not to tell you about the naughty photos of me that Gigi has? Mabel thinks. *The very naughty photos that she showed Shelby . . . and which Shelby, if she so chooses, can share with the world?*

"You told me to be the bigger woman and not involve myself," Mabel says. "I took your advice."

"Huh," Jake says.

Mabel gives a sickly smile. "A better response would be, 'Good job, Mabel. Way to go, Mabel.'"

"Good job, Mabel. Way to go," Jake recites, but Mabel can tell she's not convinced.

She hesitates, wondering how she can get out of this. "The thing is . . ." she begins. She touches the tip of her tongue to her teeth. "You want to know the truth? For real?"

"Of course."

Mabel glances around to make sure they're alone, though there's no need. David's playing golf, and Bethany left for Delilah's house shortly before Jake arrived. Mabel's surprised they didn't pass each other on the sidewalk.

"There's this story David told me, about Bethany when she was little," Mabel says. "She was four, I think."

"Toby's age," Jake says.

Mabel hits her forehead with the heel of her palm. "Oh God, I wasn't thinking."

"Mabel? Lots of people are four. I was four myself once."

Mabel pulls a face.

Jake motions for her to go on.

"Well, Bethany was at some kid's birthday party," she says, "and Slurpees were involved, and one of the kids decided to dump her cherry Slurpee on top of Bethany's head."

"What? Uncool."

"David was the parent on duty, because of course he was, so he took Bethany home and tried to make her feel better. He was all, 'That little girl shouldn't have done that. I'm sorry that happened.'"

"Poor Bethany."

"Then Gigi arrived."

"Uh-oh."

"There Bethany was, sticky and sad, but did Gigi hug her? Comfort her? Tell her everything was going to be okay?"

"I'm guessing no."

"Correct. Instead of comforting her little girl, Gigi yelled at her."

"Did she understand that another kid did the Slurpee-ing, not Bethany?"

"As a matter of fact, yes," Mabel says. "Gigi heard the whole story and said, 'And what did *you* do, Bethany, after that nasty little girl poured her Slurpee on your head?' She said if Bethany had any spine at all, she would have retaliated immediately by dumping *her* Slurpee on the other girl's head."

"You're kidding."

"She said that the next time it happened—"

"The *next* time? Did Gigi think Bethany was on *Glee*?"

"Huh?"

"The TV show about the kids in glee club. They're always getting Slurpeed? No?"

Mabel waves Jake's remark away. "Gigi told Bethany that next time, if there was a next time, Bethany better go in swinging. As in, Slurpee first and ask questions later."

Jake looks awed, but awed in the way she'd be if she was witnessing a snake swallow a rat, inch by bulging inch. "And Bethany was four?"

"Yup."

"Wow."

Mabel drums her fingers on her thigh. "So I was thinking about that, and about what you said about being the better woman . . ." She meets Jake's eyes. "Shelby's nothing, Jake. You are cooler and kinder and better than her in every way, and I guess I finally realized that she does not deserve an inch of your mental real estate, or of mine."

Jake contemplates this. "So you no longer think she should be accountable for being a shit human being?"

"Sure she should, just not by me."

"Then by whom?"

Mabel shrugs. "Not my monkeys, not my circus." Jake furrows her brow, and Mabel adds, "Not your circus, either, not anymore. I think we should both just let it go."

Jake says, "Okay, but what if . . ."

There's a clattering at the door, and whatever Jake was going to say is forgotten, swept away by a surge of happy voices as Bethany and Delilah burst in. Mabel is awash with relief.

"We decided to hang out here," Bethany announces. She spots Jake and grins. "Hi, Jake! I'm going to teach Delilah how to make friendship bracelets."

Jake smiles. "Hi, girls."

"Is Wendell here?" Mabel asks. She's never known Delilah to go anywhere without him.

"He's in the front room," Delilah says. "He's being a moody boy."

Said the pot to the kettle, Mabel thinks.

Delilah narrows her eyes at Mabel, and Mabel clears her expression.

"Why is he moody?" Jake asks.

"He's jealous that I've got Bethany and he doesn't. It's annoying."

Bethany's cheeks grow rosy. "Well, he kind of has me," she says generously. "I'm his friend, too."

"Yeah, but he wants a boy version. And speaking of . . ." Delilah scowls and jerks her thumb at Bethany. "This one is being equally annoying. Tell them who you want to make a bracelet for, Bethany."

"De*li*lah!" Bethany says giddily. "I'm going to make one for you, stupid head. And then, *if* I have time . . ."

Delilah pretends to barf, complete with sound effects. Bethany giggles and shoves her.

Jake looks at Mabel and mouths, "Billy."

"I know!" Mabel mouths back.

Bethany now has a craft basket just like Jake's, overflowing with cotton floss in a zillion different colors. She shows it proudly to Delilah, and the girls settle on the floor, pretzeling their legs and scooching around to get comfortable.

Mabel wants to shake Jake and say, "See how young they are? You were that young too, when your brother died."

She stands. "Do you want some banana bread to take home with you?"

Jake gives a startled laugh. "Am I going home?" She rises, too, ceding the great room to Bethany and Delilah. In the kitchen, she watches Mabel slice a piece of banana bread and slide it onto a plate.

"Call your stepmom," Mabel tells her. "Call Carrie." She points at Jake with the knife. "Have you ever talked to her about all this?"

"About what?"

"She still reaches out, right? She sends you birthday cards?"

"So?"

Mabel spins the knife in a circle, and the blade throws sharp, bright diamonds over Jake's face. "So *call* her. I'm guessing she's the one person who might be able to give you a different perspective on everything, or at least provide you with more information. Information you can process with your thirty-one-year-old brain, instead of your sad, scared eleven-year-old brain."

In the great room, Bethany and Delilah bicker about whether pink is a "girl color" or a "boy color."

"They're sweet," Jake says, nodding in their direction.

Mabel thrusts the plate into Jake's hands and nudges her in the direction of the front door. "I'm going to fix them a snack, and you're going to go home and call your stepmother."

Now the girls are bickering over whether to invite Billy to hang out with them on the playground. Bethany thinks yes; Delilah's opinion is hell to the no.

"Remember to ask first, before going to the playground!" Mabel calls. "And I'm not talking about Billy. I'm talking about me, the person in charge!"

There's a stunned silence. Then both girls break into manic laughter.

"Busted!" Delilah says.

"Omigod, *shh*!" Bethany exclaims. She makes her voice angelic. "Mabel, can we please go to the playground after we finish our bracelets?"

"Of course," Mabel replies, throwing a wink at Jake. "Kids these days. Am I right?"

46

JAKE

Wendell's alone on the front room sofa, knees tucked up and chin propped in his hand. I pause when I see him and say, "Hi, Wendell. How's it going?"

He smiles, his mouth pulling upward in its uneven way. "Hi, Jake. Are you going home? Can I come with you and say 'hi' to Lump?"

I hesitate, then say, "Sure, I guess." I step back into the hall. "Delilah, how long will it be before you and Bethany go to the playground?"

"Not long," Delilah calls from the great room. "Why?"

"Wendell wants to say hi to Lump. Can you swing by and pick him up when you're done here?"

"No problem!" Bethany answers for her. "We can swing by and get Billy, too!"

"Or not," Delilah says. She appears in the hall, a tangle of embroidery thread looped around her fingers. Wendell is at my side, having hopped off the sofa to join me.

"Wait for us at Jake's," Delilah tells him. "We'll be there in fifteen minutes."

Wendell nods happily. "Okay."

Mabel sticks her head out from the kitchen. "Call your stepmother!"

"We'll see!" I call back.

As Wendell and I stroll down the sidewalk, I try to sort my thoughts. I haven't forgotten about Shelby. I haven't forgotten the tea. But I put that problem aside. Maybe I *will* call Carrie. What harm could it do?

Lump hears us enter the house and trots to meet us, meowing loudly.

Wendell scoops him up and lugs him toward the sofa. "Hi, Lump! It's me, Wendell!"

Lump's enormous body sways and his front legs stick out comically. His head nearly disappears between his furry shoulder blades.

Wendell plops down, and Lump lies stretched out across Wendell's forearms, tummy exposed and limbs floppy. It reminds me of how Carrie once held me, the summer she taught me how to float on my back.

I let Wendell know I'll be in the kitchen if he needs anything, then pull up Carrie's name from my list of contacts. What do I have to lose?

"Jake?" Carrie says, picking up after two rings. "Jake, is it really you?"

Her voice is familiar and also not. I clear my throat. "Carrie! Hi!"

Her words fly out in an urgent rush. "Are you all right? Is everything okay? I'm *so* glad to hear from you! Are you all right?"

She thinks there's been an emergency. Why else would I call after all this time?

"I'm fine," I hurry to say. "Everything's fine."

"Oh, thank goodness," Carrie says, and the sound of her relief floods me with guilt.

After Toby died, she and my father split up. I never returned to that house in the forest, and now twenty years have passed.

Twenty years, and not once did she forget my birthday or leave me off her Christmas card list. *To My Daughter*, some of the cards said in embossed cursive. Others bore the message, *Happy Birthday, Daughter!* She picked those cards off the rack for me. I was her child, too, and she lost me just like she lost Toby.

"Well! Okay!" she says. "How are you?"

Oh God, a new realization. Not once, during the height of the scandal or afterward, did Carrie cross my mind. Does she know about everything that happened? Has she embraced the internet in the two decades since I saw her?

"Um . . . it's been quite a year," I say, feeling her out. "I got divorced, for starters."

"Jake, I didn't know. I'm sorry."

"It needed to happen. It's for the best."

"Well, sometimes it is," Carrie says. "Are you still in Fort Collins?"

"Yeah. New house, actually. And I seem to have acquired a cat."

"A fur baby! Boy? Girl? What's his name?"

I tell Carrie about Lump, who no one ever contacted me about, and Carrie tells me that I'm the human he was meant to be with. She has cats, too, I learn. A butterscotch kitty named Barnaby, a black-and-white shorthair named Louie, and a Maine coon named Sherbet.

She pronounces it "Sherbert" with two Rs, and the Southern drawl brings back memories. Carrie always ordered sherbet when they went to Sunshine Sammie's, an ice cream parlor whose specialty was enormous ice cream sandwiches made with cookies. I always ordered the cookie sandwich. So did my father. So did Toby, once he was big enough to hold one. Yet Carrie ordered the same thing every time: a child-sized scoop of orange "sherbert" in a cup.

"I'm watching my weight, John," she'd tell my father, patting her nonexistent tummy. "Do you want me to get fat?"

Another memory slides into place, something I haven't thought of in ages. My mom was size-zero skinny when she and my father were high school sweethearts. I've seen photos. By the time they split up, she wasn't fat, but she was no longer a size zero. She'd moved into the double digits and never looked back.

"Your father used to monitor my calories, as if that were any business of his," she once told me. "Don't ever let a man tell you how you should or shouldn't look. I mean it, Jakey. Don't even go down that road."

The doorbell rings, and I startle. "Carrie, give me one second," I say, lowering the phone and holding it to my chest. "Wendell, is that Delilah and Bethany?"

I hear the door being opened, and a new voice, but not female.

"It's Billy!" Wendell says.

I poke my head into the hall and see Billy on the porch. I feel a fresh wave of remorse for the things I said to Vanessa last night. Thank goodness Billy didn't hear. If he had, I would see it on his face.

No. If he heard what I said, he wouldn't be on my front porch in the first place.

"Hi, Jake," he says.

"Hi, Billy," I say warmly.

"I saw you and Wendell go inside, and I wondered—"

"Sure, sure," I say, beckoning him in. "You and Wendell can hang out here while you wait for Bethany and Delilah."

"Bethany and Delilah are coming over? When?"

"They shouldn't be long." I wiggle my phone. "I'm going to finish my call."

"Do you, um, have a piece of paper? I want to write Bethany a letter."

"You'll be seeing her in ten minutes."

He holds his eyes wide and still, as if not wanting to give anything away. "Yes, but . . . it's a special kind of letter."

A special kind of letter, I think, melting. Will he ask Wendell to help him pen this special letter? I can totally envision Wendell as a pint-size Cyrano de Bergerac.

"One more second," I tell Carrie, pulling a piece of paper and an envelope from the desk in my office. I grab a pen and pass everything over to Billy. "Okay, I'll leave you to it." I make eye contact with each boy. "If you need anything, just come get me!"

Back in the kitchen, I perch on a stool and hook my foot around the rungs. "I've got two neighborhood kids over," I tell Carrie. "They're sweet boys." I take a breath. "Speaking of . . . I've been thinking a lot about Toby."

The air between us changes. We're not in the same room or even the same state, but what hangs between us grows heavier, like a great felt blanket settling over us.

"Oh, Jake," Carrie says softly.

"I'm so sorry," I say, trying to hold it together. "That's why I called. I don't know if I ever actually told you that."

"Jake—"

"I never should have left him. I know that. But Dad was . . . I don't know. He was in one of his moods? I guess? Not that that's an excuse, but—"

"*Jake*," Carrie interrupts. "I'm going to ask you a question. I need you to answer honestly."

My lower lip trembles the way it did when I was little and wanted so badly not to cry.

"Do you think you were responsible for Toby's death?"

Everything hurts. Everything presses in. And then everything recedes, pulling me with it. I am the water, the creek bed, the cold and glassy rocks.

"Jake? Are you still there?"

"I'm sorry," I whisper, my voice cracking.

"Jake, no. You have nothing to apologize for."

She tells me all the things, almost exactly, that Mabel told me. "You were a child," she says. "What happened wasn't your fault."

Billy and Wendell appear in the kitchen. When Billy whispers that they're taking off, I wipe my eyes and nod my consent.

"Billy's going to teach me how to play *Final Fantasy*!" Wendell exclaims.

Billy holds out a sealed envelope. "Can you give this to Bethany?"

"Of course. Have fun. I'll send the girls your way!"

I go back to Carrie, and we move from Toby's death to Toby's life. It's like melted chocolate and the glow of a fire, sharing stories and laughing with the one person who loved Toby as much as I did.

That's not fair. My father, despite his flaws, loved Toby, too.

I say as much to Carrie.

"I suppose he did," she says, "but Toby would have been better off without him. We all would have been. I don't want to speak ill of your father, but let me put it this way. I think your mama had the right idea, moving on from him sooner rather than later."

I breathe out a puff of air. "How is he? Do you two keep in touch?" Carrie kind of snorts, and in it I hear a loose thread, a connection I'm not making.

"Should I take that as a no?"

"Jake, your father's in prison. Didn't you know?"

"What?!"

Carrie's voice is calm, too calm, as she spools out a story that makes me reel. After she and my dad split up, he got married again. Last spring he was arrested on charges of domestic violence.

"Shit," I say.

"It wasn't his first offense," Carrie says. "He's looking at five to ten years. Craggy Prison."

"In Boone?"

"Closer to Asheville. But his wife—she's from Fort Collins. Isn't that something?"

"Fort Collins? *My* Fort Collins?"

"I think your mother knew her, back in the day. Tammy? Pammy? One of those names your father always hated for no good reason."

"Nikki, Ricky, Misty, Dawn, and Nevaeh," I say, rattling off the list I learned from my mom. "I like those names just fine, especially Nevaeh."

"Nevaeh! That's it!" Carrie says triumphantly. "Your father despised that name, and what'd he do? Went and married the one and only Nevaeh he ever knew."

Unease creeps over me. Puzzle pieces hover, just out of reach, vying for attention.

"They all went to high school together—John, your mom, and this Nevaeh. Years later, he found her online and wooed her from afar. Moved her out to North Carolina, which I'm sure suited him just fine."

Memories stir, like how my father and Nevaeh dated briefly. Like how my mom's face, when she told me about it, had clouded over. "It wasn't right," she'd said. "He had that girl under his thumb."

I remember the tombstone I saw at the beginning of the summer—except it wasn't a tombstone, just a temporary aluminum marker jammed into a new grave. *Nolan*, it read. *Mother, Sister, Friend.*

"She left North Carolina after your father's arrest, and I was real glad to hear it," Carrie says. "Took the kids and moved back to Colorado."

"Kids?"

"A girl and a boy. You know, Jake, that makes them your half-siblings!"

Dizziness rolls through me.

"You should look them up. I'm sure they could use a big sister right about now."

"Carrie, I've got to go."

"Oh!" Carrie says, surprised. She recovers and says sympathetically, "Well, it's a lot to take in. But do look them up. Nevaeh Nolan, that's the name of their mom."

"Sure," I say from outside myself.

"And Jake—stay in touch, will you?"

"I will. I promise."

As soon as I hang up, I type "Nevaeh Nolan, Fort Collins, Colorado" into the search bar on my phone. I add in "obituary" and tap Go.

"Nevaeh Mae Nolan, 45, of Fort Collins, Colorado died on Tuesday, May 28, 2024," the entry reads. "She is survived by her two children, Delilah and Wendell, and her sister, Evelyn Cox."

47

WENDELL

Last year, in North Carolina, Wendell saw something bad. Delilah wasn't there. She was at school. Wendell was a kindergartner and had half days, so he was doing errands with his mom. They took the narrow mountain road that led to town because Wendell's birthday was coming up. They were making a trip to Piggly Wiggly to buy ingredients for his cake.

Wendell rode in his booster in the back seat of the car. His mom played a funny song called "Lollipop" on repeat and changed the lyrics from "Hey, Mika! What's the big idea?" to "Hey, Wendell, what's the big idea?!"

Faster cars whipped around them, even though passing wasn't allowed.

"For heaven's sake," Wendell's mom exclaimed. "They'll get wherever they're going a whole two minutes earlier. Is two minutes worth risking your life for?"

"No way, José," Wendell replied.

Halfway down the mountain, there was a traffic jam. One by one, the cars slowed to a stop, the line stretching out behind them as more and more vehicles joined the queue. Some people honked their horns. Wendell's mom shrugged and played "Lollipop" for the fiftieth time. "Hey, Wendell!" she sang. "What's the big idea?!"

Without unbuckling his seat belt, Wendell got on his knees and shuffled in a semicircle on top of his booster seat until he could see out the rear window. He watched a truck nose into the empty left lane, thinking to edge past the backlog. The guy ahead of him leaned out of his window and yelled, "Hey dumbass, we're all stuck here, same as you!"

The guy in the truck tried to reclaim his spot in line, but the vehicles behind him had filled in the gap. There was nowhere for him to go, and his truck now blocked both lanes. This led to more honking and more yelling until, finally, he threw up his hands in defeat.

High up on the road, a band of motorcycles approached.

"I sure hope they slow down," Wendell's mother said.

"Slow down, motorcycle dudes!" Wendell called, cupping his hands around his mouth.

There were six motorcycle dudes in total. Five of them, when they saw the traffic jam, slowed down and joined the line of stalled traffic. The sixth revved his engine, blew a kiss at his friends, and shot into the opposite lane.

He didn't see the truck until it was too late.

"Wendell, look away," Wendell's mom said sharply.

He didn't. His eyes stayed glued on the scene as the motorcyclist braked hard, the bike twisting and skidding sideways. Time slowed. There was a humming between Wendell's ears. Then a sickening crunch, followed by a scream so shrill and unhinged it didn't sound human.

The motorcyclist's buddies abandoned their bikes and sprinted to the man writhing on the road. When they lifted him, Wendell saw that his leg had been flattened between the motorcycle and the truck. His boot was gone, and what remained of his foot dangled from his pant leg like a wet sock, flesh and bone mashed to jelly.

Later, when Wendell told Delilah about it, she huffed. "And I didn't get to see it? No fair."

There were plenty of scary things Delilah was fine with, like snakes and spiders and bedrooms with no nightlights. But when it came to blood and guts, she wasn't as brave as she made out to be. When Wendell got shot, for example, Delilah sobbed harder than he did.

So for Delilah's sake, Wendell was glad she didn't see the motorcycle guy crash, just as he's glad she isn't here now, trapped in the shed Billy brought him to.

All the same, he longs for her. Wendell longs for his sister and he longs for his mother, whose name was "heaven" spelled backward. Which of the two is he more likely to see first, he wonders?

He shifts on his bottom, trying to get comfortable. A plastic zip tie binds his hands behind his back, and a bandana gags his mouth. His nostrils tingle with a smell he recognizes from the olden days, when his dad cooked hamburgers on the grill.

Next to him are bags of soil and fertilizer. Stacks of old newspapers are piled against the wall. The floor is littered with dried leaves and hard pellets of mouse poop, but Wendell doesn't spot any mice. It's just him and Billy, who sits on an upside-down bucket with a container of lighter fluid. He tips the container from side to side, and lighter fluid sloshes out.

"Wendell, Wendell, Wendell," he says. "What are we going to do with you?"

It's funny how calm Wendell feels, like he's watching a movie and wondering what will happen next to the little boy who left Jake's house with the bigger boy who invited him to play *Final Fantasy.*

"My mom's out shopping, she'll be gone for hours," Billy had said. "It'll be just us guys. Whaddaya say?"

Billy gestures at the door of the shed, where a metal padlock hangs from the latch. "I locked us in," he says conversationally. "I have a key, obviously." He sets down the lighter fluid, digs in the front pocket of his jeans, and produces a small metal key. "You want it?"

He extends his hand to Wendell, then laughs when Wendell leans forward.

"Nah, I've got a better idea."

Billy goes to the small window at the back of the shed, punches the pane, and uses his bloody hand to throw the key through the jagged triangles of glass.

"There," he says. "Now we'll always know where it is."

Billy shakes lighter fluid onto Wendell. He pours the rest over his own torso and legs—pensively, even sorrowfully—and Wendell's calm evaporates. Does Billy want to hurt himself as well as Wendell? Does he want to make sure that neither boy leaves this shed, ever, even if he changes his mind?

Wendell suddenly needs very badly to use the bathroom. "Mmuh!" he says, wiggling.

"What's that?"

"*Mmmuh!*" Wendell says, trying to tongue the bandana from his mouth. When that doesn't work, he uses his mind to push his words at Billy. *Why are you doing this? We're reading buddies, remember?*

"Sorry, but I can't understand you," Billy says. "I mean, duh, no one can understand you, even on the best of days." He laughs. "And, well, this isn't the best of days."

He pulls a red plastic lighter from his pocket and thumbs the striker. A flame springs up.

Wendell tries to scrabble backward, but his spine is already pressed to the wall. His sneakers skitter and squeak.

"I'd start with your shoes, but rubber stinks when it burns," Billy says. He lowers the lighter to Wendell's jeans. "This'll work."

At first, Wendell doesn't feel pain, just heat. Then the flame finds flesh. Wendell's screams are thick and clotted.

"Hey, don't cry," Billy says. "You're a big boy, aren't you? Big boys don't cry." He peers at Wendell as if trying to understand a terrible mystery. Then his face slackens. His shoulders droop. He looks exhausted.

So stop! Wendell pleads inarticulately. *If you're so exhausted, just stop!*

Wendell begs his mother to reach down from heaven and carry him away. Then pain blisters his thoughts, and fire and tears are all he knows.

48

JAKE

The world judders to a halt, then starts back up, truths shifting as reality takes on new dimensions. I have siblings? I have siblings! I have a half sister, grumpy and fierce, and a half brother as sweet as Toby, as sweet as an angel.

This cannot be.

And yet it might be, just the same?

I grab Billy's letter and step onto the front porch, desperate to gather all the kids together, Bethany and Billy and Delilah and Wendell. I spot the girls on the sidewalk and jog to meet them.

"Hi!" I call, drinking in the sight of Delilah with her beautiful, ferocious scowl. "Are you here for Wendell? He's with Billy."

"What?" Delilah says.

"They're at his house." I hand Bethany the envelope. "He asked me to pass this along."

"Billy did?" Bethany says, her eyes enormous. She opens the envelope and pulls out a piece of notebook paper. As she reads it, she grows pale.

"What's wrong?" Delilah says.

Bethany tilts the letter so that Delilah can see it. I edge closer until I can, too.

HI BETHANY!

I USED TO REALLY LIKE YOU, BUT IT TURNS OUT YOU'RE LIKE A SNAKE IN THE GRASS WHO BETRAYS EVERYBODY THEY MEET. I USED TO LIKE SNAKES. I EVEN HAD A SNAKE FOR A PET, REMEMBER?

I TOLD YOU SOMETHING HAPPENED TO MY SNAKE, BUT I DIDN'T TELL YOU WHAT. IT'S THE SAME THING THAT'S GOING TO HAPPEN TO YOUR ANNOYING FRIEND'S ANNOYING BROTHER. SMUSHED-IN HEAD? SIDEWAYS SMILE? THERE'S SOMETHING OFF ABOUT THAT KID. HONESTLY, IT'S HEARTBREAKING.

SO I'M GOING TO DO HIM A FAVOR, ONE WEIRDO TO ANOTHER.

LOVE,

BILLY

PS I KILLED IT.

:)

At the bottom, Billy had drawn a smiley face.

"What is he talking about?" Delilah says, breathing fast.

"I don't know!" Bethany says. "And why did he mention his snake? He didn't really kill it, did he?"

The ground beneath me wobbles as they talk at each other in panicked voices. All those terrible things I said to Vanessa? Billy *did* hear them.

And now he's got Wendell.

Billy's going to hurt Wendell.

I sprint across the yard to Vanessa and Billy's house, the girls on my heels. I jam down on the doorbell. I pound on the door.

"Wendell, are you in there? Can you hear me?" I rattle the knob. "Billy! Let us in!"

"Let's try around back," Delilah says. We bang and knock and rattle the back doorknob, but there's no reply.

"The door that leads to the garage?" Bethany suggests. The garage door is locked.

"Fuck!" I cry.

Bethany peers through the four-paned window. "The mudroom door is open! If we can get into the garage, we can get into the house!" She drops to her knees and uses her arm to push at a black rubber flap of a pet door, the same setup I have.

Delilah squats and yells through the opening. "Wendell!"

I'm already running back to my house. I return with the same stick I used before, the one with the loop of string on the end. "Move," I tell Bethany. "Believe it or not, I've done this before."

I lie down on the cold soil and shimmy into position, cramming my shoulder into the pet door and feeding the stick through to my empty hand. I flick the loop of string toward the door handle. It doesn't catch. Again and again, the stick thwacks the door. Again and again, no luck. I'm back at the creek, grasping for Toby as the EMTs load him into the ambulance, the bang of the doors removing him from sight.

This time there isn't a bang, but a metallic click. I scramble to my feet and fling open the door. "Come on!"

Delilah takes the top floor, Bethany takes the main level, and I take the basement. "Wendell!" we cry. "*Wen*-dell!" We search every room and every closet. We check under the beds, in the dark corners of the basement storage area, and inside every cabinet large enough to hide a six-year-old boy.

"Did you *see* him go into Billy's house?" Delilah demands, whipping toward me. "Are you positive?"

"They left my house together. Wendell said something about a video game?"

Delilah storms out the back door. Bethany and I trail after.

"Wen-*dell*!" Delilah shouts.

"Wendell!" I yell.

Bethany scans Billy's backyard, a neat rectangle of grass enclosed by a slatted wooden fence. I see nothing of interest, just the backs of the houses one street down, but Bethany draws in a breath.

"I know where they are," she exclaims. "Follow me!"

49

BILLY

A person who enjoys being cruel is called a "sadist." Billy knows this from the internet. He figures his mom is a sadist since she takes pleasure in Billy's pain. Why else would she hurt him, if she didn't get something out of it?

Billy assumes, all things considered, that he's a sadist, too. Like mother, like son. But when will the "enjoying it" part kick in?

He drops Wendell's foot after setting Wendell's jeans on fire. It's heavy, and Billy is tired. The flames will reach Billy soon, and the shed's rotting wooden walls. When that happens, *wow*. Things will happen fast.

Wendell thrashes, his legs pedaling frantically. His screams are muffled bleats.

"Shut up," Billy says dully. If Wendell keeps making those sounds, Billy will kick him, and it will be Wendell's fault for making Billy's insides feel so clenched and tight.

Or you could put out the flames, whispers a voice.

The leaves on the floor snap and crackle. One flares upward, drifting lazily before landing on a stack of newspapers. With a whoosh, the tower ignites.

Wendell drums his heels against the floor. *Thwap, thwap, thwap*, like the beats of a great winged creature accelerating to catch its prey. *Crick, creak, crack*, the creature's sharp beak slicing into the shed.

"Billy! Open the door!" he hears. Reality wavers.

"Wendell! Are you in there?"

"It's locked! I can't get in!"

"Girls, step back," the creature commands, and Billy cowers against the wall.

The door bursts open. Jake runs toward Wendell as the stack of newspapers topples, fresh flames leaping to the walls of the shed.

"Get out!" Bethany cries from the blazing doorway. "It's going to collapse!"

Delilah stands frozen behind Bethany. Her terror makes Billy's lungs seize.

Jake kneels beside Wendell, flames lapping all around. She tries to lift him but stumbles and falls on one knee.

The roof of the shed groans, flames flaring higher and brighter.

"Help me!" Jake yells, and in one stride, Billy is squatting before Wendell, whose eyes have fluttered shut. Billy wedges his arms beneath Wendell's prone form and staggers upright. A piece of sheet metal swings free. He pivots to bear the brunt of the blow, and pain roars through him. Every instinct tells him to drop Wendell and flee; to fling himself out of the shed and onto the cool soil where he can roll and twist and smother the flames that engulf him.

He plows forward, cradling Wendell like a baby. Jake navigates him through the blaze.

Delilah unfreezes at last, lunging toward them and extending her arms.

A ceiling beam creaks. Billy hunches over Wendell. He shields his charge and passes him to Delilah, just before the beam slams into his skull.

50

WENDELL

"Expect the unexpected," Wendell's mom used to say, and that's good advice except for the fact that it's impossible. You *can't* expect the unexpected. If you could, it would be expected!

But Wendell isn't the Big Boss, so what does he know?

Is there a Big Boss? If so, Delilah would probably file a complaint every day. Delilah has lots to complain about, like this morning when she grabbed Wendell's hospital tray and thrust it back at the aide not two seconds after the aide placed it on Wendell's tray table.

"He ordered French toast, not pancakes," she said.

"Delilah!" Aunt Evelyn said. "We are in a hospital, not a hotel. This isn't like getting room service, young lady!"

"Actually, it is," Delilah argued. She yanked open the top drawer of Wendell's bedside table and pulled out a laminated *Welcome to Poudre Valley Hospital!* information card.

"'We recognize the role food and nutrition play in speeding up recovery and have designed our *room service* program to answer those needs,'" Delilah read aloud. She turned to the aide. "If you want my little brother to have a speedy recovery, you'll get him the French toast he ordered."

"On it," said the aide.

If there is a Big Boss, Wendell might make a few complaints, too, but he'd also say "thank you" for all the good things, like how he has another sister now! Wendell's neighbor, Jake, turned out to secretly be Wendell's half sister, which means she's also Delilah's half sister, which made Delilah mad when she first found out.

"It is what it is," Aunt Evelyn told the two of them, after the frenzy of the fire and all that died down. Wendell suffered second-degree burns on his shins, and he'll have a cough for a while because of smoke inhalation, but mainly, he's fine. Mainly he's bummed he was unconscious for the one and only ambulance ride he's ever had in his life!

"You might have more," Delilah said. "You never know. Maybe an anvil will land on your head."

"Delilah, shush," Aunt Evelyn replied, and probably Wendell was wrong, but he thought her eyes went misty. She turned away and made a show of pouring Wendell a glass of water from the beige plastic pitcher that lives in his hospital room. When she passed him the cup, she was all business, although she took special care to make sure he didn't dribble all over his hospital gown, which ties in the back and is printed all over with green muscular action heroes.

He also has special hospital socks. He woke up in the children's wing of Poudre Valley Hospital wearing a Hulk hospital gown, gray socks, and white bandages that reminded him of other times he needed bandages.

He likes the socks, though. Last time, he didn't get socks.

After the doctors were done fussing and he was allowed to have visitors, Jake came in and sat on the edge of his bed. She explained the complicated crisscrosses that meant that her father was also Wendell and Delilah's father. It took several tellings to sink in.

Jake pulled her phone from her pocket and showed them photos from her childhood, photos that made it clear that John Nolan, who was Jake's father, divorced Jake's mom and married another woman. Her name was Carrie. Then he divorced that woman and married *another* woman, and her name was Nevaeh.

Wendell and Delilah's mom.

The whole story gave Delilah and Aunt Evelyn a bad case of scowling.

So it was Wendell who said to Jake, "That's pretty cool. I'm glad you're my sister."

"*I'm* your sister," Delilah said. Then, to Jake, "He's loopy from the drugs they gave him."

All of that happened yesterday. Today, Jake is back, rapping on his hospital door and entering with a brown paper bag.

"Who wants ice cream?" she asks, pulling out a pint of rocky road and a stack of plastic cups.

"Me, please!" Wendell says.

"I'll serve," Delilah says, striding forward and taking the ice cream from Jake. "He's my brother."

"Delilah," Aunt Evelyn says.

"It's fine," Jake says, just as Delilah says, "What?"

Aunt Evelyn humphs and returns to making clickety-clack sounds with her needles. Aunt Evelyn, as it turns out, is a knitter. Wendell didn't know that about her till now because, at home, she rarely sits still long enough to pull out her supplies.

At home. It's only since he'd been at the hospital that he's begun thinking of Aunt Evelyn's house as home. He likes knowing he has a home to go to.

Jake sits on the edge of Wendell's bed. "You're being discharged today."

"Yep."

Her blue eyes lock on his. "How do you feel? Are you ready? I could talk to the doctors and see if maybe one extra night would be a good idea."

"I'm good," Wendell says. He beckons Jake closer and whispers into her ear. "How's Billy?"

"What's that?" Delilah says, appearing in the blink of an eye. She has razor-sharp hearing, and she *hates* Billy.

Jake tells them that Billy is in the hospital, too, but hasn't woken up yet. She says it will be a long time before he's discharged, and even then, he'll never return to his old house.

"There's already a For Sale sign in his yard," she says.

"Good," Delilah says.

Wendell chews his lower lip. He knows Delilah won't like what he asks next, but he asks it anyway. "Have you gone to visit him?"

A shadow crosses Jake's face. "I haven't, but I will."

"Why?" Delilah demands. She turns to Wendell. "And why do you care?"

"I don't," Wendell says.

Delilah narrows her eyes. "I wish he burned to a crisp."

Wendell expects his aunt to object. When she doesn't, he thinks Jake will say something, surely. Neither woman utters a word.

"Here's your ice cream," Delilah says, plunking down a bowl of rocky road. To Jake, she says, "Move. I need to adjust his bed." Jake stands, and Delilah punches a button that pulls the front of the bed forward with a whirring sound.

"I'll get going," Jake says.

"Okay, bye," Delilah says without looking at her.

Jake doesn't leave. She hovers near Wendell until Delilah loudly exhales.

"Fine, you can pet him," she grumbles. "But make it snappy."

Jake's fingers are cool on Wendell's skin as she brushes his hair from his forehead.

"I'm glad you're safe," she says.

"I'm glad you rescued me," Wendell says. He glances at Delilah. "You are, too. Right, Delilah?"

"If she hadn't pulled you out, I would have." Her gaze flicks from Wendell to Jake. "I hope you know that. I hope you both do."

"Absolutely," Jake says. She gives Delilah a quick sideways hug. "That's what big sisters are for."

51

BILLY

At the hospital, Billy dreams a familiar dream. The Burrito Baby Dream, he calls it. He doesn't know where it comes from or why, only that he hates it.

In the dream, he's in a warehouse filled with babies, all wrapped burrito-style in soft pastel blankets, lying on their backs. One gazes at the ceiling with wide round eyes. Another works an arm free and tries to suck his fist. The others sleep, their perfect Cupid's bow lips slightly parted even though they don't yet breathe through their mouths. For the first three months of their lives, babies are "obligate nose breathers." Billy knows this from a nature show. They breathe through their noses because they use their mouths to suck milk from their mother's breasts.

Mommy milk.

The words pop into Billy's dream brain and fizzle away like fireworks after their burst of color. Only in the dream, Billy has always lived in the warehouse with the babies. He's never seen fireworks, so why does he think of them now?

He shakes his head the way he does when a bumblebee flies too close. (Why are there bumblebees in the warehouse, if not fireworks? It doesn't matter. There just are.)

The bumblebees won't hurt Billy if Billy doesn't hurt them. He knows that. But when one buzzes up, he shuts his eyes and shakes his head with tiny, fast shakes.

Go away, bee, Billy says. *I'm not mad at you. I just don't want you to sting me.*

Then, in the way of dreams, his mother is there. She is enormous, like God. She *is* God, even though God is a man.

The babies in the warehouse squirm and coo and suck their thumbs. Billy doesn't mind. He likes the sounds they make, the gentle schlock-schlocks.

The room turns gray. Lightning splits the air. The babies whimper, despite Billy's attempts to shush them. One baby, red-faced and furious, begins to wail.

Baby, no! Billy warns. His mother can't stand crying babies. She'll come closer if the baby doesn't stop. She'll come closer, and everyone will be punished, the burrito babies and Billy alike. She'll throw them all into the ocean. She'll hold their heads underwater.

Billy pinches shut the baby's nostrils. The baby flails and Billy's heart takes flight. *No, baby, no!*

Billy jerks awake, his body slick with sweat. Where is he? Not in his bed. Whose clothes is he wearing? Not his. His heart wallops in his chest, and a high beeping sound fills the air.

He can't breathe.

He can't see.

The beeping keeps going, and he remembers: *fire.*

Billy is in Hell. That's why he can't breathe or see. Although a whistling sound tells him he's breathing, just a little. A crescent of light appears and disappears, like a shiny moon. He can see a little, it seems.

But the fire. And the babies! He needs to help the babies!

He feels a cool cloth on his forehead and a large, rough hand on his cheek.

"Shh," says a man's deep voice. "I'm here, Billy. Don't worry."

Billy tries to blink. One of his eyelids is gooey. The other won't open at all. His hand goes to his face, and he feels gauze, miles and miles of it.

The man blurs and comes into focus. His expression is grave, but his eyes are kind.

"Dad?" Billy croaks.

"You're awake," his father says. His voice cracks. "Billy, thank God, you're awake."

Billy pats the place where his eye should be, the eye that isn't working. Why is it covered with bandages? Do bandages cover him everywhere?

His father steps away, and Billy says, "Dad, no! Don't go!"

"I'm not going anywhere," his dad says. He calls, "Doctor! Nurse! My son woke up!"

The beeping grows louder and is joined by some sort of siren. Both noises come from machines. They come from hospital machines, which means Billy is in the hospital.

The fire.

He closes his eyes. His . . . eye?

He prays to be swallowed by the deep dark sea.

52
JAKE

Online, everyone decries the boy in Colorado who locked a younger boy in a shed and set the shed on fire. Billy's name isn't mentioned, as he's a minor. People refer to him by other names: psychopath, freak, monster.

"The surprise isn't that Little Johnny turned out to be a sadistic bully because Mommy didn't love him enough," wrote someone in one of the hundreds of rants, blogs, and think pieces that sprang up when the story went viral. "The surprise is that Little Johnny hid his sadism as long as he did. One of these days, if we're lucky, he'll grab an axe and chop off Mommy's head."

I doubt it. Vanessa disappeared literally in the dark of night, leaving behind only the sign that says, Is This Your Poop? PICK IT UP!

Even that vanished when the For Sale sign appeared. It detracted from the bungalow's curb appeal, I imagine.

My name makes it into the papers, and yes, people make the connection that it's me, *that* Jake Nolan. The tide has turned, however. Everyone likes a redemption story, and this time I saved a child rather than mocking one (or so the story goes).

Billy's father stays beneath the mob's radar because no one knows anything about him. I could toss some morsels their way, but why would I?

On the day of the fire, a medic strode to me, gestured at the ambulance, and said, "You coming with or following behind?"

He assumed I was Wendell's mother, or Billy's. I hopped into the ambulance, where the boys, unconscious, were strapped on gurneys and given oxygen masks. At the hospital, Billy came to. Agitated, he fought to lower his mask.

"Is Wendell okay?" he asked. He tried to turn his head, but couldn't. The paramedics had immobilized his neck.

A nurse rushed over. Before she could get Billy's oxygen mask back in place, he clutched at me and said, "Call my dad. Please. Tell him . . ."

His face was a mess, blistered and swollen. His lips struggled to part. "Tell him I'm sorry."

Back at my house, I scoured the internet for a man who used to be married to a woman named Vanessa Stillson and had a son named Billy.

I spent hours following fruitless leads before realizing I already had the information I needed. That day with the ants, in front of my house, Billy borrowed my phone to call his dad.

I scrolled back until I found the outgoing call Billy made. The telephone number had a "602" area code, for Arizona, and seeing it gave me a jolt. I'd recently blocked this number, after it appeared on my screen for the fifth or sixth time along with the words "Unknown Caller."

When I checked my message center, I found twenty-two voicemails from 602-555-2310, all in the "blocked" bin, all unheard.

I listened to one message after another, all from Billy's father. In the last of them, his voice was jagged. "I'm literally begging you," implored this unknown man. "Please, whoever this is, just call me back."

His name was Darren Stillson, he later told me. He and Vanessa got divorced four years ago, and he hadn't seen Billy since.

When I told him Billy was in the hospital, he drew in a sharp breath. "Was it a seizure? Or did he have another asthma attack?"

"Huh?" I replied. A further back-and-forth painted a picture of Billy as practically an invalid, an image that didn't track with the tall, strong boy I've gotten to know these last few months.

"Are you sure we're talking about the same kid?" I asked.

Darren was less worried about unraveling Vanessa's lies than seeing his son. "Poudre Valley Hospital," he repeated, and I heard the scratch of pencil on paper. "1024 South Lemay Avenue, Fort Collins, Colorado."

For the last several days, Darren's been by Billy's side in the burn unit, which is where I'll be going in just a minute. Mabel thinks I'm crazy and tells me so again when I swing by her house beforehand. She's fiercely proud of me for rushing to Wendell's aid, and just as fiercely opposed to my decision to visit the boy who put him in peril.

With her arm around Bethany's shoulders, Mabel says, "You're my hero, Jake. You know that." She pulls Bethany in and kisses the top of her head. "As are you, my brave girl. But, Jake. Seriously. You owe Billy nothing."

Bethany says she thinks it's good I'm going. "I know Billy did something really bad," she says. "But . . . I still hope he's okay."

I nod and feel sad. "Yeah. Me, too." I reach into my bag and pull out the pages I brought for Mabel, a copy of Professor Lee's chapter on ethnobotany.

"Ooh, goody," Mabel says.

"Why 'ooh, goody'? What is it?" Bethany asks.

"A very thorough exploration of ethnobotany and its impact on society," I say.

"Huh?"

"Plants. It's about plants."

Bethany pulls a face. "Boring."

"Not to me," Mabel says. "Jake and I have formed a book club. This is our first selection."

"It's not even a book," Bethany points out.

Mabel accepts the pages, rolls them into a tube, and bops Bethany lightly on the head. "You are but a child and know not of womanly tribulations," she says in what is probably supposed to be the voice of a high priestess but makes her sound like a crotchety old witch.

"Weirdo," Bethany says.

“Weren’t you going to teach me how to make a fortune teller?” Mabel asks.

Bethany brightens. “Did you buy the origami paper?”

“I did, as well as some fruit-scented Magic Markers since I was at Michaels anyway.”

“I love fruity Magic Markers!”

Mabel lets Bethany drag her to the great room, and I smile, knowing we’ll talk soon.

The night of the fire, after we knew that all the kids were safe (or safe-ish), Mabel came over and we shared a couple of bottles of wine. We didn’t plant poops in anybody’s yard or make accusations about children being creepy and “off.” Instead, sensing that we’d both been keeping secrets, we laid everything bare—the hurts and pains that had been fueling our bad decisions over the past few months.

I told Mabel about breaking into Shelby and Adam’s house and described my confrontation with Adam. She admitted to going to Shelby’s panty party that morning and told me about her encounter with Shelby.

“There’s a revenge-porn clause in David’s divorce settlement,” she said, cringing behind her raised wine glass.

“Oh God,” I said. “David was a former porn star?”

Mabel did a spit take. “Ha. No. Though that could have been a career choice for him.”

She explained about the photos captured by a private detective—the very explicit photos—and we both recoiled at Shelby’s absolute lack of a moral compass.

“I mean, not that we can talk,” Mabel acknowledged.

“Oh yes we can,” I countered. “We may not be angels, but Shelby’s *way* worse. Anyway, we’ve reformed.”

Mabel sighed. “I hate that she’ll always be able to hold that over me.”

“I hear you. Same for me, with the footage Adam has.”

“What is it with those two and photographic evidence?”

I laughed. Then I poured us more wine. Then I told her about Professor Lee, my suspicions, and my plan for how to put our fears to rest.

“Well, butter my butt and call me a biscuit,” Mabel said, genuinely shocked. "I want to read it for myself, the *source material.* Think the professor would mind?"

"Are you kidding? He'll be thrilled," I predicted.

"Yes, yes, by all means!" Professor Lee said when I asked him. "This makes me feel like a bona fide writer. I'd love to meet her, your friend, and tell her about my work in person. She could meet Cindy Pawford!"

"That sounds lovely. I think you'll like her."

"More than that Shelby woman?"

"Professor Lee, there's no comparison."

53

JAKE

In the pediatric wing of the hospital, doctors study clipboards, nurses busy themselves with important tasks, and orderlies bustle past in squeaky rubber-soled shoes. It is familiar, but also foreign. At thirty-one, I feel decades older than the young woman who once worked at the gift store at Children's Hospital Colorado.

When I reach Billy's room, my resolve to visit the boy who hurt my brother hits a roadblock. Billy is ten years old, one year younger than I was when I left Toby alone in the woods. I recognize that. I do. But even at my young age, I knew better than to leave Toby unsupervised. (Carrie and Mabel can insist until the end of their days that I wasn't to blame, but what does that change? The dead are dead.)

Billy put Wendell in harm's way on purpose. And yet, I saw his resolve the moments before the beam crashed down. Billy shielded Wendell and took the brunt of the blow himself. He did that on purpose, too.

I rap on Billy's door.

"Jake," Darren says, rising from a plastic chair. His eyes are rimmed with red. His hair sticks out in tufts. "Come in. Billy's groggy, but awake."

There are no flowers, balloons, or teddy bears in Billy's room. Just Billy. A bandage covers the ravaged socket where his left eye used to be, and I know from Darren that he's unlikely to regain movement in the lower half of his face. His mouth will be forever caught between a grimace and a smile.

But. He's alive. Wendell is alive, and Billy, too.

"Hi," I say, perching on the edge of the bed.

Billy parts his swollen lips. What comes out is a rasp.

Darren is there in a heartbeat, tilting a Styrofoam cup and easing water into Billy's mouth.

"Please, don't try to talk," I say. "I wanted to check on you, that's all."

"I told him you've called every day," Darren says. "That made you real happy, didn't it, Billy?"

Billy works his throat. "How's . . . Wendell?"

"He's good," I say. "He was kept overnight, but now he's home and doing fine."

Billy grimaces, and one of the monitoring machines beeps alarmingly fast. Darren strides into the hall to find a nurse.

Billy follows his father with his good eye, then turns to me. "Tell me. Tell me all of it."

"The beam that hit you could have crushed Wendell's skull," I say gently. "A forensics team analyzed the scene, and based on where Wendell was sitting . . ."

Billy's eye wells up.

"You saved him, Billy. He's alive because of you."

A tear runs down his face. His shoulders shake.

I take his hand. "Go on. It's good to cry."

Darren rushes into the room, a nurse on his heels.

"Let's see what's going on here," she says. She hits a button that makes the beeping stop, then takes Billy's face in her hands, turning it this way and that. "Looks like we need to change these bandages, and maybe do something to address your pain. What do you say?"

I squeeze Billy's hand, then rise and slip away.

54
JAKE

After the hospital, I go to the Hemlock house for the last time. I park on the street. I'm done with hiding. Instead of going to the front door, however, I circle the house and approach from the back. I want to see the monitoring system Adam installed.

There it is, a discreet black eye peering out from the corner of the doorframe. The spiderweb I saw was higher up. It was never hiding the camera. It just served as an unintentional decoy. If I'd taken more time to listen to my instincts, maybe I'd have clocked the spiderweb *and* the surveillance camera.

But I didn't. I was too hell-bent on returning the photo of Shelby and her mom.

My instincts flare up again today, the tiny hairs on the back of my neck lifting. *Leave. Danger. Get out of here, you fool!*

This time, I override my survival instincts intentionally. Shelby will not win. Despite all she's thrown at me, I'm still standing.

I use my pilfered key and let myself in, finding it interesting that Adam still hasn't changed the locks. He said he suspected it was me, the shadow figure who'd been sneaking in and disturbing things. That's why he installed a surveillance system. And yet if his goal was simply to prove himself right—and to have damning evidence to hold over me—the camera alone would have done the job. Even with a new lock installed, Adam would have had me on film inserting the key, twisting and retwisting the key, and maybe rattling the doorknob before scowling and giving up.

But Adam left the locks as they were, which begs the question: Did Adam *want* to catch me breaking and entering? With each documented instance of my "bad" behavior, does Adam find it easier to assuage his own malfunctioning conscience?

This time, if Adam checks the footage and wants an explanation, he'll have to ask Shelby, his soon-to-be wife. I'll be able to prove her wrong if she lies, however. I take a quick peek at my phone, which I've set to act as a recording device. Everything's running as it should. I drop it back into my tote bag, empty save for a few essential items, and proceed to the kitchen. I take a seat at the table, sling the tote over the back of my chair, and wait.

"Adam?" Shelby calls from the second floor. I knew she was here, just as I knew Adam was gone. Like the locks, Adam continues to use the same uninspired password for the energy-use app.

Feet pad down the stairs. "I thought you were at work!"

She rounds the corner and draws up short. Her muscles go slack and her mug slips from her fingers, breaking into bits and spraying milky brown coffee everywhere. Shelby always did doctor her coffee with ample cream and sugar, and she drank the stuff constantly. For someone positioning herself as a tea lover, she sure craved the kick of coffee.

Then again, for someone believing herself to be of least average intelligence, I sure missed a hell of a lot of tip-offs.

"Oopsie," I say.

Shelby pulls herself together with remarkable speed. Her eyes flash as she steps over the broken crockery, and I can practically hear the snap of her vertebrae as she straightens to her full height.

"What the hell?" she practically spits. "What are you doing here? How did you even get in?"

"Would you believe me if I told you that Adam and I have gotten back together?" I propose. "I live in your basement now. Every night, your fiancé slips out of bed, tiptoes downstairs, and fucks me silly."

"You are truly a psycho," Shelby says. She's wearing tight white jeans—now streaked with brown—and she pats her pockets until she finds her phone. She swipes the screen and lets the camera analyze the thousands of data points that compose her lovely face. When the home screen changes, she gets busy with her thumbs. "I'm calling 911."

I interlace my fingers on top of the table and smile.

"I mean it, Jake," Shelby says. Splashes of color rise on her cheeks. "I'm calling the police."

I shrug. On the inside, my body is doing all the things: racing heart, fizzy blood, pricks of sweat along my hairline and on the small of my back. But outside? I'm steady.

Shelby falters.

"What?" she demands, dropping the charade of calling for help. She'll make the call if it suits her, I'm sure of that. But right now, she thinks I know more than I'm letting on.

She's right.

"Have a seat," I say.

She yanks out a chair, and it scrapes the floor. "I will," she says, sliding into it while keeping her eyes locked on mine. "By the way, you're fooling yourself if you think I didn't see you yesterday at Whole Foods. You are far less clever than you think you are."

"I don't doubt it," I say, scrolling backward through recent memories. I did go to Whole Foods yesterday, but I have no recollection of seeing Shelby. "Were you by the eggs? Or no, let me guess. Were you in the produce aisle, searching for fresh peppermint leaves?"

Shelby pulls back ever so slightly. She lifts her chin and says, "I don't know what you're playing at, but you need to stop. Oh, and siccing your friend on me at the charity luncheon? That was juvenile, even for you."

I regulate my breathing. I force my shoulders to relax. And then I study Shelby. I take a moment to really drink her in.

Her glossy hair is in the sort of messy bun I have never mastered, despite hours of practicing with YouTube tutorials. Her winged eyeliner accentuates her dark eyes, and her lips are as red and shiny as a candy apple. If I reached out and touched them, my fingertips would surely come back tacky. If I pressed a bit of dryer lint against them, or a clump of cat fur, it would cling to Shelby's wet-looking lips like a macaroni noodle pressed into glue.

Irritation flashes across her features. She doesn't like seeing me in control.

"Your *friend* came to my panty party under false pretenses," she says, framing the word in snark quotes. "You can't deny that no matter how hard you try."

"And you threatened her with blackmail," I reply. "But it was for a good cause, I suppose. The party, not the blackmail." I reach into my tote and pull out a wad of lace, tossing it onto the table. "Here, for the cause."

Shelby snatches the thongs. One is pale green, the other is the color of orange sherbet. "These belong to me, Jake. What the fuck?"

"I took them. Now I'm giving them back."

I dip my hand back into my tote, watching Shelby closely. When I pull out the handful of tea sachets, she swallows hard. I toss them on the table, too.

Shelby clutches her thongs to her chest. She shakes her head at the sachets. "Those aren't mine."

"No, they're Professor Lee's—or they were. He gave them to me, so they're mine now."

"Great. Why are you telling me?"

"They smell like peppermint, but they're not."

"So?"

"Come on, Shelby. The game's up." I lift one of the sachets. "You gave me these exact sachets, but you didn't say they were from Professor Lee. You told me you made them yourself, your special homemade tea."

Her chest rises and falls.

"Only you didn't make them yourself, and the leaves inside weren't peppermint." A pang of genuine hurt makes my rib cage tighten. I brace against it until it passes. "They were pennyroyal."

Shelby wets her lips. She blinks and says, "I don't know what that is."

"That's why you never went back to visit him with me. You visited him on your own."

Her thumb goes to her mouth, pressing her upper lip against her teeth. "Did he say that? Did you talk to him? Because if you did, you know that I was having headaches. He gave me tea for my headaches."

"And you gave that tea to me. You brought me a whole canister to celebrate my pregnancy, bags and bags of pennyroyal tea. And maybe you did have headaches. Maybe the tea eased your pain. Did it? Because you drank as much as I did, which was smart."

"It was tea, Jake. It was like drinking water, practically."

I stare at her, incredulous. "Really, Shelby?" I almost say his name—Liam, who was growing inside me, swimming in all that tea—but I don't. Shelby doesn't deserve to hear it.

"Just now, you said I'm not as clever as I think I am," I say. "I can live with that."

"Jake . . ."

"But you, Shelby—you're so much more clever than I ever imagined. And please, don't take that as a compliment."

Shelby stands. "It's time for you to go. I'd like for you to go, Jake."

I pose a genuine question. "Does Adam know?"

"Does Adam know *what*?" she says, but she's flustered. The more flustered she becomes, the calmer I become.

Or maybe I'm just terribly, terribly sad.

"While peppermint is safe for pregnant women, pennyroyal should be strenuously avoided," I say, repeating facts from Professor Lee's chapter. "Especially the oil extracted from its leaves."

Shelby's eyes dart everywhere, but refuse to land on me.

"Pennyroyal tea is used to induce miscarriages, Shelby."

She loses her cool at last. "You know what? I did you a favor!"

"Ex*cuse* me?"

"Pennyroyal causes uterine contractions, not heart defects."

"So you do know what it is."

"That baby wasn't going to live, Jake. From the beginning, that baby was going to die. Wouldn't an early miscarriage have been better than what you went through?" She comes closer. "The only thing I did wrong was not give you a stronger dose!"

I have it, her confession. It's done.

I sit back in my chair. She looms over me.

"What would people do, do you think, if they knew?" I muse. "A philanthropist, the cofounder of a charity for infants in need . . ."

The blood drains from Shelby's face.

I pull my phone from my bag. I check the screen and nod. "Good. The recording's been stored on the cloud."

"Jake," Shelby says raggedly.

"Your reputation would be ruined, and that's no fun." I widen my eyes as if to say, *Take it from me.* "You could even go to jail, with abortion laws in such a state of flux. Or be doxed, have some nutjob show up at your house." I laugh a little and glance down, gesturing at myself. "Like me! Ha!"

"You can't tell. Please don't tell."

I nibble on my thumbnail. "People online are ker-azy, let me tell you."

"Enough! Stop!" Shelby cries. "I know you, Jake, and I know you came here for a reason. You're not here to ruin my life. You don't have it in you. So what do you want?"

"It's true that it takes a special kind of person to ruin someone's life," I acknowledge. "The things you accused me of, the way you rearranged details to paint me as a monster . . ."

"I get it. Yes." She steps forward, and for a second I think she's going for my phone. I hold it out of reach.

"Omigod," she says. Speaking clearly and in the direction of the mic, she says, "I lied. Everything I said, all that #lipservice nonsense, I made it up. Okay? Are you happy?"

"Oh, Shelby," I reply, shaking my head. "'Happy' is not the word I'd use."

I rise from the table. "First of all, you will never threaten my friend Mabel again."

She rolls her eyes.

"Not about Gigi, not about her divorce, not about anything that could embarrass her in any way."

"Fine," Shelby says. "Done. Like I care about her stupid drama anyway." She presses her lips together. "What else?"

"There's a little boy who needs your help. His name's Wendell. He lives with his aunt, whose name is Evelyn Cox." I lift my eyebrows. "You're going to want to write this down."

I make sure she taps all of Wendell's information into her notes app. I tell her that he needs facial reconstructive surgery and that she's going to make it happen, at no cost to his family.

"Go to his aunt," I say. "Walk her through the process."

"Who is this kid?" Shelby complains. "Why do you even care?"

"He's my brother," I say.

Her mouth falls open. "What?!"

I sling my tote bag over my shoulder. "But I'd care even if he weren't. The thing you don't get, Shelby, is that not everyone is like you. Some people, lots of people, choose to help someone not for praise or status or likes, but because that's what humans do. We help each other."

55

MABEL

One week later, on a chilly October Saturday, Mabel and Bethany walk to Jake's house side by side. Bethany holds a cake carrier carefully in front of her, in which rests a cake Bethany made almost entirely by herself. They arrive at the same time as Delilah and Wendell, who race past their aunt Evelyn up the porch stairs and ring Jake's doorbell three times in rapid succession.

"Delilah, once is plenty," scolds Evelyn.

"Sorry, Aunt Evelyn!" Delilah says. She grabs Bethany's wrist and tugs her into the house as soon as Jake opens the door. "Hi, Jake! Bye, Jake! We're going to play Uno!"

"Ex*cuse* me!" Bethany squeals, lifting the cake carrier protectively. "I've got a cake here, in case you didn't notice?"

Jake presses her spine to the doorframe as Wendell dashes in behind them.

"I'll be with Lump if anyone needs me," he calls. He throws his aunt a meaningful glance. "Really, Aunt Evelyn, we should get that kitten as soon as possible. Okay? Okay!"

Evelyn harrumphs. To Jake, she says, "I just adopted two stinking kids, and now they want me to adopt an animal that poops in a box. I blame you, young lady."

After discovering that Jake was his half sister, Wendell proclaimed that since being a cat person runs in the family (obviously), the clear course of action is for his aunt Evelyn to get a kitten as soon as possible (obviously!).

"But kittens are so cute," Mabel says.

"*So* cute," Jake says. "You should get a Maine coon. Or a Ragdoll. Ragdolls can grow to be the size of a small horse. Did you know that?"

"That's quite enough," Evelyn says. "Not another word about cats the size of horses, thank you very much." She starts back down the porch steps. "I'll expect Wendell and Delilah back home in two hours. Don't spoil their appetite before dinner."

"Are you sure you won't stay for cake?" Jake asks.

Evelyn flaps her hand at them without bothering to turn around, sending Mabel and Jake into a fit of giggles.

"I love that she calls me 'young lady,'" Jake whispers.

"*I* love that she's getting a kitten," Mabel says at full volume. "I figure she'll hold out another week, tops?"

She follows Jake to the living room sofa, where Bethany and Delilah have already made themselves comfortable. Delilah, all legs and elbows, sits wedged in the corner of the sofa with her knees drawn to her chest, the same way Jake likes to sit. She deals Uno cards to herself and Bethany, who sits below her on the floor, spine straight and legs crisscross applesauce.

"You said you had news about Billy," Mabel says to Jake. "Let's hear it."

Jake drops into an armchair and curls one leg beneath her. "Well, his dad called me. Billy's settling in pretty well in Arizona, he said."

"I hope he dies there," Delilah says. "I hope he fries in the sun the way he tried to fry Wendell."

"Delilah!" Jake says.

"What?" Delilah says. "If nothing else, he should be in jail. Why didn't he get sent to jail?"

She has a point. Billy was charged with arson, assault, harassment, and vandalism, but the charges probably won't stick. The juvenile justice system is very forgiving.

"He lost an eye," Bethany says.

"Um, he brought that on himself, so stop trying to make me feel sorry for him. It's not going to happen."

"He also lost his mom," Bethany says. "She abandoned him, which is a crappy thing for a mom to do."

Is Bethany thinking of Gigi, who abandoned her? Mabel feels a stab of love so strong it almost hurts. Mabel isn't going anywhere. She'll be here for Bethany no matter what.

"Billy *might* never see his mother again," Delilah counters. "Key word: might. Want to know who will definitely never see their mom again? Me and Wendell, because our mom is dead. Billy's mom is just . . ." She bugs her eyes. "A really bad mom."

"It's still sad."

"Yeah, well, life is sad," Delilah says with the satisfaction of someone who knows she's won the argument.

Wendell comes into the living room with Lump dangling from his arms. He plops onto the sofa and scratches behind Lump's ears. Lump's rumbly purr kicks into gear.

"Your cake looks really good," Wendell tells Bethany. "Well, from what I can tell. It's kind of hidden by the cake lid."

"It's not a cake lid. It's a cake platter," Delilah says.

"He's talking about the part that goes over the platter. The dome thingie," Bethany says. She looks at Mabel. "What's the dome thingie called, Mabel?"

"'Dome thingie' works," Mabel says. To Wendell, she says, "It's a lemon cake. Bethany made it especially for you."

"You helped," Bethany says.

"Only a little," Mabel says. "Does everybody want a piece?"

Everybody does. Jake goes with Mabel to the kitchen, where they steal a moment to themselves.

"You're a saint to let us descend on you," Mabel says. With her back to the granite island, she braces her palms on its smooth surface and hoists herself up. "I'm referring to the kids, obviously. I am a joy to have over."

"Obviously," Jake says. She breaks into a giddy smile. "As is Bethany. As are Delilah and Wendell, *my sister and brother*. Ahh!" She widens her eyes as if she still can't believe it, then hops up onto the island next to Mabel.

From the living room comes the melody of happy voices. The girls are playing Uno, and Wendell has Lump to keep himself occupied. Mabel figures it'll be a minute before the kids start clamoring for cake.

"Where *is* Vanessa, do you think?" she asks.

"Mexico? Canada?" Jake says. "Wyoming?"

"No way. Wyoming's full of poop, with all those bears and horses, and we know how she feels about poop." She keeps her tone light. "She hasn't been online?"

Jake shoots her an amused glance. Whereas Mabel is taking a break from social media (not forever, just for a bit), Jake has cautiously waded back into those muddy waters. "The affirmation feels good," she told Mabel sheepishly, after the news of the shed fire turned her into a minor hero.

Vanessa, for her part, disappeared from GoodNeighbors weeks ago, just as quietly and cleanly as she disappeared from Sweetwater Lane.

"She's gone, baby, gone," Jake says. "Either that or she's using an alias. Either way, we've seen the last of her."

"So crazy," Mabel murmurs. "What about Shelby?"

"What about her?"

"No further interactions, accusations, or attempts to intimidate?"

"With what I've got on her? Please."

"And she'll follow through with helping Wendell?"

"She cares too much about her reputation not to. I think she considers it a payoff for my silence."

"Isn't it?"

Jake frowns, and Mabel knows what's coming. As tough as she pretends to be, Jake is a softie. Always has been, always will be.

"In theory, yeah." Jake drums her heels against the cabinet below her. "But if I'm being honest, I have a hard time seeing myself ratting her out."

"I will happily do it for you if the need arises," Mabel says. "She plays dirty, Jake. You've got to fight fire with fire."

Jake winces.

"Bad choice of words. Sorry."

Jake gazes out the kitchen window for several moments, the sunlight making her squint. She turns to Mabel and smiles. "Cake?"

Mabel hops off the island. "Yes! Cake!"

She eases the dome from the cake carrier, and the smell of sugar and lemons rises up, the perfect balance of sweet and sour.

56

WENDELL

Within a month, the swelling on Wendell's face has diminished dramatically. He's had the first of three planned surgeries and will soon go in for the second. The doctor in charge of fixing him is named Doctor Shuler, and he's really nice and not scary at all. One day in the not too distant future, Doctor Shuler says Wendell will look pretty much like he used to before his father shot him.

Wendell has started seeing a speech therapist as well, a woman named Therese who wears delicate gold earrings. She's teaching him exercises to help his tongue get stronger.

The exercises are hard, just like it's hard to go to the hospital and come out bruised and achy and not be allowed to blow his nose no matter how much he wants to. Wendell has an excellent attitude, however. Everyone says so. Doctor Shuler, Therese, Aunt Evelyn, Jake, Mabel, Bethany . . . everyone! Even Delilah.

The adults also say he's "resilient," which means he's like Silly Putty. He can be stretched in all different ways, and even snap apart, but he can be put back together, like Humpty Dumpty.

Or, *not* like Humpty Dumpty, because all the king's horses and all the king's men couldn't put Humpty together again.

Humpty Dumpty is an egg, though, and so is Wendell. Wendell is Silly Putty *and* the red plastic snap-apart egg the Silly Putty comes in.

"I am an egg," he sings under his breath. "An eggy eggy egg. And when I break, I turn into a cake!" He likes making up songs. They help when thoughts of Billy try to sneak in. Jake says Billy is gone, that he lives in a whole nother state now, and that Wendell will never see him again. Sometimes Wendell still feels scared, even so. "And when I'm a cake, I'm a-ma-zing!"

He's kneeling on the living room sofa in Aunt Evelyn's house, which is his house now, his and Delilah's *and* Aunt Evelyn's. He's supposed to just call it "our house." Across the street is Jake's house, which he's supposed to call "my sister's house." Wendell and Delilah go to Jake's often. Delilah is even starting to warm up to Lump, not that she admits it.

Wendell is kneeling on the sofa with his bottom facing the TV and his elbows on the windowsill, looking out at the house that's kitty-corner from Aunt Evelyn's house.

"Kitty-corner" is a funny word. Kitties don't have corners.

The For Sale sign in the front yard was replaced by a Sold! sign one week ago. Today, a moving van parked in front of the house, and big, burly men went back and forth in the snow, filling the house with furniture. Wendell likes the snow in Fort Collins, even though it isn't as fluffy as North Carolina snow. He likes how it makes everything look clean and new.

Will the new family know about Colorado snow already, or will they be from somewhere else? Maybe not North Carolina, but . . . Alaska! A family from Alaska would be cool. They'd definitely know about snow.

Or, Hawaii? If a Hawaiian family moved in across the street, Wendell could be their Fort Collins tour guide. "And this is how to make a snowball," he imagines telling the imaginary boy who belongs to the imaginary family who, in Wendell's imagination, moves into Billy's old house.

The imaginary boy would be a nice boy. He would be quiet and nice with wire-rimmed glasses, and he would be a first grader just like Wendell. He would never set things on fire.

"When I'm a cake, I'm a-*ma*-zing!" he sings, louder than before.

"Cakes can't talk," Delilah says from across the room. She's curled up in a chair with a book.

"Yeah-huh, because I'm a cake, and I'm talking *right now.*"

Delilah snorts.

A white Kia Sorento pulls into the driveway across the street. They're here! The family! If it even is a family. *Please let it be a family!* he prays. *With a boy my age, who's quiet and nice and doesn't play with fire.*

The car stops, and a man with jet-black hair gets out. The woman in the passenger seat opens her door and gets out, too. She picks her way around the car to join the man, taking big, high steps because of the snow. When she's close enough, the man wraps his arm around her and pulls her close, kissing the top of her head.

The back door of the Kia Sorento slides open, first a little and then more, as if someone is using their foot to push it that extra bit. Wendell holds his breath. Two blue snow boots emerge. Smallish snow boots. First-grader-size snow boots.

The mommy and the daddy smile at the stocky boy who's stomping through the snow. He wears an enormous purple-and-black puffy coat that says *Colorado Rockies* on the back, and instead of a winter beanie, he wears a baseball cap. The boy's dad sweeps his arm in a semicircle as if to say, *Look at all this!*

As the boy takes it all in, Wendell sees a round, happy face sporting a pair of wire-rimmed glasses.

"Guys! They're here!" Wendell cries. He scrambles off the sofa and hurries to the front door, where he tugs on the snow boots Aunt Evelyn bought at Goodwill.

"Who's here?" Delilah asks.

"Excuse me, Wendell, where do you think you're going?" Aunt Evelyn says, stepping out of the kitchen. She never calls him "young man" anymore.

"The *new* people," Wendell replies. "I'm going to say 'hi' to the new people!" He pulls on his winter coat and flings open the front door. "I have to welcome them to the neighborhood!"

ACKNOWLEDGMENTS

My first drafts are routinely terrible, but this one, *woof.* This one took the cake. The early drafts were so bad for so long, and yet Barry Goldblatt and Patricia Ready circled back with me time and time again until it was finally . . . not quite so terrible as it once was. And then, truth, the wonderful Dan Ehrenhaft plucked it from the submissions pile at Blackstone and decided to take a chance on it, even though it was *still* embarrassingly rough. (I know this now. I didn't at the time.) Thank you, Dan. Thanks as well to Josie Woodbridge, Lysa Williams, Isabella Bedoya, Rachel Sanders, Robert Casserly, and Sarah Bonamino, my Blackstone dream team, and to CEO Josh Stanton, who allowed himself to be worn down. I have, with enormous gratitude, given my all to proving the book worthy of y'all's faith.

Celia Johnson dove in with brilliant editorial suggestions, and sheesh, the magic she worked! With discernment and wit, Celia guided me through the labyrinth of my own weird brain, helping me figure out what this story wanted to be. Celia, you are brilliant.

Sarah Riedlinger is the creative genius behind the drop-dead gorgeous cover, and *ahhhhh,* I am obsessed. Cole Barnes pored over the manuscript with a fine-tooth comb and tried patiently to teach me the difference between "farther" and "further." I have a ways to go, but I'm sure enjoying the journey.

Dr. Jim Shuler talked to me for the fortieth time about guns—thanks, Jim! He also helped me with questions pertaining to reconstructive surgery, although anything I got wrong is fully on me. Ali Pezeshki loaned me his cat, Edwin Chong contributed his mischievous smile, and the Bennett Road Babes—Jenny, Melyssa, and Pamela—threw in the neighborhood vibes. My mom, Ruth White, helped me iron out dozens of plot wrinkles, because she is the best. My son, Al, is also the best (as are my other kids; they're just not all that into reading 😱). Thanks, Al, for your fine eye and excellent ability to cut through malarkey.

And Randy, you are the bestest of the best. Thanks for not murdering me, even as I murder others with gleeful abandon. Also, thanks for letting me borrow your fancy iPad, which read the novel out loud to me while I wielded the mighty slashing stylus. You can have it back now.